"Torrie? Y... darkness that lurked in the corners of the barn. "He's gone."

Torrie stared at Lance's hands, swollen now from the blows he had bestowed on her attacker. How was it, she wondered, that a man who possessed so much power and anger in his soul could also be capable of so much . . . tenderness?

Torrie's gaze raised up to meet the hazel eyes of the man who had saved her from harm. "I owe you, Mr. Farlo," she said. "A simple thank you hardly seems enough."

He reached up to tip the brim of his hat. He was even more handsome than Torrie had once thought.

His eyes sought hers as his tall frame towered over her; he had stepped closer to her; she could feel the heat of his body. She felt as if a flame had ignited at the core of her being. She had never been kissed, truly kissed, by a man. She wished the handsome gunfighter would gather her into her arms and . . .

Lance began to speak, his voice deep and emotional. "If I were an artist, I'd paint a picture of you. Then I could carry it with me forever."

His words left Torrie speechless. In her mind she was creating a picture of him, too. But her mind's artistic creation was interrupted when he bent his head and looked deep into her eyes. Instinctively, she closed her eyes as she felt the warmth of his moist mouth close over her trembling lips.

A simple thank you? No, it wasn't enough . . .

VERONICA BLAKE
COLORADO PASSION

ZEBRA BOOKS
KENSINGTON PUBLISHING CORP.

With love to Ortencia and Cecil Bettger.
They gave me life, love . . . and wings.
Thanks Mom and Dad.

ZEBRA BOOKS

are published by

Kensington Publishing Corp.
475 Park Avenue South
New York, NY 10016

First printing: December 1992

Printed in the United States of America

Chapter One

"He's a handsome baby. I think he looks like his father." The instant the words were out of her mouth, Torrie knew she had said the wrong thing. "I'm sor—"

"No, you're right. He does look like his father." The new mother carefully folded the blanket over the baby's head, then drew in a shaky breath. For a moment, she stared lovingly at the warm bundle in her arms. When she looked up again, tears glistened in her eyes.

"He's still alive. I feel it. I know it, Torrie." Her voice held no note of certainty, but her tone begged for reassurance.

Torrie remained silent, only nodding her head in agreement. A hard lump formed in her chest; a sense of foreboding chilled her. If Will Connor was still alive, he'd have been here for the birth of his first child. Torrie knew it, and so did Elsa. But neither of them had the energy or the courage to admit it out loud.

The night had been long and hard. This was Elsa's first pregnancy, and she had labored for nearly twelve hours before her baby was born in the early hours of the morning. At her side for nearly the entire time, Victoria Carrington felt exhausted to the bone. The doctor had been unavailable. Torrie's previous experience with birthing had been limited to helping ranch hands pull an occasional calf. Both women had been terrified, but not once did either of them speak of her fear.

Carrington wealth made Torrie's life somewhat easier, but it did not protect her from the certain knowledge the women who lived in this remote country possessed: There was little or nothing to be gained by showing weakness. Torrie had learned many valuable lessons in the eleven years she had lived on these vast ranch lands in western Colorado, but the most essential was that only the strongest survived in this brutal land.

A gurgle from beneath the blanket drew Torrie's attention back to Elsa. From somewhere in her aching body, Torrie found the energy to smile. Torrie followed Elsa's gaze to the tiny infant—a miracle even in the face of fear for Will Connor's safety.

"Thank you, Torrie," Elsa Connor said in a trembling voice. "We both would have died if you had not been here."

Torrie reached out and gently pushed a stray brown curl off Elsa's sweaty brow. Then, instinctively, she ran her fingers through the hair that hung past the middle of her back and now strayed about her face. Sometime during the night, the black velvet ribbon that had held her thick hair at the nape of her neck had slipped off.

"No thanks necessary." She searched the bureau next to the bed for a ribbon or a few hairpins. Her own ribbon, lying on the wooden floorboards beside the bed, caught her eye. She corralled her hair into a ponytail and retired the ribbon. "You know I'm always here for you and W-Will." In an effort to hide her fear for Elsa's husband, she quickly motioned toward the infant. "And for that little fella, too." She met Elsa's troubled gaze briefly, then pretended to focus all her attention on the baby.

"Will is alive. He'll be home soon," Elsa repeated, though her tired face told a different story. "And," she attempted a feeble smile, "someday, I'll be returning the favor. One of these days, Torrie, you'll meet a man and get mar—"

"You need to rest now," Torrie interrupted before the other woman could finish speaking. It was doing Elsa no good to keep thinking about Will when she should be concerned only with herself and the welfare of her newborn son. She would need all her strength when Will was found . . . and, if Torrie's fears proved true, she was left alone to raise the boy.

As for discussing the prospect of Torrie finding a man whom she would consider marrying—well that was definitely a waste of breath!

Elsa sighed and gave in to the heavy exhaustion that tugged at her eyelids and drew every ounce of energy she had left. Within seconds she drifted off, and was barely aware of Torrie when she carefully scooped the baby out of her limp arms.

For several minutes, Torrie held the infant against her breast, marveling at his perfection. In the midst of the death and mayhem running wild throughout the valley lately, a new life had begun. Torrie felt her eyes moisten and blur as she continued to stare at Elsa and Will's new son. The thought of the child's father twisted her stomach into a tight knot.

Torrie was aware of something that would be devastating news for the new mother. But so far, she had managed to keep it from Elsa, and the time was still not right to relate the tragic information.

Three days ago, Will had ridden down to the southern range to hunt for stray cattle. He had not returned. He was the second man from the Carrington ranch to ride out alone in the past week; the second to disappear.

The first, a young cowboy named Leo Mac-Farlene, had been found yesterday in a grove of cottonwood down by the river—hanged by the neck with his own rope. Torrie had not yet told Elsa about the gruesome discovery of Leo's body, nor did she intend to until she felt her friend was strong enough to cope with how it might be related to Will's unexplained disappearance.

The thought of Will Connor meeting the same end as Leo caused a shiver to run down Torrie's spine. Both were good men, but she barely knew Leo MacFarlene. Will had worked for the Carringtons for almost ten years, nearly as long as Torrie had been here. He was one of her stepfather's best

8

hands, and Will was Torrie's friend. A year ago, he'd gone to Denver to purchase cattle. He had returned with the new stock and a bride.

Torrie's mother had died a few months before Elsa's arrival, and Torrie was desperately in need of a friend. Only three years apart in age, Torrie and Elsa Connor had struck up an immediate friendship.

They were the only women on the Carrington ranch, the only women for hundreds of miles around, since Ben Carrington owned—or claimed to own—the better part of Garfield County and most of neighboring Mesa County. But their friendship went deeper than their need for female companionship; they had found a true kinship in one another. Torrie believed they would have been the best of friends even if they'd lived in a thriving metropolis among thousands of other women.

Quietly, Torrie laid the sleeping baby in his cradle and tucked the blanket his mother had knitted for him around his tiny body. Torrie had been here the night Will finished making the cradle, barely a week ago. Elsa had kidded him for days that he wasn't going to have the cradle finished in time for the baby's arrival. When he was finally finished, he boasted how he had done his job and it was her turn to get busy and have the baby.

Sometimes, when she was around Elsa and Will—where she could see it was possible for a man and a woman to be happy together—Torrie allowed herself a moment of fantasy, imagining that someday she would meet someone and fall in love just as Elsa predicted. But then she would remember her mother's life, married to Ben Carrington. Torrie would then remind herself she would never chance falling in love. . . . Never!

The baby whimpered softly in his sleep, pulling Torrie's thoughts for a second. She rocked the cradle until she was certain the infant was content again. An emptiness she had never known inched through her as she tiptoed away from the bedroom where Elsa and the child slept.

She slipped outside as quietly as possible and stood on the front stoop, hoping the fresh air would ease her heartache. But the endless acres of brown and gray sagebrush, dotted with immense herds of cattle and occasional stands of cottonwoods and cedars, only reminded her of the futility of her life. Still, it wasn't the land that she hated.

She was twenty years old and had lived on the Grand Mesa Ranch for over half of her life. The vastness of the Colorado rangelands, the muted tones of quiet mesas, and the dark waters of the Colorado River colored her soul. Rarely a day passed that she did not ride Ginger, her buckskin filly, along the river's edge or climb alone to the top of one of the flat mesas where she could see the snowcapped peaks of the distant mountains. If her life were different, she would never want to live anywhere else. But always, in the back of her mind, she knew the time was drawing near when she would have no choice but to leave.

She thought of the sprawling white ranch house, atop the far mesa and overlooking the lazy waters of the river, where she lived with her brother Gage, her stepbrother Canon, and Ben Carrington, her stepfather. A house full of men. If only her mother were still alive—it had been almost bearable then. Now the tension increased daily. Gage became more and more ruthless as he tried to win their stepfather's approval, to prove that he could fill his boots. Canon's advances grew constantly bolder. And Torrie's unhappiness and fear grew apace.

Chapter Two

Lance Farlo eyed the wide valley spread out around him. Off in the distance—on the opposite side, where the rangeland stretched all the way to the base of the far mountains—huge herds of cattle milled through stirrup-high range grass. A good-sized herd of white-faced cattle grazed or rested along the bank of the river. None of the animals paid attention to the man who had halted in their midst to water his horse.

This stop was only a stall for time.

He was tempted to swing back into his saddle, head south, and not stop until he was back in Texas where he belonged. He was a man of his word though, and he had a promise to keep in Colorado, even if he was headed straight into a hornet's nest.

Autumn tinged the sagebrush flats in shades of faded greens, grays, browns, and golds, but even this late in the season, the Colorado River flowed deep and heavy. Lance thought of the river that ran through his property on the Texas/Oklahoma border. This time of year, the Red River would be barely more than a sandy washout with a murky stream cutting a narrow gauge through its center.

He glanced toward the opposite riverbank. The silvery strands of newly-strung barbed wire shimmered unnaturally against the soft colors of the countryside.

Big ranchers versus little ranchers. . . . Murderers and rustlers and rimrockers running rampant. . . . Fences cutting up the open ranges. . . . Like the past he'd spent half his life trying to forget. Nothing but trouble.

But it was too late for second thoughts now.

The gruesome discovery he'd made at the southern border of this property was proof that there was even more trouble brewing in this valley than he'd anticipated when he accepted the position of range detective. Range detective—a glorified title given to professional gunmen hired by wealthy ranchers to protect their herds from rustlers and squatters. As a cattle inspector or range detective it was the gunman's job to see to it that range disputes were settled as swiftly and discreetly as possible. The law was of little or no concern.

In this case, however, the circumstances were slightly different. Several of the smaller ranchers in the area had banded together against the man who was trying to put claim to the better part of two counties. The man who wanted no one else to inhabit his self-declared territory.

When he received the telegram from Colorado,

14

Lance had thought someone was playing a joke on him. He had proven he was the best in the business when it came to dealing with trouble, but he rarely worked outside of Texas, New Mexico, and Arizona, where there were plenty of range wars to keep a capable man busy. In spite of his reputation with a gun, it seemed almost too ironic that of all the gunmen in the territory, the ranchers from this part of Colorado would consider him for this job.

But his own investigation revealed that the men who had contacted him knew nothing of his past association with the powerful man with whom they were about to wage a range war. Though he knew it would be a mistake to come back here, something had compelled him to accept the job. Even now, as he stood in the same spot he had stood years before, looking out over the land he had roamed as a young boy, he did not understand why he had felt such a need to return.

From beneath the wide, sloped brim of his brown Stetson, Lance studied his surroundings again. The craggy landscape was exactly as he remembered it, though he found he now preferred the wide open prairies of Texas, where a man could see as far as an eagle flew. The endless hills, plateaus, and rugged mountains of Colorado gave him the feeling of being closed in, suffocated, and made him even more anxious to finish his business in these parts and make a quick retreat back to Texas.

When he broke camp at dawn, there was a chill in the air, but the heavy brown canvas duster Lance wore was too hot now that the sun had risen high above the eastern horizon. He took off the long coat, then rolled the garment into a tight wad before tucking it into his bulging saddlebags. Besides the little plot of land on the Red River, which was his refuge when he wasn't riding the range, his belongings were on the back of his horse and on his person. Food, an extra change of clothes, and enough weaponry and ammunition to complete the job were the basic necessities of his trade. A fast draw, deadly aim—and at times—a lack of conscience were the inner resources he needed to draw upon.

Kneeling at the river's edge beside his ebony stallion, Lance scooped up a handful of the cold water and splashed it on his hot, flushed face. His thoughts were jumbled with recollections of the innocent boy he had once been and the twisted events that had determined the type of man he had become.

"You're trespassing, Mister!"

His cupped hand froze midair. The image of the dead man he had found this morning flashed through his mind. Water trickled between his fingers and dripped back into the river. His entire body tensed.

Trespasser?

The fences he had snipped in order to clear a straight pathway for himself and his horse through this range left him with no doubts he was riding through private land. That he was labeled a trespasser, however, made his return all the more ironic. He wondered if the man who had been murdered—a single bullet through his head, then

16

his body draped over the newly-strung barbed wire—had also been accused of trespassing.

His curiosity about the murder, however, was second to the anger he felt with himself for allowing his attention to be distracted with thoughts of the past when he should have been concentrating on the business at hand.

Alertness and caution were essential elements for a man in his line of work. For someone to sneak up on him without his knowledge was a rare—and lethally dangerous occurrence. Though he'd no doubt the claim that he was trespassing was supported by a loaded gun, the obvious fact that his accuser was female made him less wary now.

"Water's free," he said blandly as he stood, turned, and faced the woman. His gaze did not waver from her face, but he raised his arms in a lame gesture when he caught sight of the gun barrel aimed at his chest. The dead man hanging on the fence had been killed by a rifle slug at close range. Although this woman carried a sawed-off shotgun, Lance had learned long ago that anyone who carried a gun was likely capable of pulling the trigger.

"Not this—this wa-water," she mumbled, almost incoherently. The woman's composure, bold and righteous a second ago, faltered under Lance's level stare. In an apparent attempt to appear unshaken, she tilted her head up and steadied her gun.

For reasons Torrie could not yet conceive, the sight of the man had thrown her thoughts into a spin and left her knees trembling like the limbs of a newborn colt. His eyes were haunting and shockingly familiar—a hue of light hazel. A lump formed in her parched throat, and her heart pounded frantically. The short barrel of the shotgun shook in her sweaty palms.

"Does this land still belong to Ben Carrington?" the stranger asked.

Lance's voice was not as controlled as it had been, and he had to draw in a deep breath to still the rapid thudding in his chest. He told himself it was the odd way she was looking at him that affected him in such a disruptive manner, causing him to grow even more annoyed with himself for permitting this female to interfere with his usual common sense.

The woman's mouth opened slightly, but she didn't speak. She swallowed, then attempted to clear her throat, but a weak nod of her head was her only reply. A blush worked its way over her pale complexion.

"If this is Carrington land, then who are you?" Lance asked, assuming a belligerent tone. His gaze raked over the woman with no concern for respectability. He observed the way her black split riding skirt hugged her firm curves in all the right places, how her perfectly formed breasts strained at the material of her white silk blouse, apparent anger causing her breathing to grow fast and heavy. He noticed the way her blush deepened across the silken hollows of her cheeks when she became aware of his intimate inspection. She wore a black, flat-brimmed hat atop long, shiny russet-hued tresses that tumbled over one shoulder of her white blouse. Rebellious tendrils of the same rich red shade framed her face and complemented the gem-tones of her flashing emerald eyes, which she focused with direct clarity on him. Whoever this lovely vixen was, she was a sweet diversion for any man's eyes. His interest in her beauty, however, evaporated the instant she answered his question.

"I'm Ben Carrington's daughter." Torrie straightened her spine and gave her head a defiant toss. His rude manner of trying to distract her attention from his own guilt had not gone unnoticed. Anger sharpened her senses, relieved her disorientation. "Any further questions will be answered with this," she nodded toward the shotgun in her hand. "Now get off this property!"

Her threat was meaningless, but her identity left him dumbfounded. If she was the daughter of Ben Carrington, then the old man was more of a liver-bellied snake than Lance had always thought him to be. A snide grin pulled at the corners of his mouth as he continued to stare at the young woman. Her age, he guessed, had to be at least late teens, maybe older; Carrington must not have wasted any time after he killed his wife and ran his son off eighteen years ago.

"His daughter, huh?" Ignoring her promise to answer his questions with lead, Lance leaned forward, his arms still raised limply at the sides of his head. "Is your mother married to the bas—I mean to Ben Carrington?"

"I warned you," she retorted, placing her forefinger around the trigger of her gun and narrowing one eye as she focused on the sight at

19

the end of the sawed-off barrel.

The intruder stood only a few yards away. There was no chance she would miss at this close range. The shot would bring a cavalcade of help from all directions, since the men who worked for the Grand Mesa patrolled this range twenty-four hours a day. She would shoot him she told herself, if he refused to get off this property.

"You have one more chance, Mister, and consider yourself lucky I'm in such a generous mood today." Still, a bemused twinkle lit his eyes as his gaze held her prisoner for a few seconds longer.

It was apparent to Lance she was flustered and confused. Yet, she was full of fire, and relentless in her determination to guard what she considered her property. He liked those qualities in a woman. His mother had been a strong woman, too, before Ben Carrington broke her spirit.

A part of him felt tempted to tell this redheaded hellcat who he was, but his more obstinate nature guided him. The old man probably hadn't bothered to tell his new family the dark secrets of his past. Lance began to suspect the true reasons he had decided to come back to Colorado.

Though he still longed to reveal his identity, to watch this lovely young girl's haughty expression crumble into disbelief and shock, he figured there would be a better time. The time when Ben Carrington and all those who lived off his avarice would watch their world crumble around them. Now that he was back, Lance figured the time was rapidly approaching.

Chapter Three

"I'm here to see Ben Carrington."

The woman's eyes narrowed at first, her only reaction to his announcement. "There's a road leading to the house. How'd you get way down here by the river?"

Lance grinned again. "I rode in from the south. No need to go all the way around to the road."

An expression of confusion flitted across the woman's face again.

Torrie was certain she had never seen this man before; she'd remember a man like him. Yet, there was something so familiar about him. How was it he seemed to know whose land he was on and precisely where he was headed.

"The south range is fenced," she retorted without thinking. But as soon as the words slipped from her mouth, she drew an immediate conclusion. He wasn't merely trespassing, he was a damned rustler, and a damned thorough one. He had studied the entire ranch. He knew his way around all too well!

Lance saw the change in her expression and sensed she was seriously considering shooting him. She wouldn't succeed though. He could drop her before her finger even began to put pressure on the trigger. He could, but he decided to take the chance her foolish notion would dissolve as quickly as she had conceived it.

"My business is with old man Carrington," he stated with annoyance. He hated to waste time, and standing here letting this stubborn woman hold a gun on him was a considerable waste of his precious time! "Let me be on my way, and I won't have to get rough with you."

The expression of fear, which paled her complexion and widened her green gaze, was so clear to Lance he felt a twisting sense of guilt tighten his chest. His voice had been stern, but he hadn't meant to sound that menacing. Her fearful reaction seemed out of character for a woman who—just moments ago—had been brave enough to draw a gun on a man she thought was trespassing on her land.

Torrie fought to calm the wild thudding of her heart. The man—this stranger—had sounded just like Canon Carrington; the tone of his voice, and even the words were almost the same. . . . "Let me have my way, and I won't have to get rough with you."

From where she stood several yards from the man his eyes appeared to be almost the same pale shade as Canon's, light brown with flecks of green and gold. Without the growth of the brown beard and mustache that framed the lower portion of his face, she wondered if he would look just like Canon too. Her thoughts were spinning too rapidly for her mind to understand who this man might be. Canon Carrington was her worst nightmare, and this man's uncanny resemblance left her completely unnerved.

Still at a loss as to why this woman was behaving so oddly, Lance contemplated making a grab for her gun, which now slanted downward at an awkward angle offering little threat to him if he lunged forward. Before he had made the decision to move, however, the woman seemed to regain some of her composure. She raised the shotgun again, drew in an unsteady breath, and leveled her narrowed gaze to meet his.

"Who are you?" she asked bluntly.

Lance hesitated. His gnawing desire to make his identity known in some grander fashion still clung in his mind. But what did it matter if this young woman knew now? With a nonchalant shrug of his broad shoulders, he answered, "Guess I must be your long lost big brother."

Torrie gasped, but she stood her ground without allowing the gun to waver. This man had to be lying. He was a fool if he thought she was stupid enough to believe his fabrication. Still, he looked so much like Canon—and a moment ago he had even sounded so much like him—that Torrie's thoughts were thrown into complete turmoil.

"I'm the son Ben Carrington ran off over eighteen years ago, but I'd be willing to bet he never told you about me or what he did to my mother. Did he?''

His words rang through Torrie's jumbled mind as she fought to remain in control of her emotions. How was this possible? She searched the deep recesses of her memory, trying to recall the one conversation she could remember when Ben had spoken of his youngest son . . . the one who had been killed years ago. Had he lied about this son's death?

Torrie knew better than anyone the extent of her stepfather's cruelty, and instinctively she sensed this man was telling her the truth, which only served to increase her fear of him. Another Carrington man. A dozen questions crowded her thoughts, but the lump in her throat kept her from speaking.

"Well, I reckon my identity is as much a shock to you as yours was to me." He gave a crude chortle, adding, "It never occurred to me the old man would start himself another family."

"He-he was married to my mother. Ben Carrington is only my stepfather," Torrie said as she raised her eyes to meet his intense gaze once more. Their gazes locked briefly, but the array of emotions in her eyes bespoke something much more intense than Lance could decipher.

A stepdaughter. . . . Had Carrington been a better father to someone else's children than he'd been to his own?

"Well, now that we know who we are, do you reckon you can put down the gun and we can introduce ourselves properly?" Lance lowered his arms, confident she would do the same with her weapon. His instincts proved right.

For an instant after Torrie lowered the gun, she felt a rush of panic and uncertainty. Before she could react though, the man who claimed to be her stepbrother had come forward and extended his hand in a friendly gesture. She glanced at his hand, but made no attempt to shake it.

"I go by the name of Lance Farlo." A crooked smile tugged at his lips. "And you, little sister?" He called her that without thinking, but as the words rolled from his lips, they sounded unnatural. The knowledge she was only his stepsister, not the half sister he had thought she was at first, left him mildly surprised at the overpowering relief he felt. Just as quickly as this thought passed through his head, however, he wondered why he would think it mattered.

"Farlo?" Torrie repeated. She felt a sheen of perspiration form on her brow and between her breasts. She tightened her hand around the shotgun that dangled at her side, but she was too numb to move. Lance Farlo's reputation and impending arrival had been the talk of the entire valley. The gunfighter had gained fame as a cattle detective because of his legendary skill with a gun. The ranchers here in Colorado who had hired the gunman had made no secret of the drastic action they were taking in order to save their land and cattle.

With the crooked grin that seemed to be a permanent part of his personality, Lance added, "Didn't want anything from the old man, not even his name."

Torrie's mouth gaped open as she continued to stare at the gunfighter in disbelief. Why had Ben lied all these years about this son, and what terrible thing must have passed between this man and his father for them both to prefer such a deep web of deception? "You said he ran you off and killed—"

"Listen, little darlin', I'll tell you all about it some day." His expression grew serious as his mischievous grin disappeared. "But now, I've got to tend to business. There's a dead man hanging on a fence down at the south pasture—"

"My God!" Torrie gasped. Will Connor was still missing, and she knew he was the dead man Lance Farlo spoke of now. She had been coming from the Connor house when she encountered Lance Farlo. She could conceive of only one reason why the gunfighter knew where the body was. He must be Will's murderer. Impulsively, she began to swing her sawed-off shotgun back up to take aim at the man again.

Before she had a chance to raise her gun more than an inch or two, Lance reached out and yanked the weapon out of her hand. His patience where this woman was concerned, was exhausted. He had no intention of playing her games of captor and captive.

His swift action left Torrie stunned for an instant, but the stinging sensation that radiated from her empty hand quickly snapped her back to reality. "You killed Will Connor," she spat in a venomous tone. She attempted to step away from the man when she noticed the reaction her accusation had evoked. His anger was evident in

26

the way his narrowed brown eyes flashed inter-mittently with green and gold light as he glared down into her face.

"Damnit, woman! I didn't kill anybody in these parts—yet." His tone of voice left no room for dispute. He stepped forward. Torrie moved back. The distance between them was no more than a foot or two. Though he wasn't sure why this foolish woman aroused such feeling in him, he did know he had given her no reason to be so afraid of him, and her fear only served as fuel for his anger and impatience.

Torrie cringed visibly as the gunman continued to advance towards her. The buckskin mare she had been riding stood several feet away, but it did her no good to think she could make a run for the horse. The man had already proven he moved much faster than she did, and without a gun she stood no chance of getting away from him anyway.

"I don't intend to hurt you, either, if you'll behave yourself." With an aggravated sigh, he glanced at the shotgun he had just taken from her. He had known he would have to confront his father when he waged a war against the Grand Mesa, and he knew he would also have to contend with his older brother, Canon. He was determined nothing would interfere with the justice he sought or the job he had to complete. He was not certain, however, how he would deal with additional complications.

The woman had not made a move to run since he had grabbed her weapon, but it was apparent her only concern was for getting away. Lance suspected his father had the ranch heavily guarded. It was likely only a matter of time before one or more of the ranch hands spotted them here at the river's edge. His plan of surprise would be ruined if the old man learned of his presence before Lance rode up to the house. Now that this woman knew who he was, his only option was to proceed with her. Because her irrational behavior was also affecting him in such a strange way, however, Lance did not relish the idea of being around her any longer than necessary.

"I reckon you're going to have to accompany me up to the main house," Lance stated. "A woman shouldn't be out here alone anyway," he added as though he needed an excuse for his decision. Inwardly, he cursed at himself for sounding as if he were concerned about her safety. She was associated with Ben Carrington, Lance reminded himself. He shouldn't worry about her at all.

Torrie scowled. Somehow she felt less than gratitude for his concern over her well-being. Her stepfather had also warned her not to ride back and forth to Elsa's house alone. But Will and Elsa's house was less than four miles from the main ranch house. Torrie had felt safe going such a short distance, especially since Ben's ranch hands patrolled the area so frequently. A man was stationed to guard the Connors' house around the clock now that Elsa was alone, and Torrie was staying with Elsa to care for the infant and do the household chores. She was headed to the main house this morning to pick up a few of her personal things.

"I can take care of myself," she retorted, then felt a burning sensation creep over her face as the man cocked one eyebrow, smiled, and glanced at her gun, now in his possession.

Lance gave one quick whistle, and an instant later a black horse was at his side. He patted the animal's neck affectionately, then turned back to Torrie.

"Mount up, and don't try anything else. Old Raven can outrun that nag you're ridin' in the blink of an eye, and I don't have any more time to waste playing cat and mouse with you." He swung into a saddle Torrie was sure had to be custom-made. Elaborately carved rosettes and leaves adorned dark brown leather, which was trimmed with heavy black laces. The single letter L was tooled on the matching saddlebags.

Torrie stared up at the striking figure Lance made. Even with an aggravated expression contorting his features, his good-looks were undeniable. His wide-brimmed Stetson topped long, golden brown hair that curled slightly over the collar of his tan bib shirt. Within a rugged and handsome face, his hazel eyes gleamed with power and depth. Sitting straight and tall atop the big stallion, he threw off such an aura of danger and strength that his reputation as the most dangerous gunfighter in the country seemed grossly understated.

Torrie thought of all the talk that had circulated through the area about this man; stories of his deadly gunfights, his unequalled skill with a six-shooter. Unlike many gunfighters, who spoke only with bullets, it was said Farlo was a levelheaded man. He always attempted to reason with his opponents in an effort to avoid a gunfight. Rumor had it he had never killed a man in an unfair shoot-out.

Where there were discussions about Lance Farlo, there was always curiosity about his mysterious past. No one knew where Lance Farlo had come from. He had just appeared in Fort Worth a few years back when a range war had broken out among several wealthy ranchers. The fortunate rancher who hired the young, then unknown gunman soon discovered he had employed more than just another ranch hand.

Word of Farlo's fast draw had spread like wildfire, but also of the man himself. In spite of his unsavory profession, Lance Farlo was said to be an extremely likable man. He had the type of personality that drew men into camaraderie. For most of his employers, his mere presence brought a sense of security and inevitable victory. On more than one occasion, after Farlo had been hired, disputes were settled without gunfire simply because his opponents were intimidated by the man's legendary reputation.

"You never did tell me your name?"

The question jolted Torrie from her thoughts. She pulled herself up in her saddle, leaned over, and rubbed her buckskin's neck as a gesture of solace. When she looked up again, she met the gaze of the handsome gunfighter.

"Victoria," she stated in a brisk tone, withholding the nickname which she preferred with her friends and relatives.

Lance casually tipped the brim of his hat in her direction. Then, without further conversation, he turned his horse in the direction of the main ranch house . . . the house which he had helped his parents build when he was a young boy. He had spent so much time trying to forget his childhood, however, he found he could not remember the interior design of the house. Certain that Victoria Carrington realized she had no choice but to do as he said, Lance dwelled on his old memories and did not bother to look back until she called out to him.

"Wait!" She nudged her mare forward so that she was abreast of his stallion. Ignoring the sidelong scowl he gave her, she began to question him. "You said you found a dead man? Where is he and how was he killed?"

Without slowing his horse, Lance turned toward her again. She sure asked a lot of questions. In his business, he had learned people who asked a lot of questions were usually worried about the answers. "You know somebody who might have deserved to die?" he asked, carefully observing her reaction.

Torrie gave an indignant huff. His question hardly deserved an answer. "One of my stepfather's men is missing, and—"

"Carrington's man?" Lance interrupted with a surprised tone edging into his deep voice. "How long has he been missing?"

Torrie grew more puzzled by the gunman's questions. "Over a week. Why?"

A thoughtful frown drew Lance's heavy brown brows together.

The man Lance had found hanging on the fence had been dead at least a week, probably longer. But if the man worked for his father, it would put a new twist to his theory. He had been certain it would turn out the dead man had worked for one of his employers. For that reason, he had not wanted to remove the body from the barbed wire before the local sheriff had a chance to see how the man had been killed.

"Could be the same man," Lance said, speaking more to himself than to the woman. Victoria groaned—in pain Lance thought. If the dead man was a trusted Carrington hand, then it was possible one of Lance's employers had been involved in the murder. Usually a good judge of character, Lance found this probability disturbing. He tried to make it his practice never to work for a man he sensed was a liar or a cheat. When he met the three ranchers who had hired him, his instincts told him they were honest men.

"Will you take me to the place where you found the man?" Torrie pleaded as she gently kicked Ginger in her sides to keep up with the black stallion.

"No."

His brisk attitude infuriated Torrie, but she had a feeling it would do her no good to argue the issue. Lance Farlo was not the sort of man anyone provoked, whether they were male or female, and Torrie sensed she was already walking on a tightrope where he was concerned. Giving in to defeat, she let her mare fall several steps behind his horse, but her eyes remained glued to the form of the tall gunfighter.

Lance Farlo.

Her mind kept repeating his name.

Ben Carrington's presumedly dead son?

Canon's brother?

How much like his father and brother was this stranger? How much hatred would a man need to take a job where he would have to oppose his own flesh and blood? But most of all, Torrie found herself wondering why she felt as though her entire world was about to undergo a drastic change, and what part would this pale-eyed gunfighter play in that change?

Chapter Four

The first glimpse of the big white house on the mesa affected Lance more profoundly than he had imagined it would. It brought back a rush of memories of his mother, intertwined with ugly recollections of his departure over eighteen years ago. Though he tried to hide his lack of composure from the woman who rode with him, it was difficult for Lance to keep his emotions controlled. He was thirty-one years old, and for the first time since his mother had died almost twenty years earlier, he felt an overwhelming urge to cry. But, grown men weren't supposed to cry, he reminded himself; they evened out the score.

Torrie had remained behind the man as they traveled from the river, and she had no doubt he knew exactly where he was going. His route cut a straight path directly to the main entrance which led up the mesa where the house had been built, but his reaction to seeing the house increased her already immense curiosity about his relationship with his family. His expression was an odd mixture of sorrow and animosity, which evoked in Torrie a profusion of sympathy and fear.

"We had heard you were coming—heard about Lance Farlo, I mean, but I don't think Ben knows you're his son," Torrie said. She recalled hearing her stepfather speak about the gunman who had been hired by the men he accused of squatting on his land. Contrary to his usual undaunted self-confidence, Ben had seemed worried. Gage and Canon, however, acted as though the arrival of the famed gunfighter would be their chance to prove themselves. Torrie cringed inwardly at the thought of two brothers facing one another in a gun battle.

A crude chuckle rang out as Lance's hazel eyes drew into narrow slits. "I hope not. That would spoil my surprise." He turned and met Torrie's emerald gaze with his piercing stare.

A shiver raced down Torrie's spine. She was held prisoner once again by those luminous, mesmerizing eyes. Despite her fear of him, Torrie felt an unexplainable affinity with the man. She wondered if it was because there was no love lost between her and Ben Carrington.

From the spot where they stopped to observe the house, Lance carefully surveyed the surrounding area. From his saddlebags, he pulled out a pair of shielded binoculars so he could thoroughly scan all the outbuildings and the road leading up to the big house. Through the glasses, Lance spotted two men posted as guards along the roadway. He had figured he would have to sneak into the house, but now that he had Victoria, he decided it would be easier.

"Those men," he motioned toward the road. "You'll have to convince them I'm a friend of yours."

"They'd never believe that," Victoria huffed. She tossed her head back in a defiant manner. Her long copper-colored ponytail flew wildly over her shoulder with the brisk movement.

Lance smiled. "Why? Don't you have any friends?"

"Not the likes of your kind." Torrie hoped her tone was more confident than the mixed feelings she felt inside.

He feigned a hurt expression, but his eyes told a different story that bespoke total indifference to her lack of manners. "Are you insinuating I'm not good enough to be in your company, or do you mean you have no gentlemen friends?" His flashing brown gaze raked brazenly over her again.

Much to his aggravation, the thought passed through his mind again how relieved he was she was not his blood sister. But what did that matter?

He didn't have time for women, not for decent women anyway. Whenever he got a hankerin', he satisfied his needs with women commonly referred to as soiled doves. They represented female companionship without commitment or complications, and to Lance that was the perfect relationship. . . . It was the only kind of relationship for a man like him.

"Your first assumption was correct." Her lips

37

pursed in a pout, but her eyes glistened with sparks of anger.

Her lips were sensual, full, but not too full, Lance noticed. Lips meant to receive a man's kisses. Damnit! Lance growled inwardly.

Forcing his thoughts to focus on the business at hand, Lance turned his attention back to the house. "How many people are in the house at this time of day?"

Torrie shrugged. Why should she help him? He was, after all, hired by the men who were probably responsible for Will Connor's murder. Until Will's disappearance, Torrie had been torn with doubt about the feud brewing between her family and the adjoining ranchers. Ben Carrington claimed he owned the land where the three neighboring ranches had sprung up recently. The ranchers—Jim Larson, Shawn McLeary, and Wayne Gere—said their land was bought and paid for legally from the state of Colorado.

Ben Carrington, however, insisted he had homesteaded those areas two and a half decades ago. He said under the Homestead Act of 1862 the land belonged to him. Years ago, when the Homestead Act first went into effect, scores of men traveled to remote areas west of the Mississippi River to put down their claim on public domain lands, which could be bought for the ten dollars it cost for a filing fee. However, many of those same men had failed to file the necessary documents to clearly define their property boundaries. This had sparked more than one range war where property

38

lines were at debate. This was the major issue here in Mesa and Garfield Counties.

Lance imitated the woman's uncaring gesture and gave his broad shoulders a shrug. Her co-operation would make his entry less compli-cated, but since she was determined to be obstinate, he would have to make certain she didn't ruin his surprise. He dismounted, then tucked his binocu-lars back into the saddlebags. When he pulled his hand back out, he held a spool of thin rope. He turned around to face her.

"Get on down here, then," he ordered.

"What—why?" Terror threatened to suffocate her. The hanging of Leo MacFarlene was the thought in her head as she stared in horror at this man unwinding a long length of rope. She thought of making an attempt to get away, but common sense told her that would be a wasted effort. The man was standing close enough to reach out and grab her horse before the little filly could take a step.

"Please," she pleaded. "Don't—"

The desperate tone of her voice caused Lance to pause and glance in her direction. She was the most skittish female he had ever encountered, and at this moment she was acting as if she thought he was going to dangle her from the nearest tree. "I'm just goin' to see to it you don't interfere with my plans," Lance said as he held his hand up to help her down from the mare. "I'll come back to untie you after I've seen the old man."

When she made no move to dismount, Lance reached up and grabbed her by the wrist. He wanted to get the first confrontation with his father over with, so he would know how to proceed with the rest of his business.

Torrie stifled a gasp, and did not fight against him as he pulled her down from her horse. The stories about this man, along with the knowledge of who he really was, left her numb with fright. As she dropped to the ground, her body slid against his taut body. A new sensation united with her fear; her blood raced like quicksilver through her veins, and her heart fluttered in her chest.

The shape and the hue of his eyes were similar to Canon's but this close, she realized that was where the similarity between the two brothers ended. In Lance Farlo's expression she saw a cold detachment she felt was likely a result of his profession, but the cruelty that shone in Canon's eyes was absent. More than wariness and fear, there was a tense excitement coursing through her body as she stared up at Lance.

"I-I'll do as you asked of m-me," Torrie said in a hoarse whisper. His grasp on her wrist grew tighter. She felt the heat from his body warm her skin. At this moment, she knew he could ask her to ride off the edge of a cliff and she would obey.

He barely nodded his head, but a fire burned through his tense body. Since he had been banished from the Grand Mesa years ago, he had erected a strong barricade around his emotions. He allowed himself to feel only what was necessary to

40

keep him from being hurt and to prevent himself from hurting others who did not deserve pain. Now though, the more tender emotions he had managed to keep under such tight rein for all these years entangled with a barrage of other feelings and desires. He continued to stare down at the woman who stood so close—yet, not close enough. He wanted her soft, voluptuous curves crushed up against his own hard body, needed to feel his mouth pressed against her soft, pale pink lips that were still too far away. . . . But this could never happen. He had but one thing to offer a woman like Victoria Carrington, and he knew she deserved more than heartache.

Without permitting himself to dwell on the lascivious thoughts that had raged through him for the past few minutes, Lance dropped her arm and stepped back. He cleared his throat, but could not clear his mind completely of taking ahold of her again, of pulling her close to him.

"You'll cooperate?" His voice sounded strangely distant to his ears. The rope he held in one hand hung in a tangle from the spool and accumulated in a heap of coils on the hard ground. He felt a fevered heat inch through his body as she slowly nodded her head. His eyes were drawn to the shimmering mass of flame red hair that tumbled over her shoulder. He imagined what it would be like to run his fingers through that silken cascade. His fingers itched with yearning. He battled within himself to keep from acting upon the urges this beautiful young woman had brought to the

41

boiling point. As he struggled, he realized what it was that drew him so strongly to her, and it was not just her physical appeal—though God knew that was quite enough. It was a quality, rather qualities he sensed in her. Vulnerability and passion. And he felt kinship with her, not of family, but of will.

When Torrie drew in a deep breath, the entire length of her body trembled. The only thing that kept her from being reduced to a shivering mass of confusion, was that Lance had finally pulled his piercing gaze away from her face.

"Well," Lance said, his voice a bit breathy, "let's get going, then." He looked down at the mess of rope he held in his hand, grunted with disgust and tossed the spool into the sagebrush. He'd better get his head clear before he was completely incompetent to do his job.

He mounted his horse, then gave a sideways glance at Torrie as she climbed back up into her saddle. He took the sawed-off shotgun he had confiscated from her earlier and handed it back to her as his horse walked past her mare. He attempted not to look at her face, he did not want to take the chance of meeting her eyes again. Another episode like the one he had just experienced might well mean the loss of what little control he had left.

Torrie reached out tentatively. When he shoved the weapon into her hand, she had no choice but to grasp ahold of the gun butt. She looked to him for an explanation, but he did not even glance in her direction as he mumbled in a gruff voice, "It'd look suspicious if you didn't have your gun."

Lance kicked Raven gently and flicked the reins. The big stallion reared his head back in what Lance considered a proud gesture. He loosed his hold on the reins, letting Raven free to gallop across the sagebrush flats. The stallion was massive in stature, his legs powerfully muscled. Not a single discoloration marred his sleek ebony coat or sweeping black mane and tail. His elegantly shaped face, however, was marked with a gleaming white blaze, which started between his eyes and ran down the length of his nose. Lance had named him Raven, but on occasion would affectionately refer to him as Blacky. The horse responded to any name Lance called him, and Lance's whistle would draw him as swiftly as an arrow. Lance knew the years of training had made Raven a horse that would be the envy of any horseman or woman, but Lance also knew Raven was devoted to one man, and his precise training was geared to the profession of his owner.

Ginger, the little mare Torrie rode, was one of many seasoned old ranch horses who were pastured at the Grand Mesa. She had not permitted herself to become too attached to anything on this ranch, and now that her mother was dead, she became more detached from this place with each passing day. Still, it was usually this horse Torrie saddled when she went riding. Ginger had to trot at a fast pace in order to keep up with the easy gait of the stallion, but once they reached the narrow road that led to the house, Lance let his horse's steps slow so she was able to catch up.

Torrie had no idea what he expected of her once they reached the guards, but she figured he must trust her not to betray him. If her father's men suspected he was Lance Farlo, they would never allow him on this property. As they approached the two men who stood sentry for the house, Torrie's mind spun with uncertainty. What if she couldn't pull this off? Someone was bound to be killed, and she suspected it would not be the man who rode at her side.

"Whoa there, Miss Torrie," a burly man in his late fifties called out as the riders drew near. He squinted his eyes in the morning sun as he stepped into the middle of the road. "I thought you were staying at the Connors'?"

"That's right, but I met up with an—an old friend," she said, her words almost too fast. She forced a broad smile, then glanced at Lance with a nervous flutter of her thick auburn lashes. "An old friend of the family." Her mind groped for a false name so she could introduce the man to the ranch hands, but before she could conjure up anything, Lance began to speak.

"Name's Larry," he said with a lopsided grin. He tipped the brim of his Stetson in a gesture of greeting. His posture in the saddle had become a casual slump, as though he didn't have a care or worry in the world.

Neither of the ranch hands made the effort to

44

introduce themselves to the stranger. Instead, they scrutinized the custom-made holsters tied on each of the man's muscled thighs, his fancy mono-grammed saddle gear, and mostly, the man himself.

Stuttering with fear, Torrie attempted to ease the nerve-racking situation. "L-Larry, this here is Mac Williams," she motioned toward the big man who stood in the middle of the road, then to where the other man stood at his side, "and that's Kenny Bower."

Another deafening silence followed. Torrie's worry increased. "We're headed to the house to visit with Ben," she quickly added.

Mac Williams' eyes moved back and forth between the stranger and Torrie, distrust obvious on his unshaven face. Kenny Bower, the younger of the two men, made no movement, waiting for Williams' decision. After a moment, which seemed to drag on for much longer, Mac stepped to the side and motioned for the riders to pass by. When Kenny came forward, his mouth gaping open to protest, Mac gestured for him to stay put.

Lance noted the weapons each man carried as he passed them by. Like him, they wore Colt pistols at their hips, and on the two horses tied to an nearby cedar, hung 30-06 rifles. These were not ordinary cowboys or mere ranch hands, Lance determined. They, too, were hired gunmen.

Out of earshot from the two men, Torrie sighed heavily and glanced in Lance's direction with a look of relief. "I thought they weren't going to believe us for a second back there.''

Lance kept his eyes straight ahead, but every fiber of his body was alert to the movements behind him. ''They didn't,'' he said in a low voice. Without looking back, he knew the men were following them.

Lacking his discipline, Torrie gasped and turned around. ''They're—''

''I know,'' he interrupted. ''Act natural.'' His command was simple, but there was no denying the seriousness of his words.

As her body jerked around toward the front again, Torrie fought back the rising panic that contorted her insides into knots. ''What should we do?''

Lance was vaguely aware of the honest concern in her voice. She acted as if she was worried about what would happen to him, when in reality, Lance was certain, she probably hoped he would be shot down before they reached the house. He had no time now, however, to dwell on the woman's feelings.

''How many people will be in the house?'' he asked, repeating the question she had refused to answer once before.

Without hesitation she replied, ''Just Ben. Canon and Gage went into town early this morning.''

''Gage?'' Lance asked as he turned in her direction. The two men who followed them up the slope were closer now. He had glimpsed them out of the side of his eye when he looked at the woman.

Unless the gunmen decided to shoot him in the back and take the chance of hitting the woman, too, Lance was confident they would make it to the house without further incident.

Torrie forced herself not to look back again, but it was a difficult task. "Gage is my older brother. Ben adopted us when our mother married him." Her mind drew up the image of the short, stocky redheaded man, more a stranger than her brother lately. When her mother had first married Ben Carrington eleven years ago, she and Gage had still been close to one another. After they had been adopted, however, Gage became a Carrington progeny. His relationship with both their mother and her became distant and strained.

It was not necessary for Lance to ask the woman any questions about her brother; her voice told him all he needed to know. He suspected Gage was someone to be wary of, someone who would undoubtedly side with the old man. As they reached the flat expanse on the top of the mesa, Lance glanced out at the panoramic view of the land below.

From the plateau where the house had been built, nearly the entire floor of the valley was visible. In his vast travels since he had left this part of the country, there had been times when he had wondered why his father had chosen to settle here when there were areas in Colorado that were much more pleasing to the eye. But, looking out from this high mesa today, Lance understood why Ben Carrington had decided on this location.

47

The rushing waters of the Colorado River wound through the center of the valley like a wide ribbon of the darkest green shaded by wide-reaching branches of the cottonwood trees. On either side of the river, the land spread out in endless meadows of sage, cedars, and range grasses, broken only by the rise of the stone mesas and brush covered plateaus. Unlike the snowy ranges of the distant mountains to the east and north, this was ideal cattle country. As Lance surveyed the land, he realized that from here, his father would also have the ideal fortress if a full-blown range war did break out between the Grand Mesa Ranch and its neighbors.

Chapter Five

A long hitching post of rough-strewn logs ran along the front of the fence that skirted the house. As Torrie and Lance tied their horses' reins to the post, Lance glanced over his shoulder to check on the location of the two men who had followed them up the road. The men had stopped at the top of the ridge. They watched, but they made no attempt to keep Victoria and Lance from entering the house.

Walking through the gate and up the walkway, Lance felt as though he was strangling on memories of his childhood. Although he had not been able to recall what the house had looked like earlier, he now remembered every minute detail of the large ten room house, all on one ground floor in a huge L-shape around an open courtyard at the center of the large rooms. The entire family had worked like slaves to help build the elaborate ranch house, but the old man had never been satisfied, no matter how hard they had tried to please him.

As they reached the front porch, Lance halted to exhale the breath he had been holding since they had started through the gate.

When Torrie saw the pained expression on his face, she was overcome once more with curiosity about this man's life here at the Grand Mesa. She longed to know what had happened in this house all those years ago, but she suspected whatever it was, Lance Farlo had no intention of discussing his past—or anything else—with her.

He acted as though he could not stand to have her near him. There was little hope he would take her into his confidence. Fortunately for her, though, he had trusted her enough to dismiss his horrible plan to tie her up and leave her out on the range while he came up to the ranch house.

At the front door, a fleeting thought broke into his unhappy recollections of the years he had spent on the Grand Mesa. Lance swung around to face Torrie. "You told me your name was Victoria." He motioned toward the men who still sat atop their horses at the edge of the plateau. "That fella didn't call you Victoria."

"My friends and family call me Torrie, the ranch hands call me Miss Torrie," she answered.

"Reckon I should call you Victoria then." He had meant for his comment to lighten the tense situation, but as soon as he spoke, he realized she did not appreciate his humor. She did not even bother to reply as she shoved the front door open and stomped into the house. The look of wrath she cast over her shoulder spoke louder than words.

Her name was the least of his problems, Lance reminded himself as he followed her into the house, but the instant he was inside he stopped dead in his tracks.

Since leaving the Red River country last week, he had envisioned his first confrontation with his father over and over again in his mind. He thought he would feel pleasure when the old man realized who he had become. The look Lance expected to see on his father's face would be a part of the justice he sought.

Now though, he was cowering in the entry hall like the scared young boy he had been on the day his father ordered him to leave and never come back. He was in such a state of distress he was hardly aware Torrie had disappeared into one of the rooms.

Ben's stepdaughter had merely told him he had a visitor. When Ben had asked her who, she had said that he'd better see for himself. Her actions puzzled him, especially since he knew there were guards posted at strategic locations all over the ranch and only welcome visitors would be able to get past the lookouts.

Finally, he dismissed her odd behavior. Torrie was, in Ben's thinking, an obligation he would rather be without. Unfortunately, she'd been a part of the package when he married his second wife. After her mother had died, he'd hoped she would decide to go back to Denver where she and her brother had been born. They had lived in the city until he had married their mother and brought them all to his ranch here in western Colorado.

But then Elsa Connor had come to live at the Grand Mesa. The two young women had become close friends. Now, however, the Connor woman would probably be leaving soon, and with any luck, Torrie would go with her.

Expecting his visitor to be the sheriff from the nearby town of Rifle with word on Will Connor, Ben casually sauntered out of his office.

He froze in his tracks when he saw a stranger standing in the foyer. Ben focused on the pearl-handled guns the man wore low on his hips. His hired men never would have let an armed stranger pass by them. This man's appearance here at the house could only mean trouble.

Lance snapped out of his trance when the man he had traveled all this way to see stepped through the doorway Torrie had just entered.

"Who are you?" Ben demanded, his hand falling to the top of the holster he wore at his hips.

Lance looked into his father's eyes, brown eyes staring out starkly from beneath thick gray brows and a head of pure white hair. A huge, handlebar mustache in the same alabaster shade, drooped over his mouth, then stuck out from his chin on both sides in two stiff peaks which curled upward on the edges. His garb was that of a man who no longer had to work outside in the rough elements for his living—wearing a starched white shirt, black suede vest, black bolo tie, black jeans, and polished boots free of dust or scrapes. Ben Carrington was every inch the image of a gentleman rancher.

He was at least twenty pounds heavier than Lance remembered, but a big man who stood every inch as tall as his son, the extra pounds did not make him look overweight. The grayness of his hair was the biggest shock to Lance. His father's hair had been dark brown when he was younger.

Lance was speechless for a second. He had rehearsed this scene many times as he had traveled back to Colorado, but now he couldn't think of anything to say other than, "I'm Lance."

Ben Carrington's complexion grew noticeably pale. "Lance Farlo?" he said in a hoarse voice. His hand moved quickly away from his gun.

Ben's draw was fast, but he knew he would be no match for the famed gunman. A dozen thoughts spun through his mind. He wondered if the gunfighter had killed his guards in order to make it up here to the house? Had he used Torrie as a hostage? Was that why she had been acting more strange than usual? Or had the squatters who hired him instructed the gunman to come to his house and murder him in cold blood? Before Ben could ask any of these questions, or gather his wits about him, the other man answered Ben's first question.

"Lance Farlo—Lance Carrington—I'm one in the same." The stricken expression on his father's face was exactly as Lance had always hoped it would be when they met again. Ben's obvious shock caused his pallor to grow even more pasty. Beneath his heavy mustache, his mouth opened and closed, but no sound escaped. Lance savored every second he witnessed his father's speechless discomfort. He tried to imagine the thoughts that must be raging through the old man's head.

"That's not possible," Ben said in a gruff voice. It had never occurred to him that his own son Lance could be one in the same with Lance Farlo, the gunfighter.

Though it had not been proven, Ben had heard years ago that his youngest son died at sea, when the ship he had hired onto as a cabin boy sank somewhere in the South Pacific.

Ben studied the younger man's face for a clue to the man's true identity; his search revealed what he didn't want to know. As soon as he looked into the man's brown-green eyes, he knew that his second son had returned. "I'd thought—"

Lance felt a crooked grin lift his mouth. "That I was dead." A humorless chuckle escaped from Lance as the old man's admission added to his own sense of victory.

When he was fifteen, a tragic accident had sunk the ship Lance was working on, but he had survived, along with several others from the ship's crew. He had found his way back to America, where he had met up with an old Texas ranger named Robert Farlo. The aging ranger had taken the young man under his wing, taught him how to handle a gun, and most importantly, had been the father Lance had never had in Ben Carrington. When Robert died, Lance inherited his land on the Red River, and assumed his last name, in tribute to the man whom he had grown to idolize.

Ben licked his dry lips. He glanced toward the front door, wondering why none of his men were coming to his aid. When he looked back to his son, he saw a dangerous-looking glimmer in Lance's gaze.

"You thought I must be dead," Lance said, his teeth gritted, his voice hissing with barely contained fury. "Or else I would have come crawlin' back here, isn't that right?"

Ben shrugged and looked down at the shiny wood planks of the floor. "You were such a coward, a little weakling, when you left. I never thought you'd survive if you didn't come back right away. Then we heard you had been killed at sea."

Ben looked up again. "And after all this time, I figured even if you had survived the shipwreck, you'd never have the guts to show your face around here again." His attention was once more drawn to the low-slung guns. The boy who had left here nearly two decades ago was now a man . . . and a far cry from the sniveling little whelp he had once been.

"So now you've come to claim what you think is yours," Ben spat in a cruel voice.

"On the contrary, I've come to see to it you don't claim what doesn't belong to you. I don't want anything from you, but I don't intend to let your greed ruin anymore lives."

With a crude huff, Ben said, "You're still fighting for the wrong side, Boy. You picked the losing side last time, and you're making the same mistake again."

A nonchalant shrug shook Lance's shoulders as his mouth curled into a thin smile. "Everyone will get what they finally deserve." He knew Ben Carrington was aware of his unspoken meaning.

"I came here today only as a warning—to you and to everyone who works for you," Lance said, his scarred emotions contained for the moment, his attitude strictly business. "I've been hired by Wayne Gere, Shawn McLeary, and Jim Larson to help protect their land and cattle."

Ben Carrington straightened his slumping form. Anger colored his face. "Like I said, Boy, you're fightin' for a lost cause—for three of 'em. There's no way that bunch of squatters can beat me."

"Maybe they couldn't on their own, but now they have me," he said with an aura of confidence that sent a cold shiver traipsing through Ben's bones.

Lance stepped forward, but still kept a good distance between himself and his father as he added, "So back off, Old Man, because this time you're not gonna make me go away." His voice had barely risen above a whisper. Then, as calmly as if he were on a Sunday stroll, he turned and walked out the front door, his gait slow, swaggering.

Outside, he wished he could stop long enough to calm the frantic pounding in his chest, but he didn't dare chance staying here one minute longer than necessary. As he walked toward the front gate and the hitching post where he had left his horse, he decided coming here today had been one of the most difficult tasks he had ever faced. Still, meeting his father again had gone just as he had

56

always hoped. Lance never wanted to forget the way the old man had looked when he issued his last warning before turning to leave. Ben Carrington had been more than just a little worried. He had been downright scared!

Though his mind was savoring the image of his father's ghastly white face and wide-eyed look of fear, Lance forced himself to concentrate on his next plan of action. The two men who had followed him and Victoria to the top of the mesa were nowhere in sight, but Lance knew they were close by, watching his every move.

Approaching the hitching post, Lance cautiously glanced around at the surrounding buildings—two large barns, several storage sheds, and a couple of bunkhouses for the hired hands. There was no movement anywhere. In fact, it was unnaturally quiet. Men he faced in a fair fight were little threat to Lance, but he knew those who hid in shadows were capable of shooting a man in the back.

While Lance pondered over his precarious situation, he failed to notice that someone waited at the hitching post for him. He was surprised, puzzled when he spotted her. Though he had no idea what she was up to, his first thought was for her safety. Before he had the opportunity to voice his concern, she began to untie her horse's reins.

"I'm riding out with you," she said, her voice as determined as the expression on her pretty face. "You'd never make it alone." She swung up into her saddle, then set her emerald gaze on him with a look of impatience.

Lance quickly pulled his reins from the post and mounted his horse. It was possible he might need her help, but her reasons for helping him worried him almost as much as the enemies he could not see. Was she trying to lead him into a trap?

"Why should you care what happens to me?" He watched her closely for any indication of what she was up to. The worried expression, which clouded her pretty face, only confused him more.

Torrie did not even understand her own reasons for wanting to help this infuriating man. How could she explain them to him? She didn't care about him, she tried to tell herself. Maybe it was just because he had information she wanted, at least that was an explanation that made some sense.

"You said you found a dead man. I want you to take me to him."

Her request surprised Lance. Why was she so darned interested in his discovery of a dead man? Movement from the doorway of the barn caught his eye. The shiny barrel of a rifle disappeared from view. She would offer some assurance if she rode out with him. Surely none of Ben's men would take a shot at him if she was riding beside him. But even as the thought passed through his mind, Lance felt a tremor of anticipation shoot through his veins at the idea of being in her presence for a while longer. Damnit! He didn't have time for those kinds of thoughts!

"If seeing a dead man is that important to you, then come on." Lance gave his head a slight toss in the direction of the barn. "But I should warn you, there's liable to be some trouble."

A knowing expression crossed Torrie's face; she'd seen two of Ben's men enter the barn, two more sneaking up to the side of the house. Still, she was certain none of them would shoot as long as she was in their range. At least, she hoped so. "I've been on the Grand Mesa for eleven years." Her gaze darkened as if some buried pain had risen to the surface of her mind. "I'm used to trouble, Mr. Farlo."

"Let's ride then," Lance said, his gaze meeting hers for an instant. He saw the strange look filter through her deep green gaze. He wondered once more what secret torment those beautiful eyes cradled within their jeweled depths. Perhaps it would be better if he never knew, because if he knew too much about this woman, he might begin to care . . . might begin to think more about her than the job he had come here to do. Women and guns didn't mix well, and usually resulted in a man's downfall and a woman's tears.

Chapter Six

Lance rode beside Torrie down the steep road, but his brooding silence and grim expression made her wonder what had happened between him and his father. From the room where she had retreated, she had tried to listen to the exchange between the two men. They had kept their voices low though, and she had not been able to hear a word.

"Are we being followed?" Torrie asked when she noticed Lance glance back over his shoulder several times as they approached the base of the mesa.

Lance turned back in his saddle and stared at the road in front of them. "The same men who were guarding the road when we came in are following us again. But they seem to be keepin' their distance. I could lose them, but—" He glanced at her buckskin with a look of annoyance.

"There's nothing wrong with this horse," she retorted. She pretended to ignore his snide chuckle.

61

His obvious contempt towards Ginger was beginning to make her feel protective and defensive towards the mare. She realized that compared to his stallion, her little horse was quite ordinary, but it was no reason for his insolent attitude. She figured he was just using the horse as an excuse, but she was not leaving his side until he showed her where he had discovered the dead man.

She thought once again of Elsa and the week-old baby named William after his father. Although they had avoided the subject of Will's fate for the past couple of days, it was apparent to Torrie that Elsa was beginning to resign herself to the fact that her husband would not return. As long as his body had not been discovered, however, Elsa could still cling to a thin thread of hope Will Connor might still be a live. Torrie hoped Elsa was strong enough to handle the truth.

"Where are you going?" she asked when she realized they were headed toward the main entrance to the ranch rather than to the south range where he claimed to have found the body.

Lance tossed his head back toward the two men behind them as he spoke, "I don't intend to lead them to my discovery until I've done some investigating on my own." His eyes narrowed and one brow lifted suspiciously. "I shouldn't take anybody out there except the sheriff."

"My friend Elsa had a baby last week, three days after her husband, Will, disappeared," Torrie began in an angry tone. "Everyday, I watch her suffer, and everyday I look at that tiny baby boy wondering what happened to his father." Her voice retained a controlled pitch. "Elsa and that boy deserve to know if the man you found is Will Connor. If you refuse to take me to him, then I'll find him myself." Her expression of determination, the tone of her voice, left no doubt in Lance's mind she intended to do just as she had said.

Lance shrugged as if he were unaffected by her words, then turned away from her, consumed by a flood of emotions again. Her dauntless spirit and courage continued to impress him, and her devotion to her friend surprised him. Considering she had spent eleven years on this ranch, obviously none of Ben Carrington's coldhearted selfishness had rubbed off on her during that time.

Lance's jumble of feelings toward her was becoming more of a problem with every moment they spent together. He was infatuated with her pale, delicate beauty. Her long straight red hair still seemed to beckon for his touch, and he was almost always thinking of kissing those rosebud lips when he should be concentrating on just staying alive. So far, he had not done much to earn his pay, and the longer he was in this woman's presence, the harder it was to keep his mind on his business.

"Your friend's husband?" he said, trying once again to force his thoughts clear of images of taking this redheaded vixen into his arms. "You said he worked for Ben?"

Torrie nodded her head. "He's worked here longer than anybody else has stayed around, nearly ten years." She spoke as if she were surprised that someone could tolerate the old man for that long. "I guess that's why Ben let him and his wife build a house down by the river after they were married last year. Of course, Ben never lets anyone forget that it's his house, built on his land."

"Of course," Lance spat, his voice as cold as the expression on his whiskered face.

Lance stole a quick glance over his shoulder and noticed his father's hired gunmen were closing in the gap. "They'll never let us out of their sight as long as we're riding together. No doubt they think you're in danger as long as you're with me."

"I rode in with you, and they saw me leave with you on my own free will," she said defensively. Reaching up to wipe away a thin band of perspiration that coated her upper lip, Torrie realized how hot the autumn sun had become as the morning eased into afternoon. She glanced at Lance and noticed little beads of sweat on the tanned skin above his brown mustache and beard.

The pit of her stomach quivered with a sudden spasm of anxiety when she thought about all the repercussions that would most likely result from her association with the gunfighter. She knew she should be terrified of Ben's retaliation, and also of Gage and Canon's reaction when they learned she had been riding with the man who was their enemy in more ways than just the land dispute.

But the other unexpected feeling that had taken complete control of her emotions and made her blood burn like molten lava through her veins was not associated with the fear of being bullied and abused—she knew that type of fear all too well—

and Lance Farlo no longer scared her in the way that she had come to fear the Carrington men.

The shiver that had been only in the core of her stomach a moment ago, now radiated throughout her whole body when she chanced another quick look in Lance's direction. What she was experiencing, she realized at this moment, was a sense of dangerous excitement that his nearness aroused in her, and it was intermingled with developing feelings she knew she should be afraid of almost as much as the three men who would be waiting for her when she returned home.

"I appreciate your riding out with me. Up there at the house, I was a bit outnumbered," Lance blurted out unexpectedly, then immediately a tone of confidence edged into his voice as he added, "But those two men back there don't scare me much."

The woman, he noticed, looked over at his guns with a nervous glance. He was not always proud of his chosen profession, but the bit of recognition he had achieved because of his fast draw was his only claim to glory. Someday, there would come a man who was faster—or luckier. When that day came, Lance hoped people would remember and respect him as one of the fastest gunfighters in the west. Maybe they would even think of him as a fair and decent man.

But deep down inside, he knew there would be many who would recall the name of Lance Farlo as no more than a killer who was paid to play god with his guns.

Even today, he had made a feeble attempt to

avert a range war by making a personal visit to Ben Carrington. Lance had forewarned him, which was more than most cattle detectives would have done. But there was much more at stake this time, and when Lance finished with his business in these parts, he wanted to be able to ride away with a clear conscience . . . and an old debt paid.

Now that his father was aware of his presence, Lance knew he could not afford to waste anymore time. Nor could he permit himself to be distracted by Victoria.

"We're going to have to separate at the main gate and meet—"

"Do you really think I'm so stupid as to believe you'll meet me again once we part?"

Lance gave an aggravated grunt. Was she always so distrustful? "Well, I reckon you're goin' have to trust me if you want me to lead you to the body." He gave a careless shrug, "But you could ride on down to the south range and spend the rest of the day lookin' for yourself if you'd rather. Makes little difference to me." He noticed the way her lips puckered. . . . Damn, but those were kissable lips.

Keep your mind on business, Farlo! he reminded himself.

Although she sensed there was no arguing with this man once he had set his mind to something, and even though she knew he was right about the men who were following them, Torrie hated to agree with him. She had no choice but to trust him. "I'll try to detain them while you ride ahead," she said, motioning over her shoulder toward the two riders. "Where will we meet?"

66

Surprised by her sudden compliance, Lance took a moment to respond. He squinted his eyes toward the hot sun overhead, then glanced back at the woman. "It's about noon now. I'm headed down to the south range from here, you come as soon as you're able. If you're not there by mid-afternoon, I'm ridin' into town to get the sheriff."

"Wait," she called out in panic. "How will I know where to find you? The south range is enormous."

"I'll find you," he said. He tipped the brim of his hat in a casual gesture before sending his horse into a fast gallop, engulfing Torrie in a cloud of dust.

He was long gone before Mac Williams and Kenny Bower had a chance to catch up to where Torrie had stopped.

"Should we go after him?" Kenny asked the older man as they halted beside Torrie and stared after the trail of stirred-up dust left by the big stallion's hooves.

Mac Williams drew in a worried breath as he debated the situation. Then turning towards Torrie, he asked, "Were you his hostage? Did he threaten or hurt you in any way?"

Torrie gave her head a negative shake.

The aging gunslinger's concern for her was apparent to Torrie even in his angered and flustered state. He had been hired by Ben Carrington because he was good with a gun. Unlike the other gunmen who had been hired to protect the Grand Mesa, Mac Williams had made a real effort to befriend Torrie when he had noticed the way the rest of the men leered and made degrading advances whenever she was near.

Mac liked this little lady. Life dealt her a low blow when she had got stuck on this remote ranch. Mac had realized at once that her aloof attitude toward men had to do with the strained relationships she had with her own brother, stepfather, and stepbrother.

"Then why in the devil were you ridin' with the likes of him? Do you know who he is?" Mac asked in a tone that conveyed his worry for the woman's safety.

"Lance Farlo," Torrie replied with a faraway gaze that still followed the tiny ridge of dust, barely visible now. Her only thought was to rid herself of these two men so she could be with him again.

Both Kenny and Mac turned stunned faces toward Torrie when she said the gunfighter's name with such a strange calmness in her voice.

"You knew who he was when you rode in with him, and you let him get away with lying to us?" Kenny Bower asked in disbelief. The famed gunman's arrival had been anticipated with dread, and none of the men who worked on the Grand Mesa had spoken of anything else for the past couple of weeks. Extra guards had been posted all over the ranch as a precaution against a sneak attack on the ranch once the gunman reached the area. The last thing Carrington's men had been expecting was for Lance Farlo to be personally escorted up the road by their boss's stepdaughter, a twist that left the young gunslinger as angry as he was shocked.

"Miss Torrie had her reasons for helping the gunman," Mac said. The older man glanced at Torrie with a look that suggested he knew something no one else suspected. "And no harm was done, so instead of attacking Miss Torrie, I think we should concentrate on the fact we now know Farlo's here. Things are goin' to start heatin' up and we'd better be prepared."

Torrie drew in a relieved breath and smiled gratefully at Mac. She never knew quite how to reciprocate the man's kindness, especially since most of the men who had been hired lately were as crude and disgusting as the three men she lived with in the main house. Mac Williams had seemed different right from the start, just as Lance Farlo seemed different from any of the men she had ever met before.

"I'm going to Elsa Connor's now," she said to Mac in a voice that sounded a bit too enthusiastic, even to her own ears. She forced herself not to look in the direction Lance Farlo had just ridden, but she was unable to prevent the hot flush that she felt rise up in her cheeks again. Good grief! What was that man doing to her?

"Not alone," Kenny Bower said. His voice held a snide innuendo. His gaze traveled up and down the length of Torrie's body in a brazen manner. "I'll ride with you—just to make sure you get there without any more delays." A cruel smile cracked his tanned, rough face, and caused an icy gleam to flash in his grey eyes.

A chill whipped through Torrie's veins as she

met the man's leering eyes. "That's not necessary," she said quickly.

"I think it is," Kenny added with a chuckle. He stared at her with a look that did nothing to hide the unsavory thoughts accumulating in his mind.

"And I think you've forgotten who the boss is here," she retorted through gritted teeth. She drew herself up straight in her saddle and attempted to achieve a look of authority. "You work for the Carringtons. I'm a Carrington. It's my place to give orders, Mr. Bower, not yours." The look of fury on the man's face made her cringe inwardly, but she was determined not to show any fear. When she turned towards Mac Williams, however, she was relieved her unusually haughty attitude toward the other man did not seem to anger him. Instead, the expression on Mac's face suggested he was getting a great deal of pleasure from the entire situation.

"I would appreciate having you accompany me to the Connors', if you wouldn't mind?" Torrie asked Mac in a tone of voice completely different from the one she had used to berate Kenny Bower. Gratitude and relief washed over her when the man smiled like a Cheshire cat and nodded his head in agreement.

Mac raised his hand in the air and motioned for her to lead the way, then turned to Kenny Bower. "You'd better get on back to our lookout and make sure no more unexpected visitors get up to the house. It might not settle too good with old man Carrington if it happens again."

Before Kenny Bower had a chance to retort, Mac

and Torrie swung their horses around and headed toward the spur in the road which led to the Connors' house down by the river.

"Think he's mad enough to come after us?" Torrie asked when they were out of the younger man's hearing. The evil look in his gray eyes was still fresh in her mind, and the memory made her skin crawl.

Mac shrugged. "Nah. He's mad all right, but he's not stupid enough to leave the house unguarded, 'specially after what already happened." An understanding expression crossed Mac's weathered face as he glanced at Torrie.

She looked at him for an instant, then quickly turned away as she felt another rush of heat rise in her cheeks. He almost acted as though he knew everything she was thinking, but that was impossible, because since she met Lance Farlo this morning, she did not even know what she was thinking anymore.

"It's not an easy life," Mac Williams said suddenly. "This being a hired gunman. Can make a man feel real lonely at times."

The conversation about his profession was completely unexpected. Torrie did not know how to respond. She nodded her head in a gesture of agreement as the older man continued.

"It takes a real special kind of woman to fall in love with a man like me."

Torrie grew more perplexed with every word he spoke; what was he getting at? "W-were you ever in love, Mac?" she asked.

A poignant grin came to rest on his lips. "Oh

yeah, I was in love once. In some ways, you kinda remind me of her." He shook his head. "Prettiest little gal in all of Kansas, but she got scared."

"Scared?" Torrie repeated, growing more unsettled with the course of this strange conversation.

Mac shrugged again. He rubbed at his whiskered chin, nodding his head slowly. "Yeah, she got scared I'd get myself killed in a gunfight. Every time I left her side she was afraid she'd never see me again. That's hard on a woman."

"When did all this happen?" Torrie asked, her interest in his story growing more with every word he spoke. She had the feeling Mac was trying to tell her something beyond his own story.

Mac's brows drew together in a thoughtful manner. "Been nearly thirty years now." He turned his timeworn face toward Torrie. She saw his expression of unforgotten longings the hurtful memories had evoked. To Torrie he did not look nearly as old as Ben Carrington, but the dangerous life he led had made him old before his time. Constant sun and wind had turned his skin as hard and dry as boot leather, and set in that roughened face were eyes that had seen a life burdened with hardship and pain.

A flood of sympathy washed through Torrie as she realized Mac was still very much in love with the woman from his distant past. Had the woman loved him all of these years too? Surely Mac must regret his decision to become a hired gunman since it was obvious it had cost him the love of his life? Why hadn't he given up his guns for the woman? There were many questions Torrie longed to ask, but the man had turned away and seemed to be locked within himself, his aging face filled with pain.

As they continued to ride, Torrie attempted to figure out the reasoning behind the gunman's unexpected revelation. But her thoughts kept coming back to the sorrow she felt for the lonely man. Since she could not imagine how he would think his tragic experience would have any connection with her life, she determined he just felt the need to tell someone why he was growing old alone, and she just happened to be the one who was around.

Just as Torrie had made up her mind she should encourage Mac to talk more about his past, he brought his horse to a halt. The Connor house was just around the next bend in the river, but still out of view.

"Think you'll be all right to ride the rest of the way alone?" His knowing eyes closely studied Torrie as he waited for her to reply.

Torrie nodded her head and shrugged as if she were not concerned about her safety any longer. If it hadn't been for Kenny Bower, she wouldn't have needed anyone to accompany her at all. But to squelch any suspicions either of the two men might have had about her destination, she had felt it would be wise to have the older man ride with her. If she parted with Mac now, before they had ridden all the way to Elsa's house, it would be even better than she had hoped.

Her plan had been to let Mac take her to the Connor house, then make an excuse to Elsa about having to leave. Still, she'd worried the extra time would cause her to miss her meeting with Lance Farlo. Getting away from Elsa would not be an easy task, either, since the other woman knew Torrie all too well and would probably sense at once that there was something going on.

"Mac?" Torrie called out as the man prepared to leave. "If you'd ever like to talk about—about the past or anything, please don't hesitate to call on me."

A faint smile curved Mac's lips as he started to turn away from Torrie. "Thanks, Miss Torrie, I'll do that. And you do some thinkin' on what I told you. Might be there'll come a time when you're feeling scared, but I'm thinkin' maybe you're one of the special ones." He nodded a quick good-bye and swung his horse around before Torrie had a chance to say another word.

Torrie stared, dumbfounded after Mac as he rode out of sight. There was only one thing that scared her, and that was staying here forever on this ranch with Ben, Canon, and Gage. Mac Williams had been talking about love—a subject that did not affect her in any way.

But she did need to hurry if she was going to meet Lance Farlo.

74

Chapter Seven

Once Torrie was certain Mac Williams was out of sight, she backtracked along the river to a spot where the water was shallow enough for her short-legged mare to cross without any trouble. It was a good five miles to the southern range, but Torrie was confident she would not miss the gunfighter if nothing else detained her along the way. She knew the Grand Mesa better than most of the men who worked for her stepfather. If she chose her trail carefully, she was sure she could reach the south border of the ranch without being seen.

She had ridden only a couple of miles when she spotted trouble, however. Four riders moved south along the same route she was traveling. They were far away, but Torrie could make out the colors of the horses they rode. She knew the identity of three of the men at once. Two of the horses were shades of grey, and one, a pale buckskin similar to the mare Torrie rode. Her brother, Gage, and her stepbrother, Canon, were accompanied by the sheriff of Garfield county. The fourth man rode a dark horse that Torrie could not identify with its rider. He also led an extra horse behind the one he was riding. Instinct—and the presence of Canon and Gage—told her that all of this meant big trouble.

From the small rise where she had stopped to observe the riders, she knew she also could be seen if one of the men glanced behind them. Torrie and her horse quickly descended the ridge to take cover in the cottonwoods and cedars that blanketed the valley floor. Her body tensed with anxiety. Why were the four men headed to the south range? Did they know Lance Farlo was waiting there?

The idea that they were headed straight for the gunman ignited urgency in Torrie. She hardly knew the man who had ridden into her life this morning. She knew she should be as wary of him as she was of the other men who made her life so miserable. But she couldn't shake the feeling there was something different about this man, and for reasons she had not yet had the time to explore, she felt she had found an ally in the stranger. Maybe it was because they were both outcasts on the Grand Mesa. She sensed they needed one another.

This thought aroused an even deeper fear in Torrie's tormented mind. As much as she was drawn to Lance Farlo, she knew she had to be careful not to let herself need him too much. She had been educated on that subject by observing her mother and Ben Carrington.

A woman could be hurt emotionally by a man when she let herself care too much. Torrie was also aware of the acute pain a man could inflict on a woman when he needed to satisfy his own lustful urges. All of this and more she had learned from the men who lived in the big house. These were lessons, she constantly told herself, she could never forget, and once she finally got away from the agony she lived with daily at the Grand Mesa, she was determined she would never let another man hurt her again in any way.

The events that led the young woman to her unyielding decision about her own future dominated her thoughts as she wound through the brush-sated gully that led to the south range. There were things that had happened to her here on the Grand Mesa no one knew about, not even Elsa. If she had confided in Elsa, it would have only made things worse. Elsa would have undoubtedly felt the obligation to tell her husband, and then Will Connor would have tried to come to her defense. Will was a cowhand, not a fighter, and he would have been no match for Canon Carrington.

Torrie's only hope was to find the courage to leave here, and the desire to do so had never been stronger than it was at this moment, for she felt as if the lid was about to blow off the cauldron of trouble that simmered on the Grand Mesa for a long time now. If not for her strong devotion to Elsa Connor, she would have turned her horse around and ridden away from this place for good. But she couldn't leave Elsa and the baby until they found out what happened to Will.

Then, maybe she and Elsa could leave together.

This ideal solution occurred to Torrie just as she was approaching a thick grove of cottonwoods, which lined a nearly dry creek bed. She became engrossed with the idea of getting away from this terrible place and with not having to go alone as she'd always feared she would have to do.

Without warning, a man stepped out of the trees behind Torrie and yanked her from the back of her horse. Torrie opened her mouth to scream, but her attacker clamped his hand over the lower portion of her face. Startled by the sudden disappearance of her rider, Ginger whinnied softly.

With the suffocating hand cutting off her breath, and her attacker's other arm around her midsection crushing her against his own hard body, Torrie had little freedom to fight. But with all her strength, she kicked and struggled against the man as viciously as she could. After several seconds, the man managed to turn her around so she could glimpse his face.

The large hand of the man still held her mouth, but he had lessened the brutal hold he had around her waist. He spoke in a breathless whisper, "Keep quiet, the others are just beyond the edge of these trees." His hold on her remained taut, then grew more cruel as his brown eyes flickered with bolts of gold and green. "Or did you have it planned this way?"

The fury, which had collected in Lance's eyes and in the dark, dangerous expression on his countenance, caused Torrie to cringe with renewed fear. Her spinning thoughts clouded with no sense of direction as she tried to focus on his words and understand his sudden brutality.

He obviously thought she had set a trap for him by informing Gage and Canon of their meeting here on the south range. As she thought of this, she attempted to shake her head in a negative gesture. His tight grip on her mouth, however, kept her from doing much more than moving her eyes back and forth in a frantic motion.

Lance realized what she was trying to convey, and now that he could look into her eyes, his instincts also told him she had not set him up for an ambush. Still, he had only known this woman for several hours, and his intuition had proven wrong on one or two occasions. For an instant, he debated on whether or not he should release his hold on her, but he realized he had to take the chance. He needed to see what was going on out by the fence, and if he had to spend his time and energy holding this woman hostage, he might miss something vital to his investigation.

He straightened out his fingers and inched them away from her face. He eased his hold around her waist. When she made no move, other than to raise her gaze to his face, Lance knew his instincts had not failed him this time.

He lifted his hand up and pressed his forefinger to his lips. He quickly moved to the edge of the thick grove of cottonwoods and grabbed the reins of the mare, who still stood in the same spot. Carefully easing the filly through the thick branches, Lance led the horse to the center of the trees where his own stallion was tied to the trunk of a cottonwood, its leaves now a colorful array of golds, greens, and pale orange.

Once the mare was secured, Lance directed his attention back to Victoria. She had not moved since he had released her. Fear was apparent in the pallor of her ivory complexion. That she could be so afraid of him was unsettling, even though he normally revelled in the knowledge his mere presence evoked a total lack of confidence in most people. This woman's behavior, though, had him more than a trifle disconcerted.

When she had first held her gun on him down by the river she had appeared to be a tower of strength and courage. Again, she had showed undaunted bravery when they had ridden up to the ranch house together and encountered the guards posted at the base of the mesa. But, the more he was around her, the more Lance was convinced that her gallant exterior was merely a fragile facade, behind which she hid a deep and unspeakable terror.

Again, he motioned for her to keep silent, then gestured for her to follow him through the cottonwoods, where the low hanging branches offered a hiding place of some security.

Torrie followed without hesitation. The only protection between herself and Canon and Gage was the flimsy hope that this man would believe that she had not betrayed him. They had gone a short distance when Lance signaled for her to drop down to the ground beside him to crawl with him on their bellies, until they stopped in an area where the deep grasses beneath the trees began to thin.

The branches that had fallen from the overhanging trees, were brittle and dry. The deep grasses were no longer green and lush, but were turning flaxen. They were sharp as a razor's edge. Torrie gritted her teeth and attempted to ignore the pain caused by the biting grasses and prickly branches, which poked through her riding skirt and thin blouse and made her tender skin feel like a pin cushion.

Several hundred yards past the craggy branches of the cottonwoods, Lance saw where a barbed wire fence traced the line between the range lands Ben Carrington made claim to and the land beyond, where the foothills of Horse Mountain began to ascend toward the jagged peaks of the high country. Gathering stray cattle in the rugged mountain ranges was not an easy task, even for a skilled cowhand. Lance figured that was why his father had chosen this boundary for the southern edge of his vast ranch land.

The four men had halted at the fence and huddled around the stiff form of a man draped over the top wire. Along with Canon, Gage, and Sheriff Kearny, Torrie recognized the fourth man as John Silt, one of the sheriff's deputies from the nearby town of Rifle. From this distance, their voices were a low murmur, inaudible. Torrie held her breath as the men examined the dead man. She could not tell who the victim was as long as he was surrounded by the other men. When Deputy Silt led the extra horse over to the fence, however, Torrie had a clear view of the murdered man when they lifted his rigid and decomposing body off of the fence.

A stifled gasp made a heavy lump form in her dry throat when she glimpsed the bluish, bloated face that was barely recognizable. Still, she knew he was Will Connor by the thatch of curly blond hair that topped his head. At barely a week old, little Will Jr. already had a sprinkling of tiny blond ringlets. Torrie closed her eyes, then buried her face in the sharp grasses, uncaring of the dry thorny blades that stuck into her delicate skin. Though she had been certain Will would never be found alive, the reality of finally having her belief confirmed was tearing her apart inside.

As she fought to hold back the tears, Torrie thought of how she would tell Elsa the awful news. She knew she had to be the one who would tell her. Her face still pushed against the hard earth and dry vegetation, Torrie was surprised when she felt a hand gently touch the middle of her back in a gesture of consolation. For a moment she remained unmoving, unsure of the avalanche of feelings his touch evoked.

Along with her sorrow and anger over Will Connor's murder, emotions she had never known before were sweeping through her. Until this moment, her only association with a man's touch had been pain. But, the feel of this man's large hand resting tenderly against her back was like being wrapped in a huge quilt where she felt protected.

When her mind could no longer sort through the alien sensations that surged through her like quicksilver, Torrie slowly raised her head and turned her gaze on the handsome gunfighter. His bearded face was masked with silent pain, almost as if he truly understood the wild and conflicting emotions she was experiencing.

But that was impossible. How could a man who earned his living killing others know what it was like to feel sorrow and regret? Yet, his expression was so earnest, so tormented, it was almost as if he could look inside her mind and meld his own emotions with her torment.

For what seemed like an eternity, they stared at one another. Torrie felt caressed, soothed.

As the men rolled Will Connor's body in a tarp and loaded him on the extra horse, Lance was barely aware of anything beyond the overpowering sense of affinity he couldn't ignore. Yet, when the four men began to mount their horses, he tore his gaze away from her to pay attention to the activity outside the grove of cottonwoods.

Torrie couldn't help but to notice the cold glint that flickered in Lance Farlo's narrowed eyes as he watched his brother through the tall blades of brittle grasses. A tense concentration filled the rugged contours of his countenance as he studied Canon's every move.

Lance's observation of the brother whom he had not seen for almost twenty years was led by memories of their childhood. Canon had grown older, but to Lance he seemed like the stranger he had always been, even when they had been growing up together. Canon had never associated much with his little brother unless their mother had forced them to spend time together. Those occasions were rare, however, because Canon had been prone to fits of rage when told to do something he wasn't in the mood to do. Many times, Lance had been the source of his revenge. He had learned to stay out of his big brother's way as much as possible to avoid being used as a punching bag for Canon's anger.

Unlike Ben Carrington, whose memory had haunted Lance every day since he had fled here, Canon had rarely entered his mind. His older sibling had been seventeen when their father had run Lance off. Lance could not forgive Canon for turning his back on him when trouble had erupted. Yet, he knew there was no way Canon could have prevented what had happened even if he had wanted to come to his aid. Ben Carrington would have disowned his eldest son just as easily as he had denounced his second born. Besides, the damage had already been done by that time—their mother was dead.

Watching Canon now, Lance realized the years had changed Canon very little. Standing taller than the other men, Canon seemed constantly on edge, as if at any second he might explode into one of his fits. Lance knew he would have to be wary of his brother, but he did not feel overly threatened by him. An impulsive man with a gun was usually predictable. Most often his hotheaded enthusiasm to draw his weapon meant his own death was imminent.

Now, however, it was Torrie's brother, Gage, who caught Lance's attention. The man, whose hair was more of an orange shade than the rich copper color of his sister's long tresses, moved cautiously and seemed to calculate every movement around him. He was the shortest of the four men and strongly built. His guns skirted a stocky midsection. Yet, not an ounce of soft fat rippled on his body. Gage, Lance determined, was not a man to dismiss lightly.

None of the men seemed aware they were being observed as they prepared to haul Will Connor's body back to town. Their voices had become slightly louder when they mounted their horses, and now Lance could hear bits and pieces of their conversation, which centered around sarcastic remarks, mostly from Canon, about the three ranchers who had hired Lance to protect their herds. It was apparent the Carrington men were blaming those neighboring ranchers for Will Connor's muder as well as for the cut fence lines encountered as they had ridden down to this southern border of the Grand Mesa. It also appeared the sheriff and his deputy were buying their story.

Lance, however, was not convinced the man had been killed by his employers. His instinct still told him he could trust Wayne Gere and the others. Maybe Will Connor's murder was not even associated with the brewing range war.

Again, Lance was besieged with the feeling there was much more trouble in this valley than he had first thought. Though trouble seemed to be his middle name, he wondered if this time he might have taken on more than his fast draw, and good sense would be able to handle.

Chapter Eight

Torrie did not move until the four men had disappeared from view, and even then, she remained next to Lance in the brittle grasses for a few moments longer. Because Lance was a stranger, and worse, because he was a Carrington, there were real reasons why she should not be feeling such a rapport with him. But even before he tenderly placed his hand on her back, before their gazes had connected with such an intense desire, Torrie had been drawn to this man like metal to a magnet. From the first instant they had glimpsed one another.

Elsa Connor, Torrie reminded herself, must be her first concern. A pang of grief twisted in her chest at the thought of her friend and her new baby, now fatherless. She just had to get to Elsa before anybody else had a chance to tell her what had happened to her husband.

Torrie started to push herself up from the hard ground, but Lance was quicker to rise to his feet.

He leaned down and clasped Torrie's arm to help her stand. Once they were both upright, Torrie heard him draw in a deep breath, but she refused to look up at him for fear she would not be able to look away again. She tried to force her mind to concentrate on only one thing—the important thing—getting to Elsa as soon as possible.

The man's hand touched her face unexpectedly, which made Torrie flinch and gasp in surprise. Lance pulled back as though he had stuck his hand in a pot of boiling water. Why was she so frightened of him? "You've got some grass clinging to your face there," he said, awkwardly.

Torrie felt a fire burn through her face as she reached up and brushed the sticky grasses from her cheeks. They left a stinging sensation where their sharp edges had poked into her tender skin. She cleared her throat and mumbled a word of thanks, but she still did not look directly at Lance.

"I have to go to my friend t-to tell her about . . ." Torrie's voice faded as she glanced out through the hanging branches of the trees to the spot where Will Connor's body had hung on the barbed wire fence. Pushing the thick branches aside, she forced herself to walk from the grove of cottonwoods. She was aware of Lance's presence at her side every step of the way. Now not even his nearness could comfort her. On the fence, a jagged strip of Will's shirt—stiff with dried blood—remained, a gory reminder of his fate.

"How was he killed?" she asked in a choked whisper.

"Bullet." Lance did not elaborate on the man's

death, since he could see how badly she was affected by the discovery of the body.

"I have to tell Elsa," Torrie said, her gaze held by the shred of brown material.

Lance nodded his head, then glanced toward the grove of cottonwoods. "I'll get the horses." In the trees he found himself torn between whether he should stay with the woman since she seemed so distraught, or if he should follow the four men who had taken the body of the murder victim. Maybe their actions would lend a clue as to who had killed the man. He thought again of his own brother, Canon, and of Victoria's brother, Gage. A sixth sense told him he would be wise not to let either man out of his sight for long.

Lance untied his horse first, then dropped the reins. Raven would follow without coaxing. The little mare, however, looked to Lance somewhat dim-witted, so he led her from the trees with a tight rein.

Much to his surprise, Raven walked right next to the filly, so close, in fact, the sides of the two horses rubbed together. For some reason, this irritated Lance. He stepped from the trees with the two horses. He pushed the annoyance caused by the friendliness of the two horses from his mind and approached Victoria, who still stood in the same spot.

The sight of her slender young form standing by the fence, her beautiful face etched with sorrow, tore at Lance's usually staunch heart. What was it about this young woman that affected him in a way that no other woman had ever managed?

Without looking at Lance, Torrie reached for Ginger's reins as he approached with her horse. When his fingers brushed hers in the exchange, however, her gaze sought his of its own accord. Immediately, she forced herself to turn away. "I'd better get going. I want to be sure I'm the one who tells Elsa about her husband."

Lance cleared his throat in a strained manner and backed away from her. If she had not torn her gaze away so abruptly, Lance knew he would have been unable to control his urge to lean down and kiss those tempting lips in an attempt to wipe away all the pain in her life—if only for a moment or two.

He quickly reminded himself of the way she had reacted a moment ago when he had merely tried to wipe away the brittle grasses that clung to her face; his effort to kiss her would probably throw her into a complete state of panic. Besides, how could he be thinking about such nonsense when there was so much trouble simmering all around them?

"I'd better ride along with you," he said.

Torrie pulled herself into the saddle and tossed her head. "That's not necessary," she said, putting her attention on the black hat she wore, which suddenly felt too tight and much too hot in the afternoon heat. She loosed the leather tie from under her chin and shoved the hat back from her head, letting it dangle against her back. She ran the palm of her hand over the top of her head to smooth down any loose tendrils that might have been freed from the long ponytail that draped over her shoulder. With a sigh of discomfort, she placed the sweaty contraption back upon her head. If her pale skin didn't burn so easily, she would have left the hat off, but with her delicate complexion, the sun was a vicious foe.

"There's a killer loose, little darlin', so I reckon it is necessary." He swung up into his fancy saddle and gave his head a defiant nod. He could learn whatever information she could supply to him about the situation here in Mesa County, he told himself in an effort to justify his actions. He could confront Canon and Gage later.

Torrie felt as if all her energy had evaporated into thin air. She did not argue. She was growing tired of fighting against the attraction she felt to this man, and was sick with worry for Elsa.

"Do you reckon you could answer a few questions for me, seein' how I've only heard one side of this story so far?" Lance asked once they were on their way to the Connor house.

For the first time since their meeting earlier today, Torrie remembered she and this man were supposed to be on opposing sides. He had been hired by the men who were trying to claim her stepfather's lands, who were undoubtedly responsible for Will Connor's murder. How could she be so stupid as to have helped him before, to have placed her own safety in jeopardy for him? In spite of her lack of loyalty to the men of the Grand Mesa, she knew if she didn't make it clear where she sided, she was liable to end up being accused of straddling the fence, which in a range war meant she would be labeled as a traitor by everyone involved.

"It just occurred to me, Mr. Farlo, that your employers are paying you a mighty hefty sum of money to find out information about this land and the men they are accused of stealing it from." Her voice remained steady as she turned and faced him. "You must have thought you could play me for a real fool by pretending to sympathize with me, by making me think that you wanted to protect me, when all you really wanted was to gain information from me." She yanked on Ginger's reins, making the little mare whinny. Her anger at her own stupidity burned through her like brush fire.

"In spite of how I personally feel about my stepfather and the others, the fact remains two of the men who worked on the Grand Mesa have been found murdered. None of Wayne Gere's men or Jim Larson's and Shawn McLeary's men have been killed, have they?" Torrie's fury at this realization drew her voice into a high pitch. "I have no choice but to take sides, Mr. Farlo, and from where I sit, it looks like you're on the other side."

In his life, Lance had confronted many enemies, but to have this woman declare him as hers struck him as viciously as if she had shot a hole through his heart with her sawed-off shotgun. Even worse, she had sided with his father against him, though as the facts were stated now, she had little choice. But if it was the last thing he did, Lance vowed to himself he would prove to this woman she was wrong about him and about his employers.

"I reckon you would see things in that way, Victoria," Lance accented her name with an impertinent tone. His pride refused to let him show her how deeply her words had affected him. "And I reckon I was mistaken when I thought you were different from the old man and the others." He noticed how his words seemed to take the fight out of her momentarily, convincing him once and for all she despised Ben Carrington almost as much as he did.

"You're wrong there, Mr. Farlo. I'm nothing like any of the Carringtons. But regardless of how far you run, or what name you use, you—" she raked her eyes over his tall form, pausing for an instant on the low-tied gun at his hips before she added, "You can't change the fact that you are and always will be one of them!"

Her words were filled with so much venom, her voice so charged with rage, Lance was certain now that she had sustained as much—or maybe more— pain than he had ever endured on the Grand Mesa. An icy shard of foreboding inched through his veins as he thought of the many ways a woman could suffer at the hands of a heartless and cruel man.

Though he wanted to ask her why she hated Ben Carrington—or all of the Carringtons—with such vengeance, her state of mind seemed to be at the breaking point. Lance decided he should part company from her until he could prove he was not another enemy for her to confront.

But alerted to the possibility Victoria might have fallen victim to a similar abuse he had suffered at the hands of the old man—or maybe even something more terrible—Lance realized he could not turn his back on her.

"I reckon it's best we cut our own trails from here," Lance said as he tipped the brim of his brown hat. As he started to swing his horse around, he added, "But we'll be seeing one another soon, Torrie, real soon!"

Torrie stared at the man as his big black stallion twirled around and departed once again in a cloud of swirling dust. What did he mean they would be seeing each other soon? She had no intentions of seeing him ever again. Once she reached Elsa's house, she was going to stay there until Elsa was strong enough to travel. Then she and Elsa and the baby were all going to leave this godforsaken hellhole, and she was never going to set eyes on any of the Carrington men again!

And the next time she saw that—that man, she was going to remind him she had not given him permission to call her by her nickname either. But, she reminded herself, she wasn't ever going to see him again. She didn't have to worry about telling him anything!

Chapter Nine

Torrie arrived at the Connor house late afternoon. Sal Martino, the man who had been posted to guard Elsa and her baby today, rushed forward to meet Torrie the moment she rode into view.

"Miss Torrie, we've been worried about you." He took the mare's reins, then helped Torrie dismount, adding, "Mrs. Connor's been askin' if there's any sign of you every five minutes."

"Has anyone else been here today?" Torrie asked, praying she was the first one to reach Elsa.

The man shook his head as he tied the mare's reins to the rail on the front porch. "Not a soul." He glanced at the young woman and noticed the stricken expression on her pale face. "Has something happened? Somethin' to do with Will Connor?"

Torrie lowered her head and stared at the hard ground. She felt completely drained. "His body was found today. He'd been shot at least a week ago, probably longer."

Sal glanced out at the open range beyond the house. He had hired on at Grand Mesa just a few weeks ago, but he had moved cattle with both of the murdered men on several occasions. They had been good with cattle, good men in all aspects.

Sal, himself no more than a cowboy, found it odd the murderers killed men who would offer the least threat, when the ranch was swarming with hired gunmen. He felt a shiver of apprehension.

Torrie forced herself to head into the house. The main room—a combination kitchen, dining, and sitting room—was empty. Elsa was probably resting with the baby in the one bedroom at the back of the house. Torrie stared at the closed door. Before Torrie had taken another step, the bedroom door opened, and Elsa stepped through. Her long wavy brown hair was tousled, as if she had been sleeping—or tossing and turning in her bed. The paisley print robe she wore over her gown was wrinkled. Just yesterday, Torrie had finally told her about the discovery of Leo's body, and Torrie knew Elsa had only to look at her face to know what she had come to tell her today.

"He's been found," Elsa stated in a steady voice, belied by the tears that filled her blue eyes.

Torrie nodded her head, her shoulders sagged as if a heavy burden weighted them.

"Where is he now?" Elsa's voice was beginning to tremble slightly as she hugged her arms around herself.

Torrie cleared her throat of the choking lump that had formed there. "I think the sheriff took him into town."

It was Elsa's turn to nod her head. An odd silence filled the room. This was the first time they had ever been at a loss for words with one another.

"They'll bring him back here, won't they?" Elsa asked, at last. "I mean, to-to b-bury him, won't they?" Elsa took an unbalanced step forward, then paused to steady herself against the frame of the bedroom door.

Rushing to her friend's side, Torrie grabbed Elsa's arm. "You should sit down."

Elsa clasped Torrie's hand and peered desperately into her eyes. "They will bury him here on the Grand Mesa, won't they? I mean, he devoted ten years of his life to your father and this ranch."

Torrie met her pleading gaze, but she did not answer right away. There was a small burial plot up by the main house, but only Ben's first wife and Torrie's mother rested there. Torrie had no idea whether or not her stepfather would permit anyone outside of the Carrington family to be buried in the private cemetery. Elsa was right; after all these years of loyal service, Will Connor deserved a burial befitting a family member. He would be laid to rest on the Grand Mesa if Torrie had anything to say about it!

"Yes," Torrie replied. "He'll be buried here if that's your wish."

Elsa drew in a quavering breath, then could hold back the rush of tears no longer. In her weak state, the racking sobs made her almost too wobbly to stand. She leaned against her friend. Torrie helped her back to the bed, and once she was lying down again, the two women cried together.

Beside the bed where he had been born just days ago, little Will Jr. slept peacefully, unaware of the sorrow that surrounded him.

"Riders comin' ladies," Sal Martino called out from the front doorway.

Torrie pulled away from the other woman, then motioned for Elsa to stay put while she went out. She did not have to see who the riders were to know it was probably Canon and Gage coming to tell Elsa about her husband. As she reached the front door her suspicions were confirmed.

The moment Sal Martino began to speak, however, Torrie realized the grave error she had made by disclosing information to him when she had first arrived.

"Heard about Connor. It's a damn shame, what with his new son and all." Sal shook his head and sighed, then sat back down in the chair on the front stoop where he had been reclining as he kept guard on the house and its occupants.

Canon and Gage exchanged brief glances, yet it was Canon who spoke first. "Well now, how is it that you already heard about Will?" His expression was cold enough to freeze July, but his voice was disarmingly—unusually—calm.

"Miss Torrie rode in not long ago with the bad news."

Again, Canon glanced at his stepbrother. "Bad news travels fast."

Gage narrowed his green eyes and nodded in agreement, but he remained silent. When Torrie stepped outside, their suspicious gazes riveted. Both men nodded curtly, but there was nothing friendly in their attitudes.

"Howdy, Sis," Gage said in a gruff voice. Torrie's existence at the Grand Mesa was a constant threat to him. He worried she would say or do something that would make both of them fall from Ben Carrington's good graces. Since their ma had died, Gage had worried even more. Torrie—Gage felt—did not appreciate all that was here for the old man's heirs. As Ben Carrington's adopted children, Gage knew that they would receive only a portion of what would be left to Canon. Unless, of course . . . something unforeseen happened to Canon.

Torrie gave the men a quick nod. She shoved her hands in the pockets of her riding skirt in an effort to corral their shaking. "Howdy, boys. I suppose you've come to offer your condolences to Elsa?" She forced herself to look at each of them to study their faces. Torrie had already decided she could not afford to have these men think that she was not loyal to the Grand Mesa. After she had been seen riding with Lance Farlo, that was exactly what they would all think anyway. To fabricate too many lies would undoubtedly make her situation worse, so Torrie decided to tell the truth, well most of it.

"That's right," Canon said as his ruthless brown gaze traveled down the length of her rigid body. "But, Sal, here, says you beat us to it." He grinned slyly, "Now how is it you heard about Will?" His cold, penetrating stare leveled at Torrie as he dismounted from his horse and waited for her answer.

Before leaving for town this morning, he and Gage had told no one except Sheriff Kearny and his deputy about Will Connor's body. Once they reached Rifle with the corpse, however, they had seen to it that nearly every resident who lived in the town heard the terrible news about Connor's murder. Combined with the fact Will Connor was the second man who worked for the Grand Mesa to be brutally murdered, and the tragic timing of his demise, sympathy ran high in the valley for the Carringtons. Townsfolk and lawmen were beginning to chose sides, and since only one side had lost lives, the odds were stacking up against the smaller ranchers Ben Carrington claimed were squatters on his land. After leaving Rifle, Canon and Gage had not returned to the main house, but ridden directly here, which made Torrie's prior knowledge of the situation all the more questionable.

Torrie drew herself up to her full height, though she still had to look up to meet Canon's icy stare as he strode up onto the porch to stand before her. Gage followed close behind. "Lance Farlo told me," she said flatly. She heard false bravery in her tone, even this fled the moment Canon began to speak again.

"What the Hell! Farlo was here?" His angry gaze turned to Sal as if only a man could rationalize this development.

"No sir! I started my shift last night, and there ain't been nobody here 'cept Miss Torrie." He glanced nervously to the woman for validation.

"Sal's right," she answered in his defense. "I met

100

Farlo down by the river when I was coming here this morning.'' Inwardly, she cringed when she noticed the dark glow that had colored Canon's face. If he hated the gunfighter so violently now, how would he feel when he found out that the man was in reality his long lost brother?

Twirling around, Canon slammed his fist into the nearest rail of the porch. The porch seemed to groan with the sudden impact, but Canon's expression of rage did not alter. His anger seemed to consume his entire being.

Gage had halted on the top step when Canon flew into his tantrum. Now he stepped up onto the porch to confront his sister. His anger was evident in the purple hue of his skin, but he forced himself to speak in a level tone when he addressed his sister. ''Sounds like you've got a lot of explaining to do, and I hope, for your sake, that you haven't done somethin' stupid.'' His mouth drew into a thin line, which made his lips appear almost nonexistent.

Determined not to back down from Gage, or to let Canon know he was intimidating her with another one of his fits of violence, Torrie stood her ground and stared at her brother with an unwavering gaze. His height was barely a couple of inches more than hers, but his body was so squarely built in structure, that to Torrie he sometimes seemed a hulking bull with fiery orange hair.

''Well,'' she retorted indignantly. Facing her brother, she was able to block out her fear of Canon for a moment. Her hands drew into tight fists in the depths of her pockets. ''It's not my fault if Lance Farlo is able to sneak past your guards and roam around the Grand Mesa on his own. I tried to order him off the ranch at gunpoint. He sprung at me like a coiled rattler and took my gun away." The stricken expressions on all the men's faces filled Torrie with great satisfaction. "If he moves that fast when he draws, well—" she shook her head and gave a low whistle.

"Yeah, well we'll see how fast that low-down scum is!" Canon spat as he twisted around and kicked at the same post he had just punched with his fist. The board quivered, the whole porch vibrated.

Torrie's insides shook like a frail tree in a windstorm. She knew the extent of Canon's rages, but this time she was determined he was not going to reduce her to a trembling idiot—at least not visibly.

"So what happened after that?" Gage demanded, completely ignoring Canon's crazy, out-of-control behavior.

With a nonchalant shrug, more difficult she was sure than it appeared, Torrie pulled her hands from her pockets and threw them up in a defeated gesture. "He said he was on his way to talk to Ben, and he ordered me to ride along with him. I suppose he was afraid I'd warn somebody of his arrival."

"So you led him right up to the ranch?" Canon shouted as he pushed in front of Gage and stepped within inches of her.

"I didn't have much choice!" Torrie nearly gagged on the pulsating lump of fear in her throat, but still, she did not back down from the glowering madman. "When you meet him, you'll see he's not a man anybody would want to argue with, especially a defenseless woman." She knew her last words hit a chord of rationality in the two coldhearted men who stood before her. In their opinion, women were not much better than the dirt beneath their boots, so naturally—in their minds—she could not be expected to do anything more than what she was ordered to do.

"Where is he now?" Gage asked as Canon swung around again and stalked to the porch rail, cursing under his breath and clutching the wooden post as if he were trying to contain the fury that seethed from him.

Again, Torrie gave her shoulders a careless shrug. Inside, she was quivering like a bowl of mush. "How would I know? As soon as he left the ranch, I came over here to be with Elsa." She noticed the dark flame of anger that spread through Gage's face again. Now came the tricky part. She only hoped they would believe the rest of her story.

"That still don't explain how he knew about Connor?" Gage retorted, his patience growing thin as his anger with his sister increased. If she messed things up for him, he'd see to it she never interfered with his life ever again.

Her brother's obvious rage surprised Torrie. She was used to Canon's violent outbursts, but normally, Gage tried to keep his temper under tight rein. "He-he mentioned he found a dead man when he'd been scouting around the edge of the property s-south of the river," Torrie stuttered with uncertainty. She had to get control of herself before Gage and Canon saw through her lie.

"He said the man had been dead for a week or longer, that he was pretty badly decomposed, but then—" Torrie dropped her head down, drew in a deep breath, adding, "He said the man had a head of thick curly blond hair. That's when I knew." She kept her eyes downcast for a few seconds more, remembering the terrible sight of Will's rigid body being pulled off of the fence. Also, she was afraid to look up at her brother and Canon for fear that they would see that she was creating parts of this story as she went along. If they decided not to believe her, she had no doubt they would make her life a living hell—even more than they already did.

"We'd better get back to the house. The old man's probably so mad he's been spittin' nails."

Gage was finished with Torrie, figured her of no more use to them, so he didn't bother to look in her direction again as he stomped down the stairs toward his horse.

Canon, however, paused to glare down at her for a moment longer. "We'll talk more later," he said through gritted teeth. "I want to hear more about this—this big man who moves so fast." His lips curled in a snide grin as he reached out and pulled Torrie's chin up until she was forced to look into his cruel face. "Later, Sis," he whispered in a slow drawl before roughly yanking his hand away from her chin.

Torrie felt the sting of tears in her eyes, but she did not give in to the urge to turn and run into the house crying in fright and disgust. Instead, she glared up at Canon, made her eyes drill into his evil face until she felt the tears subside and felt her deep sense of hatred overcome her weakness.

Canon's smirking grin widened, his pale brown eyes lit with an inner fire. He had seen this transformation on a couple of occasions recently, and her newly-acquired facade of bold defiance excited him even more than her usual sniveling fear. His loins ached with the thought of what he longed to do to her ripe young body. Still, he would have to be patient, but not for much longer . . . just until tonight.

Chapter Ten

Night came earlier now as the days shortened into autumn. Torrie pulled the curtains shut in Elsa's bedroom. A shiver shook through her body. She slipped a crocheted shawl over her shoulders, but she still felt cold. The chill of autumn was beginning to invade the Colorado countryside. As the sun disappeared behind the western horizon, the night air grew brisk. Soon, winter would set in and the ranges would be dusted with snow, the high country blanketed in deep drifts that cold winds blew down through the river valley.

Torrie wrapped her arms around her waist and sighed with fatigue. Elsa finally had cried herself to sleep, and not long ago Torrie had lain Will Jr. down in the cradle beside his mother. He had been awake most of the evening. Torrie hoped he would finally fall asleep and snooze for several hours, which would give her a chance to catch some rest too. Ragged breaths, broken intermittently with lingering sobs still shook Elsa's body. But the baby was undisturbed by the noises his mother made in her sleep, and before long he was sleeping soundly.

Torrie reached down and pulled the blanket away from his cherub face, where he had managed to tug the soft material up over his head. His mouth puckered like a tiny heart, and when the air hit his face, he drew in a miniature sigh. She smiled down at the infant, once again in awe at the complete miracle.

She continued to watch the sleeping baby, losing all track of time. He was secure and safe in the little cradle his father had built for him. All snuggled up in his warm blanket, he was totally unaware of the torment and pain of the wider world. Torrie almost wished she could crawl into the cradle with him and wipe her mind clean of all the bad things she had known in her lifetime. She drew in a heavy breath and forced herself to turn away from the baby. She had no escape—yet. But it wouldn't be much longer.

Torrie walked to the front of the house and glanced out the window. Sal was dozing in the chair, oblivious to the cold Torrie felt. Soon his relief would arrive and he would be heading back to the bunk house. Every guard took a twenty-four hour shift, although none of them would have minded staying at a job like this one on a permanent basis. The assignment, which required doing only a few menial chores such as chopping wood and fetching water for the women, was a favored position among the hired hands. Torrie saw to it the men were fed three hearty meals a day when she was here, and a room in the small barn at the side of the house provided them with a comfortable bed through the night. Torrie reserved the extra cot in the house for herself on the nights she stayed. She planned to continue to stay with Elsa—tonight and every night until they were able to leave the Grand Mesa.

The memory of Canon's evil face flashed in her mind. His last foul words echoed in her ears. She shivered again, and wrapped the shawl around her tighter. Canon's threats were never made in vain. Then, without warning or invitation, the face of Lance Farlo wiped away Canon's image so completely that only the gunfighter's handsome face dominated her mind, while the remembrance of his deep, masculine voice sounded in her ears with his parting words. For some reason, Torrie did not feel a sense of menace and foreboding when she remembered Lance. Thinking about him evoked only the feeling of dangerous excitement she had experienced earlier today in his presence.

She had to be realistic.

Lance Farlo was probably just as ruthless as his brother, his father, and her own brother.

Torrie turned away from the window and attempted to force the image of the dashing gunfighter from her mind. She walked to her narrow cot and stared down at it absently. She had been exhausted a minute ago, but now that she had allowed herself to conjure up the memory of Lance Farlo, she felt recharged, too keyed-up to sleep. However, there was little else for her to do now that supper was out of the way and the baby was asleep. Before she could decide what to do, she heard the pounding hooves of an approaching horse.

Moving back to the window, Torrie hoped the man replacing Sal Martino would be Mac Williams. His departing comments today had left her confused and anxious to continue their conversation. When a grey roan and his rider came into view, however, Torrie felt as though a knife had been stuck in her gut.

Canon!

Surely he wasn't the one who was coming to guard the Connor house, her mind screamed. Maybe he had come only to relay a message, and the replacement for Sal was still on his way here. Torrie said a silent and desperate prayer that Canon's arrival did not mean he was planning to be here for the entire night. That would also mean she would be here alone with him—or the same as alone, because Elsa could be of no help to her should Canon decide to fulfill his vile threats.

Torrie twirled around and searched the wall where she had hung her shotgun on Will Connor's gun rack when she arrived this afternoon. She grabbed the weapon, stalked to the front door, and pushed it open just as Sal Martino headed for the barn where his horse was stabled. Her feet froze to the spot when she nearly collided with Canon, who reached the front door as she started to rush out.

Torrie did not have time to react as he reached out and yanked the gun from her hand. A startled cry flew from her mouth, but Canon shoved her back into the house so quickly she was barely aware of what was happening.

"Am I as fast as a coiled rattler, too?" Canon asked, his voice breathless and his eyes glinting with cruel desire. A crooked grin twisted his lips as he tossed the shotgun on the cot.

Torrie opened her mouth with the intent to scream loud enough for Sal to hear.

Canon shook his head in a threatening manner. "Now you don't want to disturb Mrs. Connor do you? I'd imagine she's not feeling real good. I don't have to get rough. Just let me have my way for once."

Torrie's bosom rose and fell rapidly as she searched the room for some way of escape. Canon was right about not disturbing Elsa, and by now Sal was probably out of earshot. She was trapped like a rabbit in a snare, but if Canon thought she would give in easily, he was grossly mistaken. She would die before she let him put his filthy hands on her again. She was about to tell him this when a knock on the door drew both Canon and Torrie's attention.

"Mr. Carrington, Miss Torrie?" Sal called from the other side of the closed door. "Will you folks be needin' anything before I leave?"

Torrie's hopes soared. She would tell Sal she wanted to ride back to the main house with him. Her plan never had a chance to evolve though, because Canon grabbed her arm and shoved her toward the bedroom door, then flung the door open and pushed her through the doorway into

111

the darkened bedroom. Torrie gasped for breath. Her hand flew over her mouth in an effort to muffle the noise. Fear made her feel as if she was going to suffocate. She swung around to glance at Elsa, who seemed unaffected by the noises. The sudden motion flung her shawl off her shoulders. It fell in a heap, unnoticed, on the floor at Torrie's feet.

The only window in the room was long and narrow. It slid open from the bottom. It was Torrie's only hope for escape. If she could just get out before Sal left, she would have the help she needed to get away from Canon. Tiptoeing across the hard wooden planks, Torrie was engulfed by a sense of impending catastrophe. Her heart felt as if it were about to explode within her chest. At the window, her panic increased when she tugged on the lower frame but could not budge the window. With all her strength, she strained to push the window up. Just as she was about to abandon the idea of escaping through the opening, she felt the frame give slightly. The tiny movement gave her hope and strength. With one more powerful shove, the window slid up.

The scraping noise made by the window caused both Elsa and the baby to stir in their sleep. Deep relief flooded through her when Elsa and her baby slept on. Torrie turned her back to the window, bent down, and scooted out through the opening. Luckily, she was still wearing her split riding skirt, which made it much easier for her to maneuver her legs through the small square in the window. On solid ground outside the house,

Torrie did not attempt to close the window again. Her only concern was being able to catch up to Sal before he left.

Luck was not with Torrie, however. By the time she ran around the house, Sal had already disappeared down the darkened road. "No, oh no," she cried in anguish, considering whether or not to run after him. He could not be far. As she debated this course of action, the front door swung open, and Canon appeared in the doorway.

The light from the lanterns in the house outlined him in a ghostly yellow glow, making Torrie think of a demon emerging from the bowels of hell.

She felt a scream well up in her throat when he charged out of the house and began to run toward her. The scream was barely more than a strangled howl. Torrie turned away from Canon, and began to run like she had never run before. The barn, though only several hundred feet away, seemed miles beyond her reach. Still, she pushed herself to the limit as she raced toward the open barn door. The building offered no sanctuary from Canon, but rather could entrap her in a place from where she would have no chance for escape. Since she knew she couldn't outrun him, however, to attempt to flee down the road would be futile. In the barn she might be able to find a weapon—a pitchfork or club . . . or anything that would stop the maniac who drew closer with each frantic beat of her heart!

A grating laugh broke from Canon when he saw she was running toward the barn. He had attempted to satisfy his cravings for her in the barn

113

up at the main house several times. Yet, every time he thought they would be alone, somebody would happen along to spoil his plans. There were always too many people milling around up at the big house, and the only time his wary stepsister chanced being alone was when she took one of her long rides. Even then she was cautious and always made sure she went out riding only when Canon was busy working elsewhere or in town on business.

He had tried to trick her a couple of times by pretending to leave, but she had grown too smart for his ploys. On a couple of different occasions he had caught her alone long enough to give her a sampling of what he had in store for the two of them.

Before she had started locking her bedroom door and bolting her window every night, Canon had managed to sneak into her bedroom as she slept. After he had crawled into bed next to her, he had been certain there was nothing that could stop him from putting his brand on this hellcat once and for all.

Canon could still recall with vivid clarity how her soft silken skin had felt as he slid his hand up under her gown along her luscious thighs until it had reached the downy moistness of her womanhood.

At that moment, she awoke. Before she had a chance to scream he clasped his hand over her mouth. But then the most horrible thing imaginable had happened to Canon. It was proof of his secret fear.

Canon Carrington could not deny that he was impotent.

To compensate for this gross injustice, his frustrations had turned to violence. He had found subtle ways to hurt women who could not make him feel like a true man, had learned how to punish them with threats of horrible consequences if they ever told anyone about his deficiency. His greatest fear was that his father would someday learn of his lack of masculinity. His ultimate goal was to prove otherwise with Torrie.

Here at the Connors, there would be no interruptions.

Torrie reached the barn only steps ahead of Canon. He was so close she could hear his footsteps, his heavy breaths. She tried to block out the horrible image of this awful man touching her again. She screamed, but deep inside her being, an inner voice told her it was useless to keep running; she was trapped. Unless she could get her hands on some sort of weapon, Canon would have her in his clutches once again.

What he had done in the past was horrible, but Torrie believed the actual act of rape could be much worse than the terror he inflicted with his verbal threats and groping fingers. And even in her innocence and inexperience, Torrie realized Canon had a serious problem related to his manhood.

Her worst nightmare was that one of these times, when the urge to rub his filthy hands on her body possessed him, he would miraculously overcome his problem.

As she charged into the dark barn, she wondered if this would be the time he finally finished what he had been trying to do for so long. She should have left the Grand Mesa, should have gotten away a long time ago! Now, it might be too late.

Canon stopped once he was inside the barn and let his eyes adjust to the darkness. Sal had left a lantern burning in the barn when he saddled his horse, but it afforded only a sparse circle of light.

She was trapped now, at his mercy. His pulse raced and, unexpectedly, his loins tightened and he felt a rise in his jeans. Was it possible?

He never had the chance to ponder over the sudden development, however, because in the next instant a hand grabbed his shoulder and spun him around. A powerful fist exploded into his chin. The force of the blow sent him sprawling back into a loose pile of hay.

Before Canon's senses cleared enough to give him a view of his attacker, the other man reached down and yanked him up by the front of his shirt. Eye to eye, the two men stared at one another for an instant before Canon was pushed back with a vicious shove which nearly knocked him off his feet again.

Canon knew instinctively this man was Lance Farlo, but he was surprised that the man seemed vaguely familiar. Canon reacted on impulse. He dropped his hand down toward his gun.

Lance Farlo palmed the gun from his right side. His movement was so swift and smooth the other man had only cleared leather when the gun-fighter's bullet hit Canon's six-shooter with a

116

crack, yanking the Colt from Canon's hand like a windstorm whips paper through the air.

Shocked, Canon realized the burning in his hand was the result of the gun being ripped from his clutch. That he had not been shot by the gunman shocked him even more. He was not given time to wonder about this stroke of good luck, however. The gunfighter charged at him. Canon realized that for some reason the other man wanted to fight him with his fists rather than with guns. Since he was already aware he could not match Lance Farlo in a gunfight, he rallied to the challenge of a battle of strength.

When Lance's weight struck the other man, Canon grabbed him in a bear hug. The men were almost the same height and body structure. They clung together for an instant before both of them toppled to the ground. They sprang to their feet at almost the same time.

Lance was quicker to throw the next punch. His aim hit Canon on the tip of the nose. When a gush of blood erupted, Canon seemed dazed for a second. He cursed and howled with rage as he shook his head, then rushed Lance.

With both fists, Canon swung at the other man; one glanced off Lance's face, but he twisted to the other side and evaded the second fist. As he ducked, he threw his head into Canon's stomach like a charging bull.. When the other man staggered backwards and doubled over in agony, Lance took another shot with his fist. The blow smashed into the center of Canon's face just as he started to straighten up.

Thunder roared in Canon's ears. He shook his head in confusion and pain. Again, his curses filled the air. His face was masked in blood, the front of his shirt was splattered with spots of red.

Lance was ready, crouched like a mountain lion. When Canon lunged, his balance was shaky. He threw his punch wild. His hand flailed as Lance crashed his fist into the middle of his chest. Lance shattered his teeth with another blow and sent him sprawling on the barn floor.

Though his eyes had grown accustomed to the near darkness in the barn, Canon's vision was so distorted from the stronger man's blows he could see only blurred flashes of movement above his head.

Lance stood over the bloodied body of his brother. He struggled to keep himself from pulling out his gun again and blowing the man's brains all over the barn.

Just minutes earlier, he had ridden up to the back of the Connor house, hoping to see Torrie again. Though he had followed her to this house earlier to make certain she arrived without mishap, since he left here, he had been plagued with such a relentless sense of foreboding he had been compelled to come back to make certain she was still all right.

That they had not parted on good terms had also plagued him. Though he still could not explain to himself why it should matter whether or not she thought of him as her enemy, he was determined to prove to her otherwise.

Knowing the house would be guarded, he had

come the back way. He arrived in time to witness Torrie's horror and flight as she tried to escape from Canon.

His brother's despicable intentions were obvious, and combined with his own suspicions about Torrie's strange behavior, the pieces fit together like a puzzle for Lance. A man who would abuse a woman, did not deserve to live as far as Lance was concerned. And he would have shot down this ugly excuse for a man in less than a heartbeat, but that was too easy a death for a man as low as Canon Carrington. He needed to suffer first, needed to know what it was like to feel the unspeakable fear Lance had seen in Torrie when he glimpsed her pale face in the dim moonlight a few moments ago. Fleetingly, Lance wondered where she was now? The thought of her cowering like a frightened animal in some dark, smelly corner of this barn made his rage boil like an erupting volcano.

"Get up, you worthless coward," he yelled down at the man at his feet. "I'm not through with you yet." His booted foot struck out and caught Canon squarely in the ribs.

Canon moaned, then cursed, spitting blood and tooth chips from his broken mouth. He made no attempt to get up. He was a man defeated in more ways than one.

He had missed the opportunity for which he had waited a lifetime—finally to prove he was a virile man. Lance Farlo had not only beaten him to the draw, he had also whipped him like a wet-nosed pup with his fists. At this moment, Canon

Carrington wished the man who hovered over him would just hurry up and complete the job.

Canon would rather be dead than have to face his father in this beaten condition. Once the old man knew what had happened to him, he would probably be so shamed he would consider finishing the job for Lance Farlo himself. The word defeat was not in Ben Carrington's vocabulary.

In disgust, Lance realized his brother was too much of a yellow-bellied coward to get off the ground. The urge to shoot the scum still raged through his tense body, but Lance was determined not to let Canon off so easily.

He bent over, grabbed Canon by his bloody shirt again, and lifted him to his feet with a vicious tug.

Canon weaved like a rag doll in Lance's tight hold as he tried to focus on the man's face, only inches away from his own. But the near darkness, and the blood that blurred his eyesight, clouded the man's image.

Lance stared into the swollen and distended face of the man he would never again claim as his own flesh and blood. Disgust seethed through his veins as he spoke in a low voice that emitted a deadly warning. "You are a real unfortunate man tonight, Canon. I could have killed you several times over, but that would have made you a fortunate man." Lance's grip tightened as he shook Canon. "But, you're goin' wish you were dead, 'cause I'm goin' be like your personal Grim Reaper, death stalkin' your every move. I'll be like the wind; you'll never know when I'm liable to blow your way, and every time you hear a strange

120

noise or see a shadow, you'll think it's me coming to take my final toll."

Canon shook visibly when Lance pressed his face so close their noses brushed together. He felt the hot breath of the gunfighter strike his blood-soaked face when he spoke again. "And, I am goin' get you. You can take it to the bank. Might be tomorrow, might be tonight, or maybe even the day after tomorrow. But I will get you." Lance shoved the limp form of the other man away from him as if he could no longer stomach the sight of him.

Canon stumbled backwards in a numb stupor, the gunman's words slicing through the jumbled thoughts in his spinning head. Fright and confusion left him wondering what was expected of him now.

"Get the hell out of my sight," Lance spat, his face contorted with a look of repugnance. Then, without warning he sprang forward again and grabbed his brother by the hair, twisting his head back as he shoved him through the wide barn door into the open yard. "You're already a walking dead man, Canon, but if you even try to come near Victoria again before I come to collect my dues, I'll see to it your death will be so hideous not even the Devil will want your mutilated corpse!"

A deep instinct for survival drove Canon forward, stumbling toward his horse. He pulled his pain-racked body up onto his horse with slow, agonizing determination. Then, without looking toward the front of the barn where the gunfighter still stood, he made a hasty retreat.

121

His head pounded almost as violently as the wild thudding in his aching chest. Lance Farlo's face floated before his blurred eyes as he struggled to remain upright in his saddle. That face, Canon knew that face from somewhere, but now he had more important things to worry about—such as his father's reaction when he showed up at the main house beaten to a bloody pulp.

A fleeting sound behind him made Canon whip around in his saddle. Every muscle, every joint hurt with the sudden movement of his bruised and broken body. But he barely felt the pain as a bolt of cold, gripping fear clutched at his heart.

"Must've been the wind," he whispered.

Chapter Eleven

"Victoria. You're safe now," Lance called out. There were several horses in the stalls, and he noticed her buckskin mare in one of them. He stopped in front of this stall and waited.

A few seconds passed before he heard a faint noise. When Torrie inched out from beside her horse, he could see she was as white as a sheet. Her obvious fear tore at Lance's heart. He opened the stall door and reached out his hand to help her out.

Torrie hesitated. She thanked God Lance had come here tonight, but her narrow escape from Canon left her shaky and uncertain.

When she finally took Lance's hand, he noticed that hers was as cold as ice in his own fevered palm.

"Are you hurt?" he asked quietly, his voice so different from the deadly tone he had used with his brother.

She shook her head, her frightened glance looking to the barn door.

"He's gone. And if he has any sense at all, he'll

stay gone." Anger was apparent in his voice again. "But it's far from over. I have a score to settle with him. I don't make promises that I don't intend to keep!"

When he felt her hand clutch him tighter his concern centered back on her. How long had she suffered from Canon's abuse? How far had it gone? He intended to find out the answers to these questions when she was ready to talk about it.

"I think it's time you got back into the house and tried to get some rest." Lance tried to lighten his tone, adding, "You have nothing to fear with me for your bodyguard."

Torrie's expression of fear did not go away. She could not imagine Canon would give up his relentless quest to torment her. His defeat tonight would probably make him more determined and ruthless, but she did not want to think about this possibility now or Lance's declaration. How could he protect her when he would be gone as soon as he finished his business here?

"What made you come?"

The trace of a smile pulled Lance's lips. "I wanted to see you."

"Why? You're working for Wayne Gere and the others."

Lance shrugged. "That has nothing to do with my wanting to see you."

"We're on opposing sides."

Again, Lance gave an indifferent shrug. Her hand relaxed in his as they walked to the house. He felt he had gained ground, although she still seemed to think of him as her enemy.

Lance opened the front door, and the sounds of a crying baby reached his ears. As Torrie rushed to the bedroom to care for the infant, reality hit Lance full force. Will Connor had been a stranger to him, a dead man. But Will Connor would never hear the sound Lance was hearing now—the crying of his son.

Lance thought of his own life compared to Will Connor. He reminded himself why he could never ask a woman to share his life.

When Torrie came out of the bedroom she carried the baby against her bosom. Lance had never paid much attention to babies, never even held one in his arms. He was speechless when Torrie walked up to him and pulled the blanket back to reveal the tiny boy.

The baby was perfect in every way . . . except he was fatherless.

"This is William Connor, Jr." Torrie said, her voice trembling. She glanced up at Lance, and was surprised to see such a tender expression on his rugged face. "Would you like to hold him?"

"No!" Lance retorted, throwing his hands up into the air, and taking a long step backwards. "Me and babies don't mix well."

A patronizing look overcame Torrie's face. She cuddled the baby to her bosom again as if she'd no intention of letting Lance touch him, anyway.

"I'm going to wake up his mother so he can eat." She looked at Lance again, her eyes wide and filled with fear again. "I don't want Elsa to know what happened here tonight. She's already got more than she can handle now."

"I won't say anything."

"Well, you probably shouldn't be here. Everybody believes your employers are responsible for the murders." She glanced away, awkwardly, when she noticed the way his face darkened with anger.

"You included?" His voice was flat, his lean body tensing with growing frustration.

Torrie stared down at the baby she held in her arms. The fleeting image of Will's body being pulled from the fence blinded her vision. "How can I believe anything else?" she replied, her gaze rising once again to his face. She noticed lines of exhaustion etched into his face, and a purplish bruise was beginning to swell up on the side of his eye where Canon's lucky punch had glanced off his cheek bone.

Lance's arms dropped at his sides. "I reckon it doesn't look good for my employers. But I aim to prove they're innocent."

The thought passed through his mind how natural Torrie looked with a baby in her arms.

He studied her for a moment. Her long hair was scooped into a loose ponytail that cascaded over her shoulder. The ends of the thick tresses were spread out along the top of the yellow blanket where the baby rested in her arms. Encased by the vibrant hue of her hair, her pale complexion reminded Lance of silk and the purest of cream.

Someday a worthy man will come along— Lance told himself—a man who will deserve a good woman like Victoria Carrington. That man will give her lots of her own babies to cuddle and love. He was not that man.

"I'd better take this little fella to his mama now," Torrie said. She was growing too weary to argue with him about his employers' guilt or innocence. As she turned to go her expression clouded with panic. "Are you going to leave now?"

Lance read her mind. "I'm not going to leave you womenfolk alone tonight. I'll fetch my horse from out back, and bed down in the barn. If you need anything, you need only to holler out the door." He turned to leave, then swung back around to add, "Be sure to close and bolt that window in the back of the house before you turn in."

Surprise shone in Torrie's eyes when she looked up at Lance. "I owe you, Mr. Farlo. A simple thank you hardly seems enough."

"The name's Lance," he said. A crooked grin tugged at his mouth as he reached up to tip the brim of his Stetson. A look of surprise crossed his face when he realized his hat was missing. He figured he'd find it lying in the barn where it must have fallen during the fight.

In spite of her grim mood, Torrie couldn't help but smile. The wide brim of the cowboy hat he usually wore hid his eyes from view, and gave him an aura of mystery and danger. Without the hat, Torrie decided he was even more handsome than she had first thought. His long, light golden-brown hair hung in thick waves down the back of his neck and across his forehead. The unusually pale brownish-green eyes were more stark without the shadow of the hat, and his light brown beard surrounded lips that were slightly lopsided. They were a welcome host for his easy grin.

By the time Torrie watched Lance disappear through the barn door, Will Jr. was asleep in her arms. He was obviously not as hungry as she thought. She placed him back in his cradle and smoothed his blanket down around his tiny body.

Elsa seemed to be in a deep slumber. She needed the rest after all she'd been through lately. Torrie wished she could sleep for a while and forget about her worries. But even as exhausted as she felt, she was not ready to sleep. She closed the window, then bent down to retrieve her shawl from the floor. A cold fear inched through her body, she straightened up quickly. She'd thought she heard a noise, but the house was quiet. Her nerves—she decided —were getting the best of her.

She felt the need to be with Lance again. Her excuse was that she was taking him a few things to make him more comfortable. She did, after all, owe him. She gathered up a pillow, blanket, and a tin cup full of hot coffee. As a last thought when she was about to head out the door, she went back and grabbed a thick chunk of corn bread left over from supper.

She glanced around as she walked to the barn. The dark shapes of the cottonwoods seemed ominous, the distant sound of the river sounded eerie. Her knees felt shaky and a nervous knot twisted her stomach. Where was Canon now?

A dim light illuminated from the post where the lantern hung. Torrie entered the little room where the extra cot was kept, but Lance was nowhere in sight. Before she had a chance to call out his name though, he slipped into view. He had been standing in the dark shadows along the barn wall. He held his gun in his hand.

"Sorry. But one can never be too careful when you're in enemy territory." His chuckle was the clue he was making a joke. However, he did not make her laugh. They didn't seem to share the same brand of humor, he decided as he holstered his gun.

"What's all this?" he asked as he took the tin cup of coffee she was holding out toward him.

"I thought you might be hungry." She nodded toward the bedding. "This might make your bed a bit more comfortable."

He smiled. "Why thank you, Tor—I mean—Victoria."

Maybe it was time they weren't so formal, Torrie decided. She started to tell him this, but he didn't give her the chance.

"Is that corn bread?" He closed his eyes and sighed. "My mama used to make the best corn bread in the world." His expression grew somber. His mood seemed to change almost instantly.

"Let me take those blankets," he said, quickly. He held his coffee cup in one hand, then he scooped the pillow and blanket out of Torrie's arms with the other. His bedroll was spread on the floor close to the barn door. He laid the extra bedding on top of his own blanket.

It was apparent to Torrie the mention of his mother was the cause of his sudden seriousness.

She was more curious than ever to learn how she had died. "Would you like to talk about it?"

"About what?" he asked. His brow lifted in a curious arch. He gingerly lifted the cup to his lips to take a drink.

"Want to sit for a spell?" He sauntered over to a pile of hay and settled himself down. There was no more mention of his mother.

Torrie debated over whether or not she should join him. But, if she stayed maybe he'd open up about his past. She approached him with slow steps, then held out the corn bread as if this were the reason she had moved closer.

He took the corn bread without saying a word. The barn was quiet as a tomb.

"I-I probably should get back to the house. Elsa might need . . ." her voice faded as her emerald gaze settled on his face. She clasped her hands together, they were empty. She had exhausted her excuse for being here.

Lance set his corn bread and coffee cup down on the ground. He rose to his feet. There was nothing he wanted more than to take her into his arms, to kiss her soft lips. But he couldn't let himself forget she was not like the women he was used to. A kiss to a woman like Victoria might mean more than he was willing to give.

Torrie felt like a flame had ignited in the core of her being. Canon's nearness was repulsive, his touch horrifying. Being close to this man felt completely different, though still a bit frightening. She'd never been kissed in the tender manner she had seen Will and Elsa Connor kiss, had never known the gentleness of a man's caress. Until now, she never wanted to know any of these things.

"You probably should get back in the h-house," Lance stammered, his voice hoarse. He considered himself a strong man, but his yearning to be with this woman was reducing him to a man with little self-control.

He cleared his throat, coughed, and glanced down at the barn floor. He felt strange—awkward. He didn't want to meet her gaze again. The expression etched on her beautiful face had bespoken longings Lance was reluctant to explore.

Chapter Twelve

Lance spent a restless night in the Connors' barn. Every time he closed his eyes, he remembered the beautiful face of Victoria twisted with terror as she raced through the darkness. His anger toward his brother continued to mount throughout the night. By morning Lance cursed himself for not putting an end to his brother's worthless existence last night. He'd never forgive himself if Canon did anything to hurt Victoria again.

He dozed fitfully for an hour or so as the night wore on. But before the sun was barely more than a gray haze on the eastern horizon, Lance was up and ready to get to work. He had a lot of business to tend to today. Before coming here last night, he had ridden into town to talk to Sheriff Kearny. The lawman was not happy to learn of the gunfighter's arrival. Lance Farlo's reputation attracted the sort of attention which usually meant trouble in one way or another. The sheriff figured there probably would be at least one man in these parts who thought his hand was faster than the draw of the famous gunfighter.

While in Rifle, Lance confirmed his suspicions. Sheriff Kearny and his deputy believed Jim Larson, Wayne Gere, and Shawn McLeary were responsible for the recent murders. Sheriff Kearny didn't buy Lance's theory that his employers were innocent.

Lance decided he would begin with his own investigation of his employers. Once he proved their innocence, he could concentrate on finding out who else might want to murder the two cowboys.

Anxious to get going, Lance called out to his horse. "Come on, Blacky. Let's hit the trail."

Raven didn't come rushing to his side as usual. A frown furrowed across Lance's face. He never worried about his horse running off. Last night he had left the stallion roaming loose in the barn. He wasn't overly concerned about the horse now either. Lance had left the barn door open so he could hear if there was any activity outside the barn or at the house next door. He figured Raven was probably outside somewhere, and did not hear his call.

Lance rolled up his bedroll, then folded the blanket Torrie had brought out to him last night. With the pillow, blanket, and dirty coffee cup he started to the house. He would fetch Raven afterward.

Outside the barn door, he heard a horse snort in one of the stalls behind him. Instinctively, every muscle in Lance's body tensed. His gaze scanned

134

the corners of the barn. He glanced up toward the loft, and listened. The bedding slipped out of his arm, and landed on the ground at his feet without making a sound.

His gun was in his hand, cocked and ready to fire. He took a cautious step toward the stall where the horse had whined. It was the stall where Torrie's mare was—the door hung open. Lance took another slow step, then growled with annoyance.

Raven stood at the open door, and the little filly was pressed against the back of the stall.

"What the devil do you think you're doing?" Lance holstered his gun. His hands thudded down on his hips as he glared at the horses.

"Did you open that door?" He focused his accusing gaze on his stallion. Lance knew the answer. He had taught the horse how to open a drop-latch like the ones used on most barn doors in case of an emergency when the animal would need to escape from a stall or corral. Now—Lance realized—his ornery horse had opened the latch on the mare's stall.

"I thought you had better taste," Lance mumbled. He grabbed ahold of Raven's long black mane and tugged hard. The horse moved out of the stall with reluctance. Lance ignored the filly as he slammed the stall door shut.

"Come on you Romeo," he growled. He shook his head as he scooped up the discarded bedding, and started to the house again. The horse trailed along behind him, his head hanging down, guiltily.

As he reached the porch, Lance couldn't resist adding, "You'd best behave yourself, or I'll be turnin' you into a gelding before too long!"

The stallion stopped dead in his tracks. He raised his head high into the air in a proud gesture, his long ebony tail curved upward. He whinnied, pawed at the ground with his front hoof, and tossed his head when the man turned to look at him again.

"Okay, you're forgiven this time." Lance's tone was patronizing. "But don't let it happen again!" He twirled around and smiled. That threat always seemed to get the horse's attention.

Lance's fist had barely tapped the wood when the door swung open.

"Mornin'," he said, grinning. "I wasn't sure if you'd be up, so I was only going to tap lightly."

He held up the bedding and coffee cup. "I wanted to return these things before I left." Torrie had not said a word, and her silence made Lance uneasy. She looked worn out as if she had gotten even less rest than he had. He noticed her green eyes were rimmed with faint purple smudges, and her complexion appeared to be even more pale than usual. Her hair was still tied with the same black ribbon she had worn yesterday, but several long strands hung loose around her face. He'd hoped she'd sleep while he was here to protect her. Now he was reluctant to leave her again.

Torrie unconsciously ran her hand along the wrinkled sleeve of her blouse. She hadn't bothered to change her clothes—she'd spent the night staring out the window. "I couldn't sleep. All I could think about was Canon." Her eyes were heavy with fear when they rose up to his face. "He'll be back you know."

Lance felt as if he were being torn in a dozen different directions. "He wouldn't dare chance coming back here." He wished he felt as confident inside as he pretended outwardly.

Torrie nodded her head. "He'll come back, especially when he learns your true identity. You haven't been around Canon for a long time. You don't realize what he's capable of!" Her voice started to rise with hysteria. She glanced back toward the closed bedroom door, and immediately lowered her voice. "When he does come . . ." her voice faded, her expression clouded with unspeakable fear. She shivered visibly.

"I have to attend a meeting at Wayne Gere's house this morning," Lance said. "Why don't you let me take you into town. There's bound to be some folks in Rifle who would let you stay with them for a day or two?"

"I can't leave Elsa alone. She has no one now." Torrie paused. She hadn't told Lance about the mistake she had made yesterday.

Lance sensed she had more to say, something she was hesitant to disclose. "Is there something you're not telling me?" he asked, impatiently.

Torrie shrugged, and backed away from the door. "You'd better come in and have a cup of coffee. There is something I should tell you." She quickly retreated to the stove where a pot of coffee brewed. "I've got fresh biscuits, too."

She turned back around, then gasped. Lance

stood only inches away from her. She was not aware he had followed her across the room.

"What are you hiding from me?" He cocked an eyebrow with speculation. As he looked down at her he noticed how lovely she was even in her tired, disheveled state. He'd like to just bend down and kiss those trembling lips. It just seemed the natural thing to do . . .

A fleeting thought passed through his mind of how angry he was when his stallion followed his natural instincts with the mare in the barn. He could excuse the horse for having no sense, but he had no excuse for himself. If he didn't know better he would think he was jealous of his horse. Lance could only daydream about the things he would like to do to Victoria. He tried to assume a stern and serious expression as he waited for her to answer his question.

Torrie held out a steaming cup of coffee. "I'm afraid I did something real foolish. It could make things worse for you." She turned back to the stove for the pan of biscuits. His nearness was once again throwing her senses in turmoil. Her hand shook when she picked up the pan.

Watching her putter around the kitchen summoned feelings Lance never experienced before— yearning for the comforts of a woman, and a sense of home and family. He didn't want to think about these things, however.

"Let me be the judge," he finally replied.

Torrie motioned for him to sit at the table. Her words practically fell over one another as she told him what happened yesterday after Canon and

Gage had arrived here. She plopped down in the chair across the table from him, adding, "I'm not sure they believed my story."

Lance showed no reaction other than his obvious hunger for her biscuits. From the way she carried on at first, he didn't know what to expect. Most of what she told her brother and Canon was true. He reached for another biscuit without hesitation. He ate too much of his own thrown-together meals. A woman's cooking was never something he declined.

"No harm was done." He popped a piece of flaky biscuit into his mouth. "But I still think that you should consider going to town for a few days. Out here you're defenseless against Canon or anyone else."

A worried frown burrowed through his face as another thought occurred to him. "Do you have any reason to fear Ben? I mean—other than the fact he's a mean, selfish old man?"

"No—well—yes. I guess I am afraid of Ben, but it's nothing like it is with Canon." Her gaze lowered toward the floor. She felt a burning sensation rise in her cheeks.

Lance stopped himself from asking the question that had been eating at him since last night. He reached out and laid his hand on her arm. He felt her tense up, but she did not pull away.

Torrie stared down at his hand—large, and capable of beating a man to death, of palming a gun with deadly intent. Yet, still able to touch her so gently.

"I-I," she glanced up to his face, the words

stopped in her dry throat. Pulling her arm out from under his gentle hold, her gaze dropped again. "I can't talk about it yet."

She rose to her feet and walked over to the stove. Her hands shook so violently she could barely pour herself a cup of coffee. The hot brew splashed over the sides of the cup onto the floor as she set the coffeepot down. She had to clasp the cup with both hands to steady it as she raised it to her lips.

Lance stared at her. Her refusal to talk convinced him his spineless brother must have succeeded in raping her sometime in the past. He knew now he had made a gross mistake last night when he had let Canon leave here.

The chair he was sitting in tipped over backwards when Lance rose to his feet, abruptly.

"I should've killed him when I had the chance!" he spat. His hands dropped to the pearl handles of his Colts. His pale brown eyes gleamed with bolts of green and amber as rage ruled his actions.

Torrie remained rooted to the spot. Her surprise over his reaction caused her heartbeat to bang against the wall of her chest, her fear made a sense of foreboding creep through her body. Something told her before this day was over, she would never have reason to fear Canon Carrington again.

Chapter Thirteen

It was still early morning when Lance reached his destination.

A dark gathering of clouds rapidly consumed the blue sky. A storm this time of year in Colorado could mean either rain or the first snow of the season.

Lance's route led him to the back of the mesa where his father's house stood. He chose this trail because he knew it would be unlikely he would be seen by any of the patrolling ranch hands or gunmen.

Thick groves of cedars, an occasional gnarled cottonwood, and an abundance of wild rosebushes carpeted the basins and gullies on the backside of the mesa. The vegetation was so dense cattle were not even pastured in this nearly impassable area.

During one of Lance's explorations when he was a young boy, he discovered a hidden path through the heavy brush. He was relieved to be able to locate the trail again, although it was more overgrown in some spots than it had been twenty years ago. In these areas, Lance was forced to dismount and lead Raven through the prickly branches of the rosebushes. Once they reached the base of the mesa, however, the slope that led up to the house was completely barren of growth. A few jagged ledges of rock jutted out from loose dirt which blanketed the backside of the mesa.

Lance stared at the slope with an avalanche of memories. Because of what happened on this side of the mesa years ago, Lance had hoped he would never return to this tragic place. But his anger over Victoria's abuse drove him here. Lance wanted to catch Canon unawares, to call him out where there would be witnesses who would hear his reasons for the challenge. They could also testify to a fair gunfight.

He remembered how simple it was for his father to get away with murder—or in Canon's case—rape and torture.

Now, however, Lance must deal with the agony of remembering the day when he had stood in almost this exact spot, and watched in horror as his mother fell from the top of the mesa and tumbled down the slope to her death. His blood chilled in his veins. The memory was as clear as if it had happened only yesterday. He remembered walking out from the thick brush—lost in whatever thoughts a boy who was just about to turn thirteen thinks—when his attention was diverted by angry sounding voices at the top of the high mesa.

What happened in the following seconds was a

blur to Lance eighteen years ago. Years later, his memory still had not cleared. He remembered his mother crashing down the jagged rocks, her arms and legs flailing around like a windmill in a windstorm. He cried out to her, rushed forward, but his mother did not fall to the bottom of the mesa. Her broken body was stopped by a protruding rock ledge a little over halfway down the slope. When Lance paused to glance up to see where his mother landed, he saw his father's face peering over the top of the cliff. He disappeared the moment he spotted his youngest son standing at the base of the mesa. From that moment on, Lance was convinced his father pushed his mother off the edge.

His parents had been fighting for several days prior to his mother's death. They'd retreat into silence whenever he was in earshot. Lance never learned the reasons for their quarrels. He suspected his mother's murder was the result of another battle, but the old man had vehemently denied he was at the top of the mesa when his wife fell. When Lance continued to repeat what he saw, Ben called his son a liar. He ordered him to stop telling lies.

Lance could not keep quiet, however. He insisted his father was guilty of murder. It was Lance's word against his father's word.

When Ben finished discrediting his youngest boy, hardly a person in the valley thought of Lance Carrington as any more than a crazed boy who invented wild tales. They shook their heads and talked about the way he drove his devoted father to the brink of despair.

Lance knew differently. He knew the old man knew, too. That's why Ben ran him off. Lance figured the old man had probably prayed his youngest son had been killed at sea.

Thunder rolled across the sky, and brought Lance's thoughts back to the present. He pulled his gaze from the top of the mesa and glanced overhead at the darkening clouds. If he didn't get up the slope before it started raining, the side of the hill would turn to mud and be impossible to climb.

"Come on, Blacky."

His voice was hoarse with emotion. For a moment there, he was that young boy again; he witnessed his mother's death, relived his father's deceit, and recalled the fear of being cast out into the world when he was hardly more than a child.

But the grudge against his father had to be put on the back burner for now.

The climb to the top of the mesa was a difficult task. Lance had trouble keeping his feet under him on the loose dirt and rocks. He was leading Raven, too, which made the climb more treacherous. By the time they reached the highest ledge, the black clouds were starting to drop huge raindrops. Lance held tight to Raven's reins as he pulled himself and his horse onto the flat ground at the top of the plateau. He undid the red handkerchief he wore around his neck to use it to wipe the rain from his face and eyes.

From this location only the back of the house was visible. So was the small cemetery plot where

Lance's mother had been buried under a large cottonwood tree. A second gravestone stood close by the cross which marked his mother's grave. For a moment the other grave perplexed Lance until he remembered Torrie saying her mother was dead, too.

How had she died? Lance wondered. It seemed the Grand Mesa was a melting pot of pain and death for its womanfolk. But if it were in his power, Torrie would not be added to the toll.

Lance pulled his gaze from the cemetery, and began to study the back of the house. Now that he had managed to get past most of the guards, he didn't intend to sneak into the house. He planned to go right up to the front door and demand to see Canon at once. If everything went smoothly, he would still have time to make it to his meeting at Wayne Gere's house later this morning.

The rain was becoming a steady downpour as the gunfighter made his way around to the front of the house. The only man he spotted was leading a couple of horses into the smaller of the two barns. Foul weather did not prevent cowboys from going about their daily work.

Drawing no attention, Lance left Raven standing at the hitching post while he proceeded to the house. When he started to double his fist to knock, he realized his knuckles were swollen and sore from the fight with Canon. He pounded on the front door with his open palm, instead. When the door swung open, his gaze looked down at Gage Carrington.

Gage stared up at the taller man with a fleeting

145

look of confusion. As was usual with most men, his gaze dropped down to Lance's guns. Gage knew immediately this stranger was not expected or invited. He suspected he was the same man who had paid a visit to the Grand Mesa yesterday. What Gage couldn't figure out was how he had managed to get past the guards at the bottom of the mesa once again?

"I'm here to see Canon," Lance stated, his face expressionless, his voice flat. Unconsciously, he flexed his hands at the sides of his holster.

Gage's mouth gaped open. His eyes caught the movement of the gunfighter's anxious hands. He thought of the guns which hung at his own hips. Yesterday he would have welcomed the chance to face Lance Farlo in a showdown. But seeing the man face-to-face, Gage realized he had no desire to test his draw.

"C-Canon's not here," Gate stammered. The red hue of his face darkened. He attempted to straighten his slumping shoulders, to appear in control of his waning bravery. Stretched to his full height, he still had to tilt his head back to peer into the face of the tall gunslinger. Gage was struck by the thought of how this man's eyes were almost the same color as Canon's.

"Where the hell is he?" Lance demanded as he glanced over the top of Gage's head. The house looked deserted, but Canon could be lurking behind the door or in any one of the many rooms. The thought occurred to Lance that maybe Canon had been too ashamed to come home after his severe beating.

146

Gage shrugged. "I'm not Canon's keeper. Why are you so concerned with his whereabouts?"

"We have a score to settle." Lance's eyes narrowed as he looked down at the man who stood unmoving before him. He could tell Gage's fleeing courage was returning. He didn't think he was foolish enough to try to prevent him from finding Canon, however. He studied the short, stocky man for a minute. Gage's red hair was damp and combed back smoothly from his round, ruddy face. His clothes were as impeccable as the attire Ben Carrington wore yesterday. To Lance, it was apparent this man did not do much in the way of the menial ranch work.

"As I already said, Canon's not here. He never came home last night." Gate's expression of contempt grew as he added, "But you're tres-passin', and if you don't leave immediately, I'll see to it that my men remove you from my property permanently!"

A chilling smirk tugged at Lance's mouth. Gage was so much like Ben Carrington. He was the son the old man had always wanted. He even acted as if the Grand Mesa was his sole possession.

"That won't be necessary," Lance retorted. His face was a mask of contempt, his voice low, threatening. "My business is strictly with Canon today. But if you see the bastard first, you tell him I've come to collect my dues."

Lance started to turn away, but the voice that rang out from inside the house stopped him dead in his tracks.

"How dare you show your face here again! I'm

goin' see to it that you never come back!" Ben Carrington stomped to the front door. He shoved Gage aside, heedless to anyone other than the man he spoke to.

Cautiously, he turned around to face his father. A fleeting sense of surprise passed through his mind. Ben's rumpled shirt, untucked, hung sloppily from his broad shoulders. The ends of the shirt were bunched up under the old man's gunbelt. Bare feet stuck out from the bottoms of his jeans. With his gray hair uncombed, scraggy strands hung over his bushy white eyebrows. Lacking wax to stiffen it, his huge handlebar mustache drooped at the sides of his chin like two limp tails. His flushed red face stood out starkly among the bushy clumps of white hair, and his eyes were bloodshot from lack of sleep.

None of the emotional turmoil that haunted Lance yesterday clouded his thoughts now.

Ben paused with indecision and panic when he met Lance's narrowed gaze. In spite of the fact he was his son, Ben knew him only by his dangerous reputation. He knew he would die if he drew his gun. He was not ready to die. His hands dropped away from his guns in limp retreat.

Lance sensed his father's thoughts. He'd experienced this with other men. A man would lose control, his mouth would overrule his common sense. One eyebrow arched as Lance's mouth curled in a sly grin. An almost sinister glint flashed through his gaze. "Smart move," he said.

Ben was not ready to admit total defeat. His anger continued to dominate him as he stepped

148

through the front door and stood before his son. "You think you're somebody important now, don't you? But you're no better than you accused me of being—you're nothing more than a cold-blooded killer!"

The smug expression did not disappear from Lance's face. "I reckon it's just a case of like father like son."

Lance was aware of the shocked gasp from Gage. He figured the old man had not told anyone yet he was the son he claimed was dead.

Now, however, he was growing tired of wasting time with these men. He would deal with them in due time.

Ben Carrington did not make another move. Nor did he make any reply to Lance's last remark as he watched his son walk away.

Gage, however, stepped out from behind Ben, his face almost purple with shock and rage. "Who the hell are you?" he demanded. He did not receive an answer. But inside, he knew, and the knowledge sent his thoughts into a panicked spin.

Droplets of rain pounded down on the hard ground, drowning out the sound of Raven's hooves as he galloped from the mesa. Overhead, the sky was completely shrouded by heavy, black clouds. Lance tilted his head back and closed his eyes for a moment. The raindrops splattered on his flushed face. His despair felt as black as the sky. He wished he were in Texas right now . . . or at least with Victoria.

Chapter Fourteen

"Who is it?" Torrie asked. She inched up to the door, her sawed-off shotgun clutched in her hands. Because of the rain, she had not heard the rider approaching. When the loud knock rang out, she thought her heart stopped beating for a moment. She looked out the foggy window, but she could glimpse only a portion of the hooded yellow rain duster worn by whoever stood on the other side of the door.

"Gage!" was the reply.

Torrie's surprise lasted only an instant. The foreboding that inched through her body and clutched at her heart lasted much longer. Gage never bothered with her unless there was something wrong.

She replaced the gun at the side of the door, and pushed up the long board that secured the door. Gage entered without invitation the moment she pulled the door open.

"This weather's not fit for a man to be out in,"

he growled as he began to tug on his hood. He glanced at his sister, then down at the rifle leaning against the door frame.

"You womenfolk had any unexpected visitors lately?" he asked. Droplets of rain rolled from the edge of his nose and dangled precariously from his copper colored eyelashes.

"No," she lied. Her emerald gaze flitted to the shotgun, then leveled back on her brother. "What brings you out in the storm?"

Gage studied her face for a moment. He noticed how tired she appeared, but he did not feel any real compassion over her well-being. In some ways she reminded him of their mother. She had the same pretty features and a similar shade of rich russet hair. But Gage always thought of their mother as a strong woman; she had to be strong to be married to a man like Ben Carrington.

Gage and Torrie's father had been the complete opposite of the tough rancher who had become her second husband. In Gage's opinion, Torrie had taken more after their father. He died when Gage was eight and she was three. Gage remembered him as a quiet man who worked as a bank teller in Denver. After he died of heart failure at the age of thirty-two, the young family struggled to survive on the measly savings left them. The money was almost gone when—miraculously—their mother met the wealthy rancher from western Colorado. Gage felt it was a shame that his sister couldn't be as grateful as he was.

"I don't suppose Canon's here?" he asked,

although the question sounded more like a statement.

Torrie's heart began to pound wildly. She felt beads of sweat break out above her lip. "No."

He pulled his raincoat off, shook it, then hung it on the coatrack. "What time did he leave this morning?"

Torrie's mouth gaped open. Her legs felt shaky, and the pounding of her heart grew more violent. "H-He left here last night. Why?"

"He wasn't here all night?"

A negative shake of her head was Torrie's reply.

Gage turned away from his sister so that she could not see the expression on his face. When he turned back to face her, he felt in control again. "Got some hot coffee on the stove?"

"What's going on, Gage?" Her voice trembled, the memory of what happened last night dominated her thoughts.

A casual shrug lifted Gage's shoulders. His pale lips puckered for an instant before he replied, "Well, it looks as if Canon is missing."

Torrie remained rooted to the spot. "W-What are you saying?"

"His horse came in this morning without its rider." Gage shrugged again. "Sal Martino said Canon relieved him of guard duty here last night." Gage's gaze darted around the room. "But he's not here now. So I'd say he's missing."

He glanced toward the stove again, where a thin trail of steam rose from the spout in the coffeepot. "How 'bout that coffee?"

Torrie's feet moved toward the stove. Her thoughts were running rampant, as was her sense of panic. She absently poured coffee into a cup for her brother without noticing when it sloshed over the sides onto the stove. Nor did she pay attention when the hot coffee spilled onto her hand as she carried the cup to the table.

Her thoughts were on Lance, and the way he had charged out of here this morning. Gage's next words fueled her fears.

"That damned gunfighter everybody's been making such a big deal over rode right up to the house early this morning—demanded to see Canon. He had nothing but killin' on his mind." Though he tried to talk calmly, Gage's voice contained an undertone of rage. His green eyes grew dark and narrow. "We'll hang the bastard from the highest tree after we find Canon's body," he added.

The image of Lance dangling from a rope made Torrie feel as if the blood in her veins curdled like sour milk. She slid down to the chair opposite her brother. So many different emotions raged through her at this moment. She hated herself for feeling glad that Canon might be gone from her life for good. More guilt crowded her thoughts—guilt over the way she'd left Lance to draw his own conclusions about the extent of her abuse. Most of all, she felt afraid . . . afraid she'd never see Lance again.

Lost in her thoughts, Torrie cried out when Gage slammed his coffee cup down on the table. Her startled gaze rose to his face. She cringed when she noticed the way his anger made his face splotch with streaks of purple.

His mouth curled into a snarl as he spat, "And that's not all! It seems this—this Lance Farlo is claiming to be Ben's long lost son. The one who was supposed to be killed at sea years ago!"

Torrie recoiled in her chair as his spittle sprayed through the air. She had seen this sort of rage in Canon, but never in Gage. For a moment she was too shocked to speak.

"Y-You said he c-claimed to be Ben's son?" she finally managed in a stuttering voice. "Don't you believe him?"

Gage slumped back in his chair as if his outburst left him drained of all his energy. He rubbed his hand back and forth across his forehead in a frustrated gesture. He remembered the gunfighter's eyes. "There's no doubt he's Lance Carrington."

Gage quickly looked down at the tabletop, and pretended to stare into his coffee cup, almost as though he worried Torrie might be able to read his mind if he met her gaze.

The bedroom door opened and drew Torrie's attention away from the tense silence that held her captive.

Elsa Connor stepped slowly into the room. Her long, wavy brown hair was combed back away from her face, and she had changed into a clean robe. In her arms was her eight-day-old son.

"Let me help you," Torrie said. She sprang to her feet and rushed to her friend's side. After she took the baby, she reached out to Elsa with her other hand.

"No, I'm all right," Elsa said, casting her friend a feeble smile. She continued to walk forward with a slow shuffle until she reached the table where Gage Carrington sat.

"Howdy, Mrs. Connor," Gage said. His voice strained with a forced tone of politeness.

Elsa gave her head a curt nod. She had never liked any of the Carrington men. But for Will's sake she had tried not to make her feelings obvious.

"Has my husband's body been brought back to the ranch for the burial yet?"

Gage rose to his feet, and stared at the woman with a blank expression on his homely face. "I would imagine he's to be buried at the cemetery in town."

"I planned to talk to Ben about having Will buried at the ranch," Torrie intervened. She glanced at Gage with a look of silent pleading. "I'll see him today and take care of all the details." Looking down at the chubby baby in her arms, she added, "But maybe I shouldn't leave you two alone."

"No," Elsa retorted quickly. "We'll be fine. Please talk to Ben before it's too late."

She sounded so distraught Torrie did not have the heart to deny her friend anything. But when Torrie's gaze looked to her brother, she could tell Gage had doubts that Ben would allow a hired hand to be buried on the ranch.

Torrie kept her face tilted down. She didn't want Elsa to see the uncertainty in her eyes. "I'll ride back to the main house with Gage so I can

156

talk to Ben."

She walked over to the window. An almost solid sheet of rain shrouded her view. The thought of traveling in the foul weather was no more appealing than traveling with Gage.

"Thank you," Elsa said, her weak grin still intact. Her hollow cheeks made a deep indent in the sides of her face, and dark circles hung heavy under her listless blue eyes. She'd lost far too much weight since the birth, but food made her feel queasy. On several occasions Torrie threatened to force-feed her if she didn't eat, but Elsa usually refused. The baby was a healthy eater, however. He sapped every ounce of his mother's reserve strength as his appetite increased.

Torrie turned from the window, and met her friend's gaze. A pang of sympathy shot through her chest. Elsa had been through so much heartbreak, she didn't need more. Will would be buried at the Grand Mesa. That is, if Torrie had anything to say about it.

Gage was anxious to leave. He paced back and forth in front of the window while he waited for Torrie to tend to Elsa and the baby.

Torrie was reluctant to go until she was sure there was nothing left for Elsa to do. She banked the fire in the stove, and threw extra logs in the fireplace in the bedroom. The rainy weather brought a chill into the house. Torrie feared her friend could not ward off the cold in her fragile state.

She changed Will Jr. into clean, dry clothes, and put fresh bedding in his cradle. Elsa balked at going back to bed, but she lacked the energy to argue with Torrie. Once she was settled under the quilt, Torrie was finally ready to leave.

The four mile ride to the house was miserable. The relentless rain continued to pour down on the Colorado countryside without mercy. The chilliness in the air suggested it could be snowing by nightfall. The thought of an early snowstorm increased Torrie's state of gloom and depression.

They passed several ranch hands who were scouting the area for Canon on their way to the main house. So far, there were no signs of the missing man. The rain washed away all tracks, leaving the searchers with no particular direction to conduct their search.

To make matters worse, the huge herds were growing restless, beginning to gather in masses. The cowboys feared lightning would spook the cattle, and one or more stampedes would occur.

Once they reached the main house, Torrie's first task was to dispatch a man to the Connor house. She had an abundance of volunteers for the job, but she chose Mac Williams without hesitation. When he went to saddle his horse, Torrie followed him out to the barn.

"Got somethin' eatin' away at you, don't you, Miss Torrie?" He went about saddling his horse. But he kept glancing in her direction when she didn't answer right away.

She pushed the hood of her raincoat back from her head and met the knowing gaze of the man. Her head nodded slightly.

"Does this concern Lance Farlo?"

"Yes—and—Canon." She looked down to the ground as she groped for the right words. There was only one way to tell the story if she hoped to ask for advice from Mac Williams—she had to start at the beginning. She related every detail about her encounter with the gunfighter down at the river yesterday, about meeting him out on the south range. None of this was difficult.

Her voice faltered, though, when she started to reveal the events of last night. She knew she had to trust Mac enough to tell him everything—but, she didn't trust herself enough to meet his gaze.

Mac made no attempt to interrupt her story. His anger over Canon's behavior made him speechless. He was even more angry at himself for not putting a stop to it when he had first noticed the way Canon acted around her. Her decision to confide in him was the only thing that soothed his rage. He only hoped he was worthy of her trust.

"You're a strong woman, Miss Torrie, but I suspect you're gonna have to be a lot stronger before this is over. If it turns up Lance Farlo killed Canon, you're the only one who can defend him against a murder charge, and a noose. Even a man in Farlo's line of work has to walk a fine line where the law's concerned."

She had never been called strong by a man before. Yet, she'd never felt as weak as Gage, Canon, and Ben tried to make her out to be. A bitter taste coated her mouth, she swallowed hard. A sense of gratitude shone in her gaze when it rose up to the rugged countenance of the man.

The sagging skin on Mac's forehead grew taut,

159

his eyes narrowed, his hands twitched nervously at his sides. "When there's been a wrong done against a woman, there ain't no decent man on God's earth who'd blame Farlo for what he did."

Heat soared in Torrie's face. She cleared her throat, still, her voice was grave when she spoke. "Even if Canon never actually . . ." she stopped, unable to say what she was thinking.

"You said he tried."

Torrie closed her eyes, and nodded. A visible shiver shook her as the memories of Canon's repeated attempts blurred her thoughts.

"Tryin' is just as bad, Miss Torrie," Mac said, his voice just above a whisper. He stood, mute, while he waited for her to regain her composure. When her eyes opened, Mac was not surprised to see the glimmer of determination in her emerald gaze.

"I won't let him hang." Her chin squared, her fists clenched at her sides.

A deep admiration overcame Mac, a fleeting memory of the girl he'd lost flashed through his mind. His suspicions were right—Torrie Carrington was special. Mac wondered if Lance Farlo knew this, and if he realized what a damn lucky man he was!

Chapter Fifteen

Ben Carrington's office was a realm of masculinity. Women were not allowed in this room unless they wished to discuss something of a business nature.

Two elaborate gun cabinets held an extensive collection of pistols, shotguns, and rifles, as well as an assortment of hunting knives. All the furniture in the room was of a dark rich mahogany. The walls were decorated with several mounted heads of wild game from the local region. Over the fireplace hung a massive elk head, another wall sprouted the head of an antelope, and a third stuffed head was from a mule deer. Their glass eyes seemed to follow visitors around the room.

Torrie hated this room. She felt suffocated by the overpowering odor of cigar and cigarette smoke that always lingered in the air. It reeked of Ben Carrington.

She sat in one of the huge brown leather chairs

and stared at the burning logs in the large rock fireplace. She'd washed, and changed into a clean riding suit, but she didn't feel refreshed. The speech she'd rehearsed for her discussion with Ben was already forgotten.

Her thoughts kept returning to Lance Farlo.

"I never thought you'd have the nerve to show your face around here again." Ben Carrington's deep voice boomed through across the room as he stalked through the doorway. His disposition was obvious, his face contorted with fury. Kenny Bower had made sure he heard all the details about Torrie's alliance with the gunfighter.

Torrie's mind went blank the instant she heard Ben's voice. Abruptly, she rose from the chair. She stared, wide-eyed, across the room. The way this man intimidated her was something else she hated. "I-I wanted t-to—"

"To apologize for yesterday."

"N-no," she stammered. She clenched her hands, straightened her sagging posture. "I wanted to talk to you about Will Connor's funeral."

"What about it?" He began to shuffle through a stack of papers on his desk. His encounter with Lance this morning had turned his mood more foul than usual.

His oldest son's disappearance infuriated him almost as much as it worried him. Canon was never too bright when it came to making rational decisions. Ben knew Canon had no business going over to the Connor house last night to take Sal Martino's place. He also knew why he went there.

He glanced at Torrie. He was disgusted by the way she cowered on the other side of the room.

He'd known for a long time she'd bring trouble to the Grand Mesa, had known Canon would, too. He realized now he should have done something about it long ago.

Torrie didn't notice the strange look in Ben's gaze. She was trying to keep her thoughts focused on the reason she had come here. "Elsa feels Will should be buried at the Grand Mesa. I feel the same."

Ben shrugged. He returned his attention to the papers he held in his hands. "He's not family. Only Carringtons will be buried on this land," he stated, dispassionately.

Torrie stared at him for a moment. A slow burn fired in her stomach. Why did she let this man frighten her, and dismiss her as if she were nothing more than excess baggage?

She stalked forward.

Ben glanced up when she stopped in front of his desk. His brown gaze flashed with a look of surprise. The papers he clutched in his hands made a slight rustling sound.

"Will Connor deserves to be buried on this ranch as much as any Carrington," Torrie said, her voice unusually steady and forceful.

Ben's surprise clouded over with a mask of fury. He glared down at Torrie, expecting his mere look to send her into her usual cowardly state. When she returned his narrow-eyed stare he was stunned —and mildly impressed.

"I will not discuss this any further. Connor will be buried at the cemetery in town." Again, he glanced down at the papers.

Torrie's pent-up frustrations erupted inside her

like a broken dam. Before she took time to consider her actions she reached out and ripped the papers from Ben's hands. They scattered over the top of his desk, some floated down to the tapestry carpet that covered the floor.

"I won't take no for an answer," she spat.

When Ben's look of stunned disbelief wore off, his expression grew wrathful.

Torrie watched the transformation on his face as she realized how rash her actions had been. Her chest tightened, her knees felt like jelly. But, this time, she was determined not to back down.

The urge to slap the defiant expression off her face tore at Ben. He reminded himself, however, of the repercussions that could occur if he did. With the range war taking on steam he could not do anything that would alter his position. His anger, though, would not allow him to retreat altogether.

"You," he pointed one threatening finger to within inches of her face. "Get out of my house, and get off of my land. And don't come back!" Ben's mind was vaulted back to the day when he had said those very words to his youngest son. Then, like now, he would allow no one to oppose him when it affected the Grand Mesa.

For an instant the depth of his words escaped Torrie's spinning mind. When she realized he was ordering her to leave the Grand Mesa for good, her first reaction was a sense of relief. She'd always planned to leave—someday. Now, there were no more excuses.

She took a stumbling step backwards. Her gaze never left the old man's face. He still had his finger aimed at her face.

"Is this the way you ran your own son off years ago?"

Ben fought to control his growing rage. What did Lance tell her about the past—the past Ben wanted buried forever? "He's a liar! Nobody believed him years ago, nobody's gonna believe him now."

He stepped around his desk. His voice contained a low hiss as he added, "Lance is gonna pay for starting up those lies again. And he's gonna pay for Canon, too. You tell him that when you see him."

His next step brought him within inches of Torrie. A strange glint flickered in his eyes. "You'd be smart to get out of this valley just as fast as your feet can make a path."

"Are y-you threatening me?"

"You could take it as such." Ben nodded, slowly. His mouth curled in a snide grin. He stared at her for only a second more, then he bent down and began to gather up his papers. When he heard Torrie flee from the room his gaze never looked up.

Torrie paused in the hallway outside the office. She needed to collect her thoughts and catch her breath. It had been a waste of time to come here. She wondered why she'd ever thought Ben would do anything decent.

A sick feeling washed over Torrie when she thought of the news she must relay to Elsa. The selfishness of Ben's decision made her deaf to his last words for a moment. She turned back toward his office, thinking she would go back in, and try to reason with him. She peered through the open door.

Ben was at his desk. His head was bent over the papers again. But even from this angle, his victorious smirk was still visible.

She twirled on her heels, and stomped to the coat tree where her raincoat hung. She wanted nothing from him, nothing from the Grand Mesa—except to be rid of them.

At the front door she noticed the rainy drizzle had turned to a wet snow. She returned to the coat tree and grabbed her heavy winter coat. She might need it, and she had no intention of coming here again. When she got back to Elsa's place, she'd ask Mac to come and get her clothes and personal belongings out of her bedroom.

She pulled on her rain coat and raised the hood over her head. The heavy coat was in her arms as she headed out to fetch a horse, but she took the time to put it on once she reached the shelter of the barn. The weather was growing nastier as the day wore on. She planned to saddle one of the fastest horses in the stable. Ginger was in the first stall, however, and for some reason, Torrie felt the urge to take her again.

As Torrie started down the road, she glanced back over her shoulder toward the house. Ben stood on the porch. She couldn't make out his face because of the falling sleet. But she knew he was smiling.

She thought of his final words, his threatening words. Although she needed to get back to Elsa, there was someplace else she needed to go first.

Chapter Sixteen

"Half the valley already thinks we had a hand in the murders of Leo MacFarlene and Will Connor. With Canon Carrington missing, we'll have a hellva time trying to prove our innocence."

Shawn McLeary nodded his head in agreement with Jim Larson's words.

In a chair in the corner of Wayne's den, sat Lance Farlo. He remained silent while he listened to the conversation between his employers. His intent gaze studied each of them closely.

Nearing fifty—Lance guessed—Jim Larson was the oldest of the men. A tall, and extremely thin man, his appearance reminded Lance of a shopkeeper. He didn't see Larson as a weak man, though, and he knew the rancher was prepared to fight for his land.

"In town this morning," Shawn McLeary began, "I couldn't even get one person to talk to me who wasn't looking over their shoulder. Even Sheriff Kearny acted as if he was afraid to be seen talking to me." Shawn shifted his weight nervously in his chair, and drew in a worried sigh.

Of the three ranchers, Shawn was the youngest —close in age to Lance Farlo. He was affected the most, too. His small acreage ran to the south of the Grand Mesa. The only source of water for his herd was a narrow section of the Colorado River. Late yesterday, Ben Carrington's men strung a fence line along that portion of the river.

"What did Kearny say he was gonna do about the fence?" Wayne asked.

Shawn shrugged. "He didn't say he'd do anything."

Lance noticed the men kept glancing in his direction. When he told them he was Ben Carrington's son, their initial reactions were a combination of mistrust and anger. They felt he should have told them his true identity when they had hired him. Lance understood their feelings. When he explained to them about his past relationship with his father, though, they calmed down.

Wayne Gere wanted to circulate the story about how Carrington ran off his son, wanted to dig up the speculation surrounding his wife's death. Wayne figured Ben's sympathizers would see him in a different light then.

Lance almost regretted telling Gere about his mother. He wished he would have kept the range war separate. He didn't want a repeat of what happened in the past.

Wayne Gere—in Lance's opinion—was almost as tough as Ben Carrington. He looked to be in his early forties, and he was a man who seemed to face conflict with enthusiasm. Recently retired from the U.S. Cavalry, Wayne had fought in the last of the Indian wars. He told Lance he thought Ben Carrington was a minor foe when compared to the likes of Geronimo and Sitting Bull. He also made no bones on how he felt about hiring a cattle detective to protect his cattle and land.

Lance knew Ben Carrington—and the Grand Mesa—were too powerful for Wayne to fight on his own. Wayne knew this, too.

He was forced to band together with his neighbors if any of them hoped to win. In part, Lance attributed Wayne's attitude toward hiring him to the fact that the ex-cavalryman was unmarried. Jim Larson and Shawn McLeary had families to consider. Hiring a gunfighter seemed more sensible than facing Carrington's bunch of henchmen on their own.

"What's your opinion on all this? You've hardly said a word since you got here," Wayne Gere said, turning to face Lance.

Lance leveled his pale gaze on Gere's face. His thoughtful expression drew his eyebrows close together. "I think somebody's being set up."

"Damn right. We are!" Wayne retorted. He motioned around the room with a wide sweep of his arm. Then, he huffed with disgust. "We're not paying you to tell us what we already know. Your job is to keep it from happening."

Lance's eyes narrowed slightly. He was not surprised by Wayne's reaction.

"We've got to find a way to convince Carrington we're not squatting on his land," Shawn McLeary said. He wanted the range war to end before any more lives were lost.

"I've tried. I showed him the receipts to prove

my land was bought and paid for," Wayne said. "Carrington refuses to accept it. He says the damn government sold his land."

Shawn nervously rolled an unlit cigar between his thumb and forefinger. He directed his question to no one in particular. "Why don't we take it to court? A judge would surely rule in our favor."

"Maybe," Wayne answered. "Maybe not. Twenty-five years ago when men like Ben Carrington came out here and laid claim to all the land they wanted there was no reason for them to worry about boundary lines. They ran their cattle where the best grass grew, and wherever there was plenty of water. Now, all that's changed. The men who didn't clearly define the property lines of the land they homesteaded back then are finding out they don't own as much land as they originally thought."

"Carrington wants it all," Jim Larson added, then grunted with aggravation. "A judge might decide he owns the whole damn valley!"

"I won't be pushed out," Wayne Gere's voice was as determined as the expression on his tanned face. He sat down in the chair behind his desk. On the desk was a fancy wooden box with the cross sword emblem of the U.S. Cavalry engraved on its top. Wayne opened the box and took out a cigar. As he struck a match and lit the cigar, his gaze settled on Lance. He took a long puff on the cigar, blew out a stream of smoke, then said, "It's also your job to see to it that none of us gets pushed out."

Lance met his penetrating gaze. "Eventually you'll have no choice but to get a court ruling. Ben will not give up. But, if one—or all of you—go to jail for murder, most of his problem will be solved."

The gunfighter's words left a heavy silence hanging over the room, but it was interrupted by a banging on the front door.

Wayne stalked from the den to answer his door. When he returned, Torrie Carrington was at his side.

She paid no attention to anyone other than Lance. A shiver of excitement raced through her body as she watched him rise from his chair. She thought she detected the same reaction in him when he looked across the room at her.

"Your father has ordered me off his land," she blurted out, "and Canon's missing. Ben and everybody else at the Grand Mesa is blaming you." She pushed her wet, dripping hood back from her forehead. Her damp hair clung closely to her head.

Her words made an impact on Lance Farlo that was not felt by any of the other men. His memory fleetingly dredged up the day when his father had ordered him to leave the Grand Mesa.

"How do they know that Canon Carrington is really missing? Maybe he's just holed up in some saloon or whorehouse." A snide chortle followed Wayne's insinuation.

He missed the deadly look Lance cast in his direction.

"His horse showed up this morning not long after you were at the ranch looking for him," Torrie retorted without looking away from Lance. "They're saying you killed him—saying his body will turn up just like Will Connor's and Leo

MacFarlene's." She made no effort to hide her concern over Lance's predicament.

"Is that true?" Wayne asked. "Did you go after Canon Carrington?"

"I did, but I didn't find him." His pale gaze narrowed as Lance stepped to the center of the room. "If I'd found him, I would have killed him." His words were spoken without a note of sarcasm or malice, just a definite tone that left no doubt.

Lance crossed the rest of the room in a couple of long strides and stopped before Torrie. "Did the old man threaten you in any way?" His voice was filled now with a tone of compassion as he reached out and gently touched the wet sleeve of her coat.

"He told me I'd be smart to get out of the valley," Torrie gave her shoulders a shrug, adding, "but he doesn't scare me anymore."

"Don't underestimate the old man," Lance replied. He noticed how hard she was trying to convince herself of her own words. This was something else he understood. Ben Carrington didn't scare him anymore either—but if he did, he would never admit it.

"What do we do now? If Canon does turn up dead—" Jim Larson began.

"We don't know that he will," Lance interrupted. He realized his impetuous behavior this morning was backfiring on him. "But I'm gonna do some checking around on my own. I don't have much faith in Sheriff Kearny."

Shawn grunted and nodded his head in agreement.

"I'll keep a low profile while Ben has his men lying for me," Lance added.

"Does that mean you're going into hiding?" Wayne's voice was taunting. He wondered if Farlo's reputation was overstated.

Intense aggravation lined Lance's face as he turned to Wayne. "If you're having second thoughts about hiring me or about the way I'm handling things, maybe we'd better settle up now."

The two men stared at one another for several seconds. Finally, Wayne hung his head and nodded. "I suppose we'd be smart to stick together."

Lance's tense expression lightened. He heard the sounds of relieved sighs coming from the other two men.

Victoria stood at his side. She had not moved since Wayne confronted him. He turned to her again. "I think you should let me take you to town now." A strange fluttering erupted in his chest. He probably wouldn't see her again.

"I won't leave Elsa Connor and her baby alone on the Grand Mesa." Torrie's tone of voice, and the stubborn tilt of her head did not invite dispute.

Relief flooded through him, irritation, too. He had a job to do, he reminded himself.

"Is Mrs. Connor able to travel—even a short distance?" he asked. He glanced around at his employers.

"The women and the baby are welcome to stay here," Wayne offered, sensing Lance's thoughts.

"I think Elsa's strong enough to travel," Torrie said, still looking at Lance. "When she hears what Ben did, she won't want to stay one more minute on that selfish old bas—" Torrie stopped. She felt a

173

hot blush work its way through her face.

"My wife wouldn't mind if the women stayed at our place," Shawn McLeary offered.

"Same goes for us," added Jim Larson. A meek smile curved his lips. "We've got a big house, and my daughter can help with the baby."

"Thank you—all of you," Torrie answered as she looked to each of the ranchers. She turned back to Jim Larson. "Elsa would appreciate the extra help," she added. She knew Elsa would feel most comfortable at the Larson's home. Their house was the most logical choice. Jim and his wife had built a large two-story home on their property. Their only child—Linda—was fifteen years old.

The McLeary house was considerably smaller. It barely accommodated Shawn, his wife, Abby, and their four young children.

Wayne Gere's house had plenty of room. But he was a confirmed bachelor, and Torrie knew he was not accustomed to having women and babies in his home.

"It will only be temporary," Torrie said to Jim Larson. "As soon as possible we'll be going to Denver."

Lance made a point of thanking the ranchers for their generosity. At the same time he was overcome with an odd mixture of consolation—and disappointment—over knowing Torrie's future plans.

Denver.

What did it matter where she was going?

When he finished with his business he was headed back to the Red River country. Texas was a long way from Denver.

Chapter Seventeen

Lance planned to ride to the Connor house before daylight faded, spend the night, then transport Elsa and her baby to the Larson ranch the first thing in the morning. Victoria rode at his side.

The weather, though, did not cooperate with Lance's plan. Sleet had given way to a heavy, wet snow as the afternoon began to fade to dusk. The hooves of the horses sank into the layer of snow, and were sucked deep in the murky ground. Torrie's mare could barely pull her hooves out of the muck. Lance did not say a snide word, even when he had to stop constantly to wait on them.

To carry on any sort of conversation was impossible, anyway.

A freezing wind accompanied the autumn snowstorm. It whipped the breath out of the riders' mouths every time they attempted to speak. They wrapped the lower portions of their faces with handkerchiefs for protection.

Because of the storm, darkness crept across the

countryside long before it was due. Torrie and Lance had gone less than half the way to the Grand Mesa when the fading daylight, and the growing intensity of the storm forced them to stop and consider their options. A grove of cottonwoods offered them meager sanctuary.

"We'll never make it to the Grand Mesa in this weather," Lance said, his voice breathy. He pulled the scarf away from his mouth while he spoke. The brim of his Stetson hung low over his eyes, heavy with a mixture of snow and water. He pulled the hat from his head and shook the snow from the brim and crown. A worried frown tugged at the corners of his mouth.

Torrie untied the handkerchief from the back of her head, then wiped it over her eyes. Wet snow had accumulated on her eyelashes and made her vision blurry. She was grateful she was wearing her heavy coat under her raincoat. But even two coats didn't keep her warm.

"I need to get to Elsa's," Torrie finally said. She immediately realized she was being foolish to think they could continue to travel in this foul weather. She had lived in this country long enough to know riding in a storm as violent as this one was not possible. Nightfall reinforced the impossibility.

Lance looked past the cottonwoods. Snow hung heavy on their branches and made them droop almost to the ground in some places. He was alarmed at how fast darkness was swallowing up the land. Only the starkness of the falling snow illuminated the ground, but following the road was no longer feasible. There was no road to be seen . . . just endless white. Even that was devoured by darkness within a few yards. Lance carefully calculated the direction they were traveling, but during a blizzard—and at night—even the best tracker could get lost.

"There's a line shack over on Piceance Creek," Torrie said. Her teeth chattered together when a blast of icy wind whipped through the cotton-woods.

A look of relief passed through Lance's face. He thought she would insist they keep going.

If he remembered correctly, Piceance Creek was only a couple of miles from where they were now. With the constant intensity of this storm, finding some sort of a shelter was their only hope to survive the night. Lance gave his head a quick nod before pulling his scarf up over his mouth again. In the faded light he could not make out her expression.

Torrie quickly retied her scarf. There were a dozen thoughts crowding into her mind. Most of them centered around the idea of being in the line shack—alone—with Lance Farlo. Her thoughts were as unsettling as they were desirable.

They reached the shack in complete darkness, and they might have ridden right past the building if both the horses hadn't whinnied when they smelled the hay stacked in a lean-to beside the small building.

Torrie was sure she'd never been as happy as she was to see the dark outline of the line shack through the falling snow. Her entire body felt numb from the freezing cold, and she was no longer able to focus on the direction they were traveling. Only moments before the horses had alerted them to the shack, she had been ready to admit they were hopelessly lost in the blinding blizzard. But now, her hope was renewed, and her thoughts diverted back to the idea of being alone with Lance through the long, cold night ahead.

The horses did not hesitate to go directly to the lean-to, and the hay. In this country, where a horse was almost as necessary as food and water, the animal's needs came first.

Torrie did not complain about her own discomforts as she went to work beside Lance. When the horses were rubbed down, fed, and tied up so they couldn't wander out into the snow and become lost, she followed him from the lean-to. Her blood felt as if it had turned to icicles in her stiff limbs as she hauled her saddle and bedroll into the shack.

This line shack was typical. A mattress was thrown in the middle of the floor. A single chair sat in front of a long shelf, which had been built on one wall and served as a table. A stove and a lantern completed the furnishings. Others exactly like it could be found scattered along the open ranges and up on the high mountain meadows. The purpose of these crude structures was for the same reason Torrie and Lance welcomed its shelter—to survive the ever-changing weather in this temperamental land. Many a cowboy found himself stranded out on the range when an unexpected storm blew in. A line shack was sometimes their only chance to beat the elements.

All the shacks built in this part of the country were kept well-stocked with firewood and kindling. After Lance lit the lantern, he discarded his wet duster, then tackled the job of starting a fire in the potbellied stove. The walls of the sturdy shack contained no cracks, and there were no windows to allow the heat to escape. In no time the interior of the temporary dwelling was warm and toasty.

Torrie had not moved the entire time he worked over the fire. She'd taken off the scarf from her face, but not her wet raincoat or the heavier coat underneath. A circle of water stood around her feet where the snow melting from her clothes was accumulating.

"I reckon you'd best rid yourself of those wet clothes." He wondered if he sounded as awkward as he felt.

He'd had his share of women—whores who worked in saloons, mostly. He'd once had a brief affair with the lovely wife of one of his employers. It was not something he was proud to remember. Victoria was different. She made him feel as flustered as a schoolboy who was about to ask her to his first dance.

Torrie did not notice his agitated state. She was concerned with her own strange feelings. The lantern cast a cozy glow through the interior of the little room, and she felt as if the flames in the stove were licking at her body. She was no longer cold, no longer aware of her wet, uncomfortable clothes. She was vitally aware of Lance, however.

She cleared her throat. The loud noise seemed to echo across the room. The heat soared through her body with more intensity. He was staring back at her.

She turned away and tried to concentrate on

ridding herself of the wet coats. She gasped when she felt Lance's hands clasp ahold of her shoulders. For a moment she froze, uncertain of his motives. With ease he pulled both her coats off. In the process he managed to turn her around so they were facing one another.

There was barely more than a few inches separating them.

Torrie forced herself to stare at the top button of his shirt, rather than raise her gaze to his face again.

Another deafening moment of silence followed until Lance cleared the lump in his throat in the same type of loud, uncouth noise as Torrie had made a moment ago. He backed away, taking her coats with him. He bent over to grab his saddlebags and bedroll, then retreated the short distance to the opposite end of the tiny room. He pretended to busy himself with hanging her raincoat and the heavier one up by the stove.

Now, the mattress in the middle of the floor separated them.

Torrie tried, but did not succeed in keeping her gaze from watching Lance as he began to strip his wet shirt from his muscled chest. He acted as though he were oblivious to her inquisitive stare while he bent down and undid the saddlebags at his feet. She noticed how his sinewy muscles rippled like a fine-tuned machine across the broad expanse of his back as he dug through his bags. When he straightened up again he held a grey shirt in his hand. Torrie was captivated by him—and shocked by the thoughts ravaging her mind.

A fiery, unknown sensation was radiating from

the core of her being. It worked its way through her entire body like wildfire. Her hands tingled with a burning ache to rub themselves along the smooth tanned skin that encased his strong shoulders. The long, brown hair that hugged his neck almost seemed to beckon her fingers to entangle themselves in the wet curls.

Torrie could not believe she was capable of summoning up such wanton thoughts about this man. Good grief! He was only changing his shirt. She forced herself to look away from him again.

Stumbling to where she had dropped her own saddlebags, Torrie tried in desperation to divert her thoughts. Her gaze moved toward the mattress. It was an old mattress, fairly clean, and it appeared not to be too lumpy.

It seemed innocent.

This was, after all, a matter of survival, Torrie reminded herself. If he was as worn-out as she was, it wouldn't take long for them to fall asleep—side by side on the mattress—and him with those strong muscles and tantalizing curls and . . .

"Do you have dry clothes to change into?"

Torrie jumped at the sound of his deep voice intruding into her increasingly wanton thoughts. In spite of her determined attempt not to look in his direction, her gaze immediately sought him. He was wearing the shirt, but he had not bothered to button it yet. She was afforded a teasing glimpse of the golden-brown ringlets that blanketed his chest and trailed down his flat belly before disappearing into the waistband of his snug-fitting jeans.

"I-I—no," she stammered.

"Well, I have an extra change of clothes." He pretended not to notice her fidgety behavior. However, he was aware of every move she made—or rather, every move she didn't make. He wondered if the drumming sound of his heartbeat could be heard above the crackling din of the fire.

He chuckled as he held up a shirt and pants. He thought his laughter sounded high and unnatural. "I reckon you'll get lost in these duds, but you're likely to catch pneumonia in those things."

Torrie's mouth opened slightly, then clamped shut. She focused on the clothes for several seconds, then her gaze disobeyed her frantic inner voice and rose to meet his. Not one tangible thought raced through her head. . . . He expected her to take off her clothes—right here, right now—and they were probably going to sleep together on the mattress. . . . How come she never had noticed the little dimple below his bottom lip, the one that was almost hidden by his closely-cropped beard?

Good grief!

Then, without warning or invitation, Canon's face flashed through her mind. She saw his brown eyes—so like Lance's—yet, so very different.

The fleeting look of terror that crossed her face was undeniable, and so devastating Lance felt as though he had been doused by a bucket of ice water. An instant before, he knew he had glimpsed a boiling cauldron of desire and rapture in her gaze. He did not need to ask her what or who stole away the ecstasy which should have belonged solely to him. He wondered if Canon's abuse would affect everything she did for the rest of her life.

"I'll wait over by the stove while you get those wet things off," his voice sounded strained, hoarse. He shoved the clothes toward her, stalked to the stove, and busied himself with removing his gunbelt. He hung the belt and holsters over the back of the chair. All the while keeping his back to Torrie.

She stared at his back, still lost to the sense of fear Canon's memory evoked. She found it hard to believe she could compare this man to Canon in any way.

As she fumbled to get out of her damp blouse and riding suit, Torrie continued to think about Canon. Because of him she had been convinced she would never experience the types of tender emotions she had witnessed between Elsa and Will Connor. Now, she realized how he had almost cheated her out of ever knowing what it felt like to desire a man. Not that it mattered, she told herself.

She couldn't forget who Lance Farlo was or that soon he would be gone from her life forever.

This made her want him even more. She realized tonight might be all they would ever have . . . a beautiful memory shared with him would be worth the lonely tomorrows she would have to face once they went their separate ways.

Chapter Eighteen

This time it was Lance's turn to jump when Torrie walked up to hang the rest of her wet things by the stove.

"T-Thanks for the clothes." She noticed that his gaze surveyed the way his baggy shirt and pants fit on her slender form. She'd rolled his denim jeans up around her ankles, and secured the waist with the black leather belt from her riding skirt. His white cowboy cut shirt hung almost to her knees, and she'd folded the shirt cuffs up so her hands were freed of the excess material from the long shirt sleeves. Practically every inch of her was covered up by his oversized clothes, but he was looking at her as if he thought she'd never looked better.

Torrie tried in vain to divert her attention away from him. She glanced down and noticed he was still clad in his wet jeans. "I guess it's my turn to look away while you get outta your wet pants."

A sheepish grin tugged at his lips. He shrugged.

"That's not necessary." He motioned towards the blue jeans she was wearing. "I only had one extra pair."

"Oh, you should have kept them for yourself," she said. She slapped the open palms of her hands against her thighs, then added before thinking, "I'll take them off."

Her attempt to reciprocate his kindness painted vivid pictures in Lance's mind. He knew she had not meant anything with her innocent comment. Still, it summoned up the image of her wearing no pants at all.

"I didn't mean. . . ." she gasped when she noticed his lopsided grin. Her words were cut short by the unexpected laughter which burst from him. She stared at him for a second, confused by his obvious mirth. But then she found herself laughing with him.

Lance reached out and tenderly clasped his large hands on each side of her flushed face. His laughter faded away.

Torrie's mouth closed. She swallowed the lump in her throat.

Lance began to speak, his voice deep and emotional. "If I were an artist, I'd paint a picture of you laughing. Then I could carry that picture with me forever."

His tender words left Torrie speechless. His warm hands still encased her face. Her gaze made no attempt to look away from him again. In her mind she was creating a picture of him—one, she too, could retain for the rest of her life. Her mind's artistic creation was interrupted when he bent down. Instinctively, she closed her eyes as she felt the warmth of his moist mouth close over her trembling lips.

This was her first kiss—Canon's slobbery attempts did not count. This was nothing like she had ever imagined. The feel of his beard and mustache were unexpectedly soft against her face. She found her own lips returning his fevered kiss. Her arms rose up to encircle his neck as if they'd been invited.

When Lance finally pulled away, he experienced a moment of surprise over his own actions. "I reckon I shouldn't have . . ." He never finished. In the next instant a deep moan echoed from his parted lips as he pulled her against him once more. He brought his mouth down upon her lips, urgently.

He couldn't resist her—not when she stood there looking up at him with such a look of rapture on her lovely face. His mind kept trying to remind him of his vow to never let desire for this woman overwhelm his common sense.

Lance knew desire. It was like a drink of whiskey, and he sated his thirst for both when the need arose. Victoria awoke something in him entirely different, confusing . . . and thoroughly undeniable.

Torrie felt her lips being pried apart with little resistance. She allowed Lance's darting tongue to explore the interior of her sweet-tasting mouth. Soon, her own tongue danced and entwined with his as if they were old friends. Her head swam with conflicting thoughts—protests struggling with yearnings. Her body pasted itself up against his hard body as though there were no doubts about its intentions. She revelled in the way his strong arms completely enveloped her in their tight embrace.

She felt her spine curve as easily as a limp noodle as he bent her backwards to leave a hot, fiery trail of kisses on her mouth and down along the column of her exposed neckline. She felt weak, dizzy—not sick—excited. Dangerously excited . . . a million times more than she'd felt the other day when they had ridden side by side across the vast ranges of the Grand Mesa.

Sometime—amidst the fevered moments—Lance straightened his stance. He pulled Torrie with him until they were upright again. He leaned back slightly to look at her face in the flickering light of the lantern. In her green gaze he could see his own miniature reflection. Her complexion flushed crimson with unrestrained desire, her rosy lips were swollen from his recent kisses. Beneath the loose material of his large white shirt, he noticed the rapid rising and falling of her breasts. Her excitement was infectious.

His head tilted to one side, from between his beard and mustache, his lips curved with a gentle smile. His voice broke softly into the pervading quiet in the line shack. "I want to make love to you tonight, Victoria. I reckon I want it more than I've wanted just about anything." He paused and drew in a deep sigh. "But I won't lie to you. I won't tell you that if we make love tonight—or tomorrow— or a dozen more times, well—" he shrugged his shoulders, adding, "What I'm trying to say is that

I'm not gonna' make you any promises I can't keep."

Torrie choked back the rising sensation in her parched throat. She nodded her head. She understood, but she still wanted him. "I-I . . ." her voice trembled. She didn't want him to know how deeply she was affected by his words. She ran her tongue over her lips, then attempted to speak again.

"I won't think it means you've fallen in love with me or expect you'd want to make a respectable woman of me or anything else." She felt the burning of tears sting the corners of her eyes. Desperately, she willed them not to fall as she tried to keep her gaze from wavering from Lance's face.

An uneasy silence followed her half-accurate description of his blundered attempt to voice his feelings. Lance knew he could not promise her marriage or any sort of a future which would require a commitment. Sometimes, he thought of himself as a walking deadman. What woman would want a man that smelled of death?

As for falling in love with her—well—that was something altogether different. He realized he was beyond falling, he was already tumbling down into the bottomless pit defined as love. He couldn't tell her this, though.

His silence confirmed what Torrie believed. Still, she clung to him like a dying woman clings to a single thread of life. She tried to convince herself that nothing mattered but tonight.

"I don't know what to say," Lance said at last. It surprised him that he felt the need to say anything at all.

"You've already said it." Torrie let her arms drop back down to her sides as she glanced down toward the rough floorboards. He'd given her a taste of passion, a morsel of love. She was grateful to him for these things. She would learn how to live with the heartbreak of losing the love she thought she would never find. What more could either of them say now?

"No! There's a lot more to be said," Lance blurted out. He was usually so confident about his actions, so certain he could control every facet of his life. Victoria threw him into complete turmoil. He felt as lost as a homeless puppy. Reaching out and clasping onto the loose material of her shirt sleeve, he stopped her from turning away from him again.

As always, she found it impossible to prevent her gaze from succumbing to the lure of meeting his. Hope soared in her breast as she stared up at him.

Outside the intensity of the wind began to howl around the walls of the little shack. Lance was vaguely aware of the wailing sounds of the wind. He felt trapped by the storm, and by his own restraints.

"I have to at least try to explain to you what I meant," he said. He held onto her sleeve, tightly, as if he actually thought she could escape from him. Torrie did nothing. Several more seconds of nerve-racking silence followed before he began to speak again. "When I said I couldn't make you any promises it wasn't because I don't want to—it's because I can't.''

He exhaled a burdened sigh, and turned loose of his tight hold on her shirt. A tortured expression washed through his tanned face as he started to speak again. "You know what I am, the way I live because of it. A woman would have no future with a man like me." He paused. His arms hung limply at his sides. "I can't change the way things are . . . not any more than I can prevent myself from falling in love with you."

Unconsciously, Torrie had been holding her breath. She exhaled in a loud gasp. She did not expect promises from this man, but his love was more than she ever expected. Her conversation with Mac Williams produced itself in her mind almost word for word. The old gunslinger had been trying to tell her something, after all.

She stepped forward and tilted her head back so she could look in Lance's eyes as she spoke. "I can accept the way things have to be between us. You've already given me more than I ever dreamed possible . . . and we will have tonight."

Lance did not give her the chance to change her mind as he swept her back into his arms. How could he help falling in love with a woman like Victoria Carrington? He only wished he would not have to hurt her.

If it was possible to love a lifetime in one night, then Lance intended to make this his ultimate goal. When he kissed her again, her response suggested to Lance she had made the same vow to herself about the night that awaited them.

Chapter Nineteen

Not knowing the extent of the abuse Torrie had suffered, Lance felt a certain responsibility to be extra gentle with her.

She didn't seem to have any problems with kissing, though. His touch grew bolder as his hand moved down along the curve of her hip, then up under the loose material of her shirt. He felt her body grow rigid. His hand stopped above the waistband of her jeans.

"It's all right," he said, his voice a whisper. He removed his hand from beneath her shirt, and raised it to her face. He cupped her chin gently in his grasp so he could look into her eyes when he spoke. "Tonight, I want to wipe away all the bad memories, Victoria."

The spot where he had just removed his hand felt as if he had lit a match there. She thought she was doing a good job of hiding her nervousness, but obviously he could sense her uncertainty. A timid smile tugged at her lips. "The name's Torrie."

She saw a change in his worried expression almost at once. He seemed so grateful for the simple privilege of using her nickname. His mouth curved into a smile, his pale gaze appeared to darken. Torrie did not resist when he pulled her to him again.

His hand traveled the same path up under her shirt, intent now to reach its destination. His mouth devoured hers with demanding kisses. Torrie felt a choked gasp rise in her throat when his hand closed over the mound of one breast. She was wearing a cotton camisole under the shirt, but he managed to push her undergarment out of the way. Her skin tingled beneath his kneading hand, her breast responded to his touch without a moment's indecision. Swollen with desire, the tiny kernel at the tip of her bosom hardened against his palm. His proficient fingertips flicked at the little bud, taunting and enticing it until Torrie's body swooned against him.

He was barely getting started . . .

With the mattress at their feet, Lance easily pulled Torrie down with him. His devoted kisses continued to entertain her lips as his fingers expertly undid the buttons running down the front of her shirt. He slid her shirt open, but was still confronted with the camisole. The undergarment could be removed only by pulling it over her head. Lance dragged his lips away from hers, groaned with impatience, and sat up. He gazed at Torrie for a moment. The lantern cast a golden glow over her face. A tremor of desire shot through his body.

Her eyes opened slowly. She looked up at him, expectant, trusting. She still lay on the mattress, but her arms stretched to encircle his neck. Her lips were parted, slightly trembling.

A pang of guilt clutched Lance's chest. He couldn't stop now. But, it would be so damned hard to leave her after tonight.

"You're beautiful," he whispered, his voice quavering.

Her mouth closed, her gaze remained on his face. She wanted to find a way to tell him how beautiful he looked to her, but her fumbling mind could not locate the right words.

He clasped ahold of her arms and unwound them from his neck, then pulled her up. She did not move while he began to pull her thin camisole up over her bosom. Her arms hung limply at her sides until he pushed them up as he continued to slide the garment over her head. The small fingers on his hands brushed lightly against her skin as they moved upward. They left a tingling trail on her skin. A slight shiver shook through her body.

"Your turn," Lance said.

Torrie didn't move. She was aware only of the fact that she was completely exposed on top. Her embarrassment held her captive, unable to do anything other than stare at his face. Her only consolation was that his gaze was staring back into hers.

When she still made no attempt to move, Lance clasped ahold of her hands and placed them against his chest.

For a moment her hands did nothing. He had

195

never buttoned his shirt. She felt the soft curls of his chest hairs sticking out from the material of his shirt. Her mind began to function again. She pushed the shirt away from his chest. Her gaze traveled over the smooth skin along his shoulders and over his muscled chest. She noticed there were no interruptions of his dark tan, which suggested to her that he frequently worked out in the sun without a shirt.

Her fingers stretched out with a sweet ache as they moved to gingerly touch the downy hairs on his chest. Lance did not give her the chance to fulfill this longing.

He captured her in his embrace again, his lips enslaved her mouth. Their bare chests crushed together. He pushed her back on the mattress again.

Torrie felt his fingers fiddling with the clasp on her belt. He unfastened the buckle, then went to work on the snaps on her jeans. His fingers were nimble and able. In no time he was sliding the baggy jeans—along with the rest of her undergarments—down her hips, her legs, and past her feet.

Torrie's body stiffened. There was nothing to shield her from his hands as they charted a fevered path back up her legs, her hips, and around to her buttocks. She could not move, his hands held her tightly against him, his kisses prevented her protests—or lack of protest. Torrie's thoughts were quickly lost to the new sensations her body was discovering. Every inch of her being seemed to be alive—on fire—and more desperate for his touch with every passing moment.

His mouth released hers, and began a tantalizing descent over her chin, down her neck. He stopped when his lips encased one hard kernel at the tip of her breast. His tongue lavished it with swirling, teasing swipes until Torrie cried out in ecstasy. He pulled away and looked up at her face. She tried to avoid meeting his gaze. One side of his mouth curled in a crooked grin as he sat up.

"Your turn," he said again. He tugged his tall boots off and tossed them by the stove. Then he motioned to the snaps on his jeans, and leaned back.

Torrie ran her tongue over her parched lips. She slowly pushed herself. She noticed his gaze move along the entire length of her body. His nostrils flared slightly, his chest rose and fell more rapidly. Instinctively Torrie drew her hands over her bosom.

He gave his head a negative shake from side to side.

Torrie cleared her throat, swallowed, and forced herself to lower her arms. She followed his gaze down to his waist again. His jeans were still damp, the snaps difficult to undo. But he didn't help her as she clumsily struggled to unfasten them. Her fingers noticed right off that he wore no underwear under his jeans. Shooting spears of heat soared through her hands, up her arms and throughout her body.

Suddenly, Lance grew impatient. He tugged his jeans down and kicked them away from his feet. He reached over and pulled Torrie to him. He pushed her back into the mattress. His body pinned her beneath him.

A startled cry issued from Torrie when she felt the unmistakable pressure of his hard manhood pressing against her abdomen.

He silenced her with more demanding kisses. Almost at once, Lance felt her body begin to relax, grow placid beneath his own feverish loins.

He pried her tightly clamped legs apart with his hand.

She attempted a protest. His lips stole away her words with another ardent kiss.

His fingers wasted no time burying themselves in the moist, warm crevice. He felt her body wiggle beneath him as she weakly fought against this intrusion. He continued to work his fingers back and forth until he felt her relax again.

Torrie was shocked by his intimate touch, but not enough to ignore the way it made her feel. The gentle, probing motion of his fingers was creating a building sense of wild abandon in her being. When he eased his fingers out, she wanted to cry out for him to continue.

Before she was aware of anything else he slid his hips down between her limp thighs. She felt the tip of his rigid manhood pressing against the moist chasm where his fingers had just explored.

Lance felt her grow stiff and tense again. He heard her inhale sharply. "I promise I'll be gentle."

"You don't make promises." Her voice was raspy, low.

"Only ones I can keep," he reminded her. His

lips sought her mouth in another kiss as he positioned himself, then plummeted downward. He buried his manhood deep, felt her tight— almost unyielding—resistance. Her startled cry reached his ears. In spite of the pain he knew she had just experienced, he felt a rushing sense of relief wash over him.

Without thinking he blurted out, "Canon never . . ." he stopped himself.

But Torrie heard. She was so wrapped up in the pleasure of his loving, it hadn't occurred to her that he might still think Canon had raped her. The pain of losing her virginity was only minor compared to the anguish she felt over not telling Lance everything.

Lance felt the moisture of her hot tears against his face. He also felt a dampness form in his own eyes. A strange sensation flooded through him—a powerful sense of bonding with this woman, and it went far beyond his urge to make love to her.

He clutched her slender form, tight, kissed her lips with a slow, engulfing kiss. Then he began to make gentle love to her.

Torrie's pain faded with each plunge of his hips. The brief intrusion of Canon's memory disappeared completely. She began to return each of Lance's thrusts with a natural urge to raise her own hips up to meld with his. She felt like firecrackers were exploding in her body as his movements intensified. Something akin to molten lava spread through her entire being when Lance spilled his life-giving seeds into her with abandonment.

was one of Elsa's dresses—on her friend and not woman becoming pregnant. Elsa was lighter built, and Torrie felt the dress was not right

Chapter Twenty

Lance woke with a start. He'd sensed a movement close by. His instinct was to go for his gun. For the first time in years his weapon was not in his reach. His chest tightened. The feeling evaporated as his sleepy gaze focused on the chair where his gunbelt hung.

Torrie moved again. An unconscious smile tugged at Lance's mouth. He felt strange being here like this—waking up beside her. He let his gaze wander along her sleeping form. She looked younger when she was asleep—he noticed—and more vulnerable.

The way she'd been last night reminded him of a ripe young bud hanging on a vine, slowly opening up. Lance felt like a gardener who had pruned away all the bad weeds and unveiled a beautiful blossom. He smiled to himself. Lately, it seemed he was full of poetic thoughts. His satisfaction was short-lived, however.

He glanced back down at Torrie. She slept on

peacefully. Lance's smile drooped into a frown when he realized he would not be around to appreciate the bounty of his harvest. The idea of another man touching this woman caused something explosive to erupt inside him.

Torrie stirred again. She rolled over on her side and surprised Lance by snuggling up against him. He thought of a little girl cuddling up to her teddy bear. Her long tousled hair lay in wild abandon around her face and shoulders. Even in the dim light its vibrant color shimmered like sun-kissed copper. Lance closed his eyes and listened to her soft, even breaths.

The shack was still warmed by the fire in the stove. They had made love until the wee hours of the morning, and Lance stoked the fire right before they had drifted off to sleep. He figured he should get up now, and check outside to see if the weather had cleared. But he wanted to prolong this peaceful feeling for a little longer.

He knew it was likely he would not see her much after they left here. He had things to do, she did too. By the time he finished with his business, she would probably be in Denver. He shivered, in spite of the heat emitting from the stove. Lost in his thoughts, Lance was not aware Torrie was observing him.

"Was last night that awful?" she asked in a sleepy voice. A teasing smile curved her lips.

"Last night—" he said, pulling her against him. His long legs entwined with hers. "Was too wonderful for words." There was not one inch of her body he had not explored. The mere remembrance made his manhood swell, throb with a renewed desire.

"What are you doin' to me woman?" he said, his tone husky. Already, he was positioning himself between her legs again.

"What are you doing to me?" she retorted, innocently. She accepted him with eager anticipation. She wondered if it was possible to ever tire of this ritual.

For a time, everything—and everyone—outside of this dwelling was forgotten again. Torrie was consumed by Lance's loving. She noticed a difference in him this morning, however. His loving seemed more intense, almost driven by desperation. Torrie understood, though. Their time together was running out.

At last, they were forced to draw apart.

Lance rose from the bed and began to put on his clothes, while Torrie watched his every move. She couldn't seem to get enough of him, his touch, his musky male scent—and most of all—the memory of what he felt like when they were melded together as one. A sweet, torturous yearning worked its way through her loins as she tried to savor each of these feelings and memories.

She wanted to cry out to him how much she loved him, wanted to cling to him and beg him to never leave her. But she could not allow herself to forget what he had said to her last night.

No promises . . .

A cold gust of wind blasted into the shack when Lance opened the door. A foot-deep snowdrift straddled the front of the shack. The storm had blown over, though. The sun was even shining faintly through a break in the clouds. Snowstorms this early in the season usually didn't last long. Before long the sun would soon melt the snow on the ground.

"We'd best be on our way." Lance's attitude assumed a sense of urgency. He began to gather their gear quickly, quietly.

Torrie kept glancing over at him. She scooped up her riding suit and began to get dressed. Her fingers fumbled with the buttons on her shirt, she tried to put her vest on inside out. Lance did not seem to notice her sudden clumsiness. He acted preoccupied, irritated. Torrie wondered if he regretted what happened between them. She bent down and shoved her feet into her tall riding boots.

She let out a startled gasp when she straightened up. Lance was behind her. His arms slipped around her waist. He rested his chin on the top of her head. Without a second thought, Torrie relaxed into his embrace.

"Once I know you, Mrs. Connor, and her baby are all safe at the Larson's, I'm gonna be tied-up with business." He buried his face in the profusion of her hair. He thought he detected a faint, sweet odor of roses.

"I understand," Torrie answered. His voice held a melancholy tone, and it infected her with a sense of sorrow. She could feel the warmth of his breath against her hair, but inside, she had suddenly grown cold.

"We're wastin' time," Lance said. He released her and headed for the door. Without another glance around the shack he stalked outside.

Torrie, however, cast a last look over her shoulder before she left. She tried to memorize every detail of the room. She stored the picture with her memories of Lance.

Once outside she turned her attention to saddling Ginger. The wind was not nearly as cold as it had been last night. But it still penetrated through her clothes, and made her anxious to get moving again.

She couldn't help but notice how friendly Ginger was with Lance's stallion. As they saddled them, the two animals continuously nudged one another with their noses, and whinnied softly as if they were talking sweet nothings into each other's ears. Torrie just wished Lance was still acting as chummy with her.

While they rode toward Elsa's house, Lance surprised Torrie by talking about his childhood. He told her only minor things about his growing up on the Grand Mesa. But she welcomed any information he disclosed about himself. When he pointed towards Horse Mountain and mentioned a cave where he and Canon had played when they were young, Torrie wondered if he was ready to talk about some of the other things in his past.

"Were you and your brother close when you were children?" she asked.

"No," he retorted in a blunt reply. Then to Torrie's surprise, he turned toward her, abruptly. In another sharp tone, he asked, "How did your mother die?"

Torrie was caught off guard by his question.

"She—she got a high fever. Nothing would bring it down. Why?"

His mouth drew into a thoughtful scowl. When he spoke again the bluntness had faded from his tone. "I was just curious if she had been—well—I was just curious." He drew in a heavy sigh. "I reckon sometimes I'm not too sensitive. I'm sorry."

Torrie remained silent. She wanted to talk about his past. There were few memories she held dear about the Grand Mesa. Her mother's marriage to Ben Carrington was among her unhappiest. Although her mother used to say she loved Ben, Torrie never understood why. It seemed to her the old man had made her mother's life a living hell.

"My mother was murdered," Lance blurted out. He looked straight ahead, his voice sounded strange, controlled. "My father pushed her from the top of the cliffs on the backside of the mesa."

"My God!" Torrie gasped. Her mind painted a vivid picture of the rugged cliffs and ledges on the back of the mesa. She kicked Ginger in the sides so she could get abreast Lance's horse. He didn't turn to look at her when she rode up beside him.

"Are you sure?" she asked.

He shrugged. He tried to appear nonchalant, but his actions only intensified his pain.

"I saw him do it." His clenched teeth barely permitted the words to escape.

All the questions Torrie intended to ask vanished from her mind. She was beginning to understand almost everything.

"He denied it. He called me a liar," Lance

offered, guessing her thoughts. "It was my word against his. He won."

Torrie was confused again. "What brought you back?"

He glanced at her, then quickly looked ahead again. "I'm not sure. I reckon I thought I could even out the score somehow."

"An eye for an eye?"

His shoulders lifted in a shrug again.

Torrie was surprised by his uncertainty. She figured him for a man who was always in control of his life. Before she had a chance to question him further, though, he leaned forward in his saddle and stared off in the distance.

"We've got visitors," he said, motioning toward the approaching riders.

Torrie's gaze followed his. Dread inched through her as the riders drew nearer. Then, she recognized them. Although she knew them by sight, she did not know their names. "They're Shawn McLeary's men."

They were riding hell-bent across the open range. Lance figured they were running away from something or someone.

The two riders skidded to a halt several yards in front of Torrie and Lance. Their faces were bright red from the cold wind. The horses they rode blew white vapor from their noses as if they had been running for a long distance.

"McLeary's got trouble," one of the men shouted. "His herd's all bunched up at the river. Some of 'em started chargin' the fence to get to water."

"Lead the way," Lance answered. But before he urged Raven on, he glanced at Torrie as if he didn't know what to do with her.

"I can ride the rest of the way to Elsa's alone," Torrie said.

"You're comin' with us," he retorted. His voice was as firm as the expression on his face. He diverted his gaze back to the two McLeary men, and gestured for them to move out.

Torrie did not try to argue with his decision. She wanted to get to Elsa as soon as possible, but it was still a good ten miles to the Connor house. Normally, that would not seem like a long distance to Torrie. Today, though, she was glad she did not have to go on alone.

Chapter Twenty-One

Shawn McLeary's herd gathered at the fence was an unsettling sight. The slightest disturbance could set the animals into a frenzied stampede, so none of the riders were anxious to get too close. Lance joined Shawn McLeary and the rest of his men on a hillside above the herd.

Torrie followed, and halted Ginger beside the others. She shivered when a blast of cold wind whipped across the top of the hill.

"Have you seen any of Carrington's men in the area?" Lance asked. He glanced at each of the men. All of them shook their head in a negative gesture.

"The only activity is when some of those ornery old steers charge at the fence," Shawn McLeary said. His face was flushed as though he'd been out in the wind for a long time. Under his eyes were heavy dark circles induced by lack of sleep.

Torrie was shocked by Shawn's haggard appearance. He looked like he'd aged ten years overnight. She glanced down at his herd, then over at the new fence line along the river's edge. She thought of how her stepfather's cattle outnumbered McLeary's herd by thousands. Carrington's acreage was even more immense when compared to the small section Shawn McLeary claimed title to. Ben's selfishness had never been so evident.

"I'm going down," Lance announced after studying the situation in silence for a few minutes. "Alone," he added.

A look of relief flooded over Shawn's face. "What do you got in mind?"

"The cattle need water."

"You're gonna cut the fence then?"

Lance gave his head a quick nod. He turned away from Shawn, then dug a worn pair of wire-cutters out of his saddlebags. He nudged Raven down the slope.

Shawn's hesitation to go down to the river didn't surprise Lance. He knew he'd been hired to take the risks, and there could be more than just thirsty cattle waiting at the fence. He eyed the thick brush on the opposite side of the river for any signs of trouble. Nothing moved.

It was difficult for Torrie to understand why none of Shawn's men went down to the fence with Lance. A sliver of dread inched through her as she watched his lonely figure approaching the angry cattle. She wanted to turn to the men beside her and scream at them to go down and help him. Instead, she forced herself to remain silent.

Several loud snorts rang out from the herd. Without warning one of the steers flung himself forward, rushed at the fence with his head bowed and his heels flying through the air. The wire almost seemed to spear the cow on its sharp barbs for a moment. With a loud bellowing the animal pulled away from the fence—leaving chunks of reddish brown hide on the fence where he had been gouged and torn by the barbed wire. The cow's encounter with the fence drew the attention of the rest of the herd. It seemed to increase their uneasiness. Snorting, mooing, and the sounds of stomping hooves filled the air. Each passing second made the cattle more impatient to reach the water on the other side of the fence.

"He shouldn't be down there alone," Torrie spat, unable to contain her feelings any longer. She received no reply. When she glanced at the other men's stony faces, she had a feeling nothing she said would influence them to help Lance.

"Don't you do anything foolish," Shawn McLeary finally said, glancing at Torrie briefly. "If you take off down this hillside the added commotion might be too much for those nervous steers."

Torrie stopped herself from telling Shawn what she thought of him—and the rest of his cowardly men. She turned her attention back to the activity at the river.

Lance had reached the fence. He cautiously inched his horse along the boundary line until he was only several yards away from the edge of the herd. Using slow movements Lance leaned down with his wire-cutters and began to snip through the top strands of the wire. He practically had to hang from his saddle horn to cut the bottom wire. The fence sagged, but it still stood. To open an area large enough for the cattle to get through without too much injury, Lance had to cross in front of the entire herd and cut the fence again.

The cattle appeared more restless with the intrusion. The entire herd pushed closer to the fence. Their insistent mooing and snorting grew continuously louder.

The uneasiness in Torrie also increased as she watched her man inch farther along the fence line. Anything could send the mass of cattle charging through the fence—and over Lance. He did not take long to reach his next destination. To Torrie, however, it seemed to take him forever.

She exhaled the breath she had been holding, yet, she still did not breathe much easier. Lance would not be out of danger until he was far away from the herd. He appeared to be just as anxious to finish with his risky task. He leaned over the side of his saddle again, and began to snip the strands of wire. His actions were much more brisk this time. When he finished cutting the fence, he gently shook the nearest post until the entire length of wire running between the two areas where he cut began to sag over to one side.

Lance nudged his horse backward until they were a safe distance from the herd. He alternated his attention between the cattle and the bushes on the opposite side of the river.

The cattle standing nearest to the fence noticed at once the wire barrier was no longer in their way. They took several slow steps forward, sticking their necks out to make certain their heads would not meet with the sharp barbs again. The bravest of the animals moved forward with little caution. Still, even lying flat on the ground, the wire posed a dangerous threat. When the cows began to stomp over the long strands lying on the ground their hooves and legs kept becoming entangled in the sharp, curling lines.

Lance noticed several of the lead steers were already badly cut and bloody from their previous encounters with the fence. He hated to see cattle torn up by barbed wire. More than once he'd known of cases where these types of injuries became infected or attracted screwworms—both could be fatal to the cows. When large numbers of a herd contracted screwworm infestation ranch hands were kept busy doing nothing else except doctoring the sick cattle, and skinning the dead ones so the hides could be sold. Then, the death of the cows would not result in a total loss. Lance knew of instances where ranchers had even killed one another when their cattle had been injured on each other's fences.

He continued to keep a close eye on McLeary's herd until all of the cows had managed to reach the river. As the numerous hooves trampled over the wire it was eventually pounded flat into the murky ground where it no longer posed a threat. The panic ceased to exist. The cattle quieted as they began to spread out along the snowy, muddy riverbank to lap at the cold water.

The gunfighter was still not at ease, however. He felt something was awry. It seemed strange his father did not have any men guarding this section of fence. This would have been the perfect opportunity for men from the Grand Mesa to catch him out in the open.

While Lance was contemplating this, he noticed

the arrival of another man on the top of the hill. He knew the horse—and its rider. His eye caught the flash of silver that glistened on the ex-cavalryman's saddle. Gere's saddle was adorned by two oval conchos, which decorated each side. Lance had noticed the fancy saddle hanging on a rail in Gere's barn.

Lance made it a practice never to decorate his gear with silver. Shiny decorations could reflect light or draw unnecessary attention.

Raising his arm up into the air, Lance returned Wayne's wave. He sensed his arrival was not just coincidental. "Now what, Blacky?" he said as he patted the stallion's neck. He nudged the horse in the sides.

The cattle appeared content now. Most of them were still spread out along the riverbank. Others no longer seemed interested in the water now that it was easily attainable again.

Lance rode his horse through the middle of the herd. He knew their attitude could change with the blink of an eye, so he made certain Raven's steps were not too hurried.

Once he was away from the cattle, however, he urged Raven to speed up. A sense of uneasiness clutched at his chest again. When he was close enough to glimpse all the grim expressions, he knew his intuition was right.

"Jim Larson's place was set on fire early this morning," Wayne announced as soon as Lance was in hearing range. "The barn's gone and most of the house."

"Damnit!" Lance said between clenched teeth. "Larson's family—are they all right?"

Wayne Gere nodded, "Nobody got hurt. But Jim's fit to be tied. Says he's gonna go after Carrington himself."

"That's my job," Lance replied, flatly. His pale gaze studied the other man for a moment. He turned away from the cold stare of Wayne to look toward Shawn McLeary.

"Leave a couple men to guard the herd," Lance ordered. "Spread the rest of your men out. Tell 'em to keep alert." He met Shawn's worried gaze, and added, "You'd be wise to stay close to your family. It looks like things are gonna turn ugly."

The pallor of Shawn's complexion told of his panic. He nodded in agreement. He made no attempt to hide his fear that his place could fall victim to the same fate as Larson's. His greatest worry was for his family, though. Except for cattle drives when he hired more help, he employed only four men. He'd brought all four of them to the river with him this morning. His wife was alone with their four children.

"Anything strange happening around your place?" Lance questioned Wayne once the rest of the men were gone.

"Nope. But then, I've got a hellva a lot more men workin' my spread than McLeary and Larson. It'd be tough for Carrington's men to get close to my house without being spotted."

"We don't know if it was his men who started the fire at Larson's," Lance retorted. A thoughtful frown creased his bearded face.

His remark seemed to throw Wayne off guard. "W-What do y-you mean? Who else would want to do something like that?" He glanced from Lance

215

to Torrie, then back to Lance again as he waited for an explanation.

Lance lifted an eyebrow in a speculative gesture. His gaze leveled on the other man. "It's just a gut feelin'. I could be wrong. But nothing fits." He glanced out toward the expansive river valley as he added, "Down in Texas I've hired on as a cattle detective for ranches as big as the Grand Mesa— even a couple that were bigger. Things usually follow a set pattern."

"Looks to me like things are going according to plan—to Carrington's plan, anyway," Wayne retorted. He motioned towards McLeary's herd. "He tried to keep Shawn's cattle from water. Now he's tried to burn Jim out. That selfish old bastard won't quit until somebody stops him!" Wayne pushed the brim of his black cowboy hat up on his forehead, and stared at the gunfighter. His eyes narrowed. "You just said that was your job. Well, when are you gonna start earning your wages?"

The look Lance cast in the other man's direction was not friendly. His grip tightened around the reins he held in his hand, his eyes flashed with anger. He figured Wayne would be his strongest ally when the range war got rough. But if the rancher kept insinuating he was not doing his job, Lance knew they would eventually come to blows. Now wasn't the time for a showdown, however.

"We've got to get over to Larson's," Lance said. His gaze riveted to Torrie. It occurred to him that if they'd made it to the Larsons' last night as planned, she would have been there when the fire broke out. Things had turned out for the best—in more ways than one.

"What about Elsa?" she asked.

"I take it you didn't get far in the storm last night?" Wayne's question was directed to Torrie, but she didn't have a chance to reply.

"We can't take her to Larson's place now," Lance answered. He spoke to Torrie, and ignored Wayne's question.

"Mrs. Connor and her baby will be safe at my place," Wayne said. The sarcasm was gone from his voice. "You're still welcome too," he added as he looked toward Torrie.

She nodded her head gratefully, then glanced at Lance as if she needed his approval. He met her gaze for an instant, then his head gave a quick nod.

The gestures did not go unnoticed by Wayne. His eyes shifted back and forth between the couple. He wondered how close they'd become since leaving his house yesterday.

"Could you go for Mrs. Connor?" Lance directed his question to Wayne. He noted the strange way the man was looking at them, but he told himself he was too suspicious. Women had a habit of doing that to a man.

"I'll head over there right now," Wayne said. He turned toward Torrie. "You want to come with me?"

"She's staying with me," Lance stated in a firm voice. He fidgeted in his saddle. They were wasting time sitting here.

When Torrie started to voice her opinion, she was greeted by a silent warning from his pale gaze that made the words stick in her throat.

"The Connor woman's had a rough time of it," Lance said as he turned back to Wayne. He caught

217

Torrie's grateful expression out of the corner of his eye.

A shrug shook the shoulders of Wayne's dark blue coat—a remnant from his cavalry days. "I'll try to make it as comfortable for her as I can." He looked at Torrie again.

Torrie attempted to smile at him, though her heart wasn't in the gesture. A feeble curve touched the corners of her mouth, she met Wayne's blue gaze in a brief glance.

His face was of a man who had lived hard—like most men who spent the better part of their time in a saddle. When he smiled back at her his smile seemed out of place. Torrie thought it was because the look in his eyes did not match the smile on his lips.

"There will be a room waiting for you if you want it." He tipped the brim of his hat. Without another word he turned his horse in the direction of the Grand Mesa, and rode away.

Alone with Lance again, Torrie was overcome with unexpected emotions. But since meeting Lance, these feelings were becoming almost common. The responsibility she felt toward Elsa was put to the back of her mind for the moment. A sense of building excitement caused a quivering in the pit of her stomach. Her face felt flushed—in spite of the cold wind. She glanced at Lance to see if he could tell the way he affected her. But he was not looking in her direction. His complete attention was focused on the disappearing sight of Wayne Gere.

Chapter Twenty-Two

"Aren't we going to the Larsons'?" Torrie asked, alarmed. At the bottom of the hill, Lance turned toward a trail that bordered the river.

"Nope. We're gonna' find out what happened to Canon."

Torrie's eyes widened as she turned in her saddle. "But . . . that means we have to go back to the Grand Mesa." Her mouth remained open, her eyes wide. She kicked Ginger in the sides in an effort to catch up to Lance again. The mare lowered her head and took one long stride, then fell back to her usual slow pace.

"He didn't disappear into thin air."

Another cold wind blew across the Colorado River, making the surface of water ripple with miniature waves. Torrie shivered and pulled her hood lower on her forehead. "Gage and the other men searched the entire area."

Lance glanced at her as an eyebrow arched with suggestion. "Maybe they didn't know where to look?"

Without taking the time to sort through the thoughts that crowded her head she blurted out, "How would you know where to look, unless you killed . . ." she stopped herself. She slowed Ginger with a slight tug on the reins. She did not want to see Lance's reaction.

A brittle-sounding laugh rang out from him. He halted his horse. Ginger lumbered up next to them. Lance reached out and grabbed ahold of Torrie's reins, stopping her at his side. His piercing stare drilled into her eyes.

Torrie tried to look away, but she could not make herself move. His face was masked in anger. She didn't want him angry with her, not when they had so little time left together.

As if the same thought crossed Lance's mind, his tense expression faded. He attempted to smile again, but the fleeting effort was lost to a look of regret that consumed his face. "Maybe you'd be better off to catch up to Wayne Gere and help him get your friend and her baby over to his place." He dropped her reins, and turned around in his saddle so he was facing straight forward.

His words surprised Torrie, especially since earlier he had been so determined for her to stay with him. But she was more hurt than anything by his suggestion that they part. Without warning she felt the burning of tears well up in the rims of her eyes. She blinked them away before they had the chance to fall. "If that's what you think I should do—" she began, but she was interrupted before she could finish speaking. He let out a moan, almost as if he were in pain.

"No," he said. Then he shook his head as if he were confused over his own actions. He grunted and kicked Raven in the sides. As the stallion stepped forward, he added in a hoarse tone, "Let's get moving."

He didn't offer an explanation, mainly because he didn't have one. It was beyond his understanding why he insisted that she stay with him, even though he knew it would be best for her to be somewhere safe. He had no idea what they would encounter once they reached the Grand Mesa again. It seemed nothing good ever came from going back there. He thought of the beautiful woman who rode at his side, however, and decided that not everything associated with the Grand Mesa was bad.

It was past noon by the time they reached the Grand Mesa, and since neither of them had eaten all day, Lance decided they should take the time to grab a bite before he began scouting around. He stopped at the base of a long mesa. The ground was littered with rocks and large boulders and allowed them to escape from the mud.

"It's not much, but we need to put something in our bellies," he said as he handed Torrie a strip of hardtack. They were not far from the Connor house, and after they ate the dried beef and washed it down with the water from Lance's canteen, he planned to follow the route he had seen his brother take on the night he had left the Connors' barn.

The wind had finally subsided. The clouds that lingered were rapidly being consumed by the blue sky, and the snow was melting fast. Only a few snowdrifts remained, but the ground was muddy and puddles of murky water stood in every low spot. The wind and snow had stripped the trees of their colorful leaves. Now only stark, barren branches were left as a reminder of the impending winter.

Torrie finished the meager meal in silence. Lance's mood seemed to have improved, somewhat, but she was wary of angering him again. He seemed distracted as he gnawed on a strip of hardtack. Not once, did Torrie see him glance in her direction as they ate.

The temperature was still not warm enough for Torrie to discard her heavy coat, but she no longer needed the raincoat. As she started to remove the outer garment, she was once again surprised when Lance came to her side to help her pull the coat off her shoulders. When she thanked him their gazes met briefly before he surprised her even more by leaning down and gently brushing his lips against her mouth. He pulled back quickly, however.

His attitude appeared more aggravated than before as he shook his head and grumbled something inaudible as he stomped over to the horses. He took her raincoat with him, then stuffed it in with her bedroll.

His temperamental behavior was beginning to grate on Torrie's frazzled nerves, and when she sprang up from the rock where she had been sitting she did not attempt to curb her aggravation. "Look," she spat. "I didn't ask to come with you today, and I think your suggestion earlier that I catch up to Wayne Gere and Elsa was a good idea.''

Lance had his back to her, and for a moment, he made no movement. When he did turn around to face her, he wore a strange expression on his face. "I-I don't know why—" he drew in a deep breath and stepped forward. His voice was hesitant as he shrugged, adding, "Well—it's just that I'm not sure how I should treat you after last night."

Torrie ignored the heat she felt rise in her face as she forced herself to look into his eyes. "How do you usually treat a woman after—after . . ." Torrie's words faltered as she glanced down at the muddy ground. Last night they had been as close as it was possible for a man and a woman to be, yet, now she could not even speak to him without growing embarrassed and tongue-tied.

"I'm usually long gone before the sun's up," Lance admitted.

"I could've went with Wayne Gere, and you would have been rid of me."

Again, Lance's broad shoulders shrugged. His face became a deep scowl. She was saying the same things he had been saying to himself all morning. So why didn't he just admit to her why he wanted—no needed—her to stay with him? Because, he angrily told himself, he refused to admit his feelings to himself . . . he could never admit them to her.

His silence only fueled Torrie's determination to make him speak to her. "What are you afraid of?" she demanded.

Lance's head snapped up as his flashing eyes leveled at her face. "Afraid!" A snide laugh escaped from his pouting mouth. He started to speak, but Torrie beat him to it.

"I know what you're afraid of." Her chin set in a stubborn tilt, and the anger she was trying to control flashed from her darkening emerald gaze.

"Well, if you know so damned much, why don't you explain it to me?"

Torrie stared up at the tall gunfighter without blinking her eyes or faltering when she spoke. Inwardly, her emotions were in a turmoil. "You're still afraid that I'm going to use last night to try to corral you."

His bearded face drew into a deeper frown as he mulled over her words. Was she right? Since he had not been able to understand his own feelings lately, he decided her reasoning was as good as any. When he slowly nodded his head in agreement though, he noticed her anger seemed to fade into an expression of hurt and disappointment. Maybe she wasn't right, after all. Maybe it was his own emotions and actions he feared, but he never had the chance to say another word.

Off in the distance a low rumbling sound could be heard. It grew closer with every passing second. Both Torrie and Lance looked around in confusion. The noise seemed to be coming from the top of the mesa that rose above them.

"What is it?" Torrie asked as a feeling of panic rose in her breast. It sounded like thunder rolling across the sky, yet, it seemed too loud—too close—to be thunder.

"Stampede!" Lance hollered. He was already dragging her toward her horse. His mind envisioned the endless herds of cattle that roamed on the Grand Mesa. The threat of Shawn McLeary's entire herd stampeding the fence this morning was minor when compared to the havoc that could be wrought by only a fourth of the cattle owned by Ben Carrington.

Torrie swung into her saddle, then she glanced up toward the ridge of the mesa. A horrified cry rang out from her mouth as she spotted a dark mass of cattle cresting the ridge.

Lance noticed the approaching threat at almost the same instant, but there was not time to consider anything other than escaping. Cattle began to stumble over the edge of the mesa. The slope was not steep, but the herd was running too fast to control their descent. The side of the mesa became a mud slide. As the animals slid down the slope many of the leading cattle disappeared under the weight of the ones who were following them, and all of the animals were tumbling down the slope out of control.

"Let's get outta their way!" Lance yelled. He kicked Raven in the sides as he glanced at Torrie's horse with a look of panic. He wondered if the little mare had enough speed to clear the area before the stampede reached the bottom and regained their footing. The animals could start charging off in every direction.

Torrie did not need to be told what to do when hundreds of cattle were heading her way. She'd seen the destruction of the land after a stampede. She would never forget seeing what pounding hooves could do to a man, either. A few years back a cowboy on the Grand Mesa had been trampled to death when lightning had startled the cattle he was watching. There had barely been enough of the man left to bury after they had scraped him out of the beaten-down ground. This gruesome memory was foremost in her mind when she twirled Ginger around, and dug her heels in the mare's sides.

The horse lunged forward in a blind panic behind the flying hooves of the retreating stallion, but the horses and their riders barely cleared the path before the first of the cattle thudded to the bottom of the mesa.

As Torrie's horse ran through a scattering of boulders and rocks, the mare tripped over one of the protruding rocks. Ginger crashed down among the rocks, throwing her rider as she fell. It happened so fast Torrie was not sure what was happening until she felt her knees slam against the hard boulders. She opened her mouth to cry out in pain, but only a stunned gasp escaped.

The horse fell on her side against one of the largest of the rocks, and whinnied shrilly. With her legs flailing through the air, she finally managed to roll upright. Ginger did not wait for her rider to regain her composure. The instant she was back on her feet, she galloped away.

Torrie—still in a state of shock—was unaware of the throbbing pain in her knees. Her only concern was the cattle, whose thundering hooves were closing in all around her. Before her thoughts could concentrate on the immense danger she was in, Torrie felt herself being yanked up by one arm. She forced herself to push herself to her feet as

Lance continued to pull her up into his saddle. Now, she realized the acute pain in her legs.

Just as she managed to swing one of her injured legs over the saddle horn, the stallion began to lunge over the boulders. The cattle were already plowing through the boulders where Torrie had lain seconds ago.

She didn't realize her narrow escape. She was too busy trying to hang on to the saddle horn.

Once they had cleared the rocks and boulders at the base of the mesa, they did not have to go far until they were out of the danger zone of the stampeding cattle. The last of the herd was sliding down the slope and the majority of them were already charging out through the open field. Their pounding hooves flung mud in all directions as they raced on. They had no destination, and it could be miles before they calmed down enough to stop. Anything in their path would be trampled.

Lance had been fighting his own battle to cling to the back of the saddle after he had pulled Torrie onto his horse. As soon as he was able to get Raven slowed down, he let himself drop from the back of the horse. The animal stopped almost immediately when he felt him slide from his hindquarters.

"How bad are you hurt?" Lance asked. He pulled Torrie down to the ground. She shook her head, faintly, almost as if she were in a daze.

"I'm not hurt," she mumbled. But as her feet hit the ground, her knees buckled under her weight.

"Not hurt, eh?" Lance scooped her up into his arms when she fell against him. His gaze scanned the area for a dry spot where he could lay her down and examine her injuries. The only place not solid mud was the rocky spot where she had fallen from her horse. The cattle were moving fast, and now were no more than a disappearing dot in the distance, so Lance carried her back to the nearest boulder.

"Let's have a look at those knees," he said as he gently placed her down on the rock. He kneeled down and began to pull her torn and bloody riding skirt up. His fingers were careful not to scrape the material against her injured legs.

Torrie did not make a move as she watched him unveil her bloodied knees. Although she felt a little dizzy, she was surprised to see how badly her skin had been gouged and bruised by the impact with the rocks. She was even more amazed how concerned Lance seemed as he carefully wiped away the blood with the red handkerchief he had taken from around his neck.

"We'll need to wrap that knee," he said, pointing to the deepest cut. He glanced up and met her eyes for an instant. The aggravation he had been feeling with her before the stampede was completely forgotten. "I'll need to find something to use for a bandage." He stood up and scratched his beard in a thoughtful manner as he glanced toward his horse. "I reckon I've got something in my saddlebags we can use for now. But you'll need to have those cuts cleaned out. You should probably stay off your feet for a day or two."

"I'm not hurt that bad," Torrie retorted in a defensive tone. He had been trying to find a way to rid himself of her then, and now it looked as though he had found a way. "If you'll just help me find my horse, I'll get out of your way."

Lance dropped his arms down at his sides and grunted. He motioned toward the distant horizon with a broad sweep of his arm. "With any luck that stupid horse is in the next county by now."

"Just what do you have against my horse?" Torrie demanded. Her knees were beginning to throb, and she didn't feel like engaging in a heated battle over anything right now—especially a horse—but her temper was short.

Lance swung around as if he were prepared to tell her exactly why he thought the mare was nothing more than a worthless piece of horseflesh. His mouth opened, then drew shut quickly. His head slowly began to shake from side to side. He knew the sooner he made up his mind to part company with Torrie, the better off it would be for both of them. He clamped his hands on his hips, his steady gaze still focused on her pouting face.

He was irritated at himself, aggravated with her . . . in love with her, too. He tried to force himself to concentrate on business—on anything besides his out-of-control feelings for this woman.

He glanced up toward the top of the mesa . . . something or somebody had run those cattle over the edge. Had it only been a coincidence that he and Torrie had been directly in their path or were the animals purposely chased to the edge of the mesa because somebody figured they would be able to hide a couple more murders under the deadly hooves of the stampeding herd?

Chapter Twenty-Three

As Elsa nursed her son, Torrie sat in a chair beside the bed. The cradle Will had made stood in the corner of the room. Wayne Gere had loaded up as much of Elsa's belongings as he could carry in the wagon. What he couldn't bring, she said she no longer wanted.

"It's settled then," Elsa said. She absently rubbed Will Jr.'s downy blond head as she spoke. "We'll move to Denver after the funeral."

"When you're well enough to travel," Torrie added. The sight of Elsa nursing the baby caused her heart to twitch with emptiness.

"I'll be able to travel by then."

"The funeral's in two days."

"I can travel in two days." Elsa's voice remained determined. "When we're in Rifle for the funeral, I'll wire my parents and let them know we're coming."

Torrie didn't argue. Since their arrival here yesterday, Elsa seemed to be regaining her strength.

Her apparent hatred of Ben Carrington was fueling her with energy to leave the area. Torrie worried about Elsa's mental state, though, almost as much as she worried about Elsa's physical well-being.

"I think I'll try to get some sleep," Torrie announced. She felt drained, and the cut in her knee still ached. Pete Wheeler, one of Wayne Gere's ranch hands, had taken her to Rifle today to make the arrangements for Will's burial. Elsa wanted to do it herself, but Torrie managed to convince her she wasn't strong enough. Elsa finally agreed, but only because she wanted to save her strength for the funeral, and for the trip to Denver.

"What's wrong, Torrie?" Elsa's voice was soft, caring. "I mean—other than the trouble with Ben and all."

Torrie started to rise from the chair. She sat back down with a thud. "I do have something I want to tell you," she said after a long pause. She stared at Will Jr., and did not meet Elsa's gaze. "I'm not even sure where to begin."

"What is it?" Elsa's voice took on an edge of panic.

A pang of guilt shot through Torrie as she thought about Elsa's recent loss. "I've fallen in love," she blurted out.

Elsa gasped. "Who?" A smile parted her lips, then almost immediately her smile began to fade. "You can't leave here if you've fallen in love."

Torrie tried to appear calm. She absently clutched at the skirt of her dress with her hands. It was one of Elsa's dresses—one her friend had not worn since becoming pregnant. Elsa was slighter built, and Torrie felt the dress was too tight. However, she had not been able to retrieve any of her own things from the Grand Mesa yet, and before they left for Denver she knew she had to figure out a way to get back to the ranch.

"He's not from these parts." She drew in a heavy breath. She was sure Elsa would think she was crazy to fall in love with a gunfighter.

"Well—who is he, and what does it matter where he's from?" Elsa glanced down at her son. He was finished nursing, and he was staring up at her with wide blue eyes. A sense of comfort and love moved through her being. She pulled her robe together, and looked back at Torrie. She noticed the worried expression on her pretty face. "Who is he?" she asked again.

Torrie tried to smile when she met Elsa's gaze, but it was a weak imitation.

"L-Lance Farlo." She barely managed to whisper his name. Her mind envisioned his handsome face as clearly as if he were standing right before her.

"Good grief!" Elsa gasped. She had no idea how Torrie had met the famed gunslinger, but she knew she must have missed a lot in the past few days. "How—I mean—" she paused and shook her head. She was at a loss for words.

"It doesn't matter. Soon, he'll be back in Texas and I'll be in Denver." Torrie felt fiery tears spring into her eyes. She rose from the chair and turned away from Elsa. It had only been one day since she had seen him, and already she missed him more than she ever thought possible.

"Are you sure you love him, Torrie?" Elsa's thoughts were still in turmoil. She wanted Torrie to find the kind of love she had known with Will. But, she had heard talk about the dangerous gunfighter. It was hard for her to imagine Torrie being in love with a man like him.

Torrie swung around to face Elsa. Her emerald gaze glistened with unshed tears, a rosy glow colored her cheeks. "Oh yes, I do love him."

Elsa stared at her. Her mouth gaped open, but she still could not think of anything to say. Torrie's love for Lance Farlo was so evident it gushed from her like a flood.

"L-Lance Farlo?" Elsa managed to gasp. Questions were beginning to spring into her mind.

Torrie nodded her head, a single teardrop shook loose from the corner of her eye and rolled down her cheek.

"How far has it gone?" Elsa asked. She didn't care if Torrie hated her for asking this question. Her only concern was for Torrie's welfare.

Torrie turned away again. She walked to the window and stared out. Dusk was closing in, and the autumn evening was clear and cool. There was no evidence of the snowstorm from a couple of days ago on the valley floor. Only the tops of the highest mountains had retained a few patches of white. Torrie ran her tongue over her lips—they still felt dry. The bodice of Elsa's dress seemed to grow tighter around her bosom as her breathing grew heavier. Elsa's blunt question summoned up the memories of the night she spent with Lance in the line shack. In remembrance, her insides were quavering, her knees felt weak.

A gnawing ache tore at Elsa's breast as she stared at her friend's back. Torrie's silence answered her question. The other questions she wanted to ask seemed unimportant now. Before Elsa could collect her thoughts, Torrie swung around from the window. Her face was even more flushed than before, her gaze glowed like candles in the dark.

"Lance is here! He just rode up," she said. Her voice exposed her sense of excitement. She met Elsa's gaze, briefly. But she did not take the time to discuss the worried expression on her friend's face.

"I'll be right back," Torrie said over her shoulder as she rushed from the room. She was barely to the top of the stairs when she heard the knock on the front door. Her steps halted. From here, she could see the door. Her heart felt as if it were trying to crash through her chest, her legs shook, and a slow, yearning ache inched through her body. She was not aware she was holding her breath.

Torrie saw Wayne Gere walk out of his den. He didn't glance toward the staircase. She watched as he opened the door, then she listened to the exchange of greetings between the two men.

"I have some information you might find interesting," Lance said as he entered the house. He wore his long brown duster and Stetson of the same color.

"Come into the den." Wayne led the way.

Lance started to follow him. He took a couple of

235

steps when his gaze riveted to the second floor. His footsteps slowed, and then stopped. A lopsided grin crossed his mouth as he looked up at Torrie. His head motioned toward the front door. He held up five fingers, then silently mouthed, "five minutes."

A radiant smile captured Torrie's lips. Her head nodded an enthusiastic reply.

Lance stared up at her for an instant longer. She was wearing a green dress. He thought it matched her eyes, and that it hugged her curves perfectly in all the right places. He forced himself to turn away from her and follow Wayne. His mind retained her beautiful image. His chest tightened around his pounding heart. He fought to control the building sensation of excitement in his whole body. His business with Wayne would not take long; he wished he'd told her two minutes instead of five.

Torrie exhaled the breath she had been holding in one heavy gust. Fleetingly, she thought of telling Elsa she was going outside to meet Lance, but she decided against it.

Pete Wheeler was leaning against the rail. He was staring off into space. His face hosted a deep frown, and his thin shoulders slouched as if he were weighted down by a heavy burden. When the front door swung open his head jerked around in an abrupt manner. "Miss Torrie? What are you doing out here?"

A smile reclaimed her lips. She didn't hesitate to tell him. "I'm meeting Lance Farlo out here when he's through talking to Wayne." She ignored the troubled glance he cast in her direction as she

236

stepped down from the porch. There was a slight throbbing pain in her knees, but she could feel Pete watching her, so she forced herself to walk as normally as possible as she made her way to the hitching post where Raven stood.

The night air was cool. Torrie wished she could have thought to grab a shawl. She wrapped her arms around herself in a tight embrace. A shiver raced through her, but it was not caused by the temperature. Knowing she would be with Lance in a few minutes made her shiver with anticipation.

The stallion watched her—curiously—from the side of his eye. In a slow gesture she reached out and waited until Raven stuck his neck out and sniffed at her hand. He nudged her open palm with his nose. She began to scratch his neck and the areas behind his ears. The large stallion stepped closer, he whinnied softly.

"Now if that don't beat all!" Lance said as he walked toward the hitching post. Raven was usually aloof with anyone other than him.

"He likes me," Torrie retorted as she abruptly stopped lavishing attention on the horse. She stepped forward. Her mouth opened as she started to speak, but she never had the chance.

Lance had dreamt of kissing those lips for the past twenty-four hours. He didn't intend to wait one minute longer. He pulled her into his arms, crushed her against him, and ravished her with hungry devotion. His tongue slipped between her lips without invitation, his hands charted a familiar path along the curve of her hip, her waist, and up to her rapidly heaving bosom. The material of her dress strained against his hand as the tiny bud on the tip of her breast immediately responded to his touch. Her entire body seemed to be on fire, he was sure he could feel the heat radiate from her underclothes.

He pulled away from her, and took a deep breath. She was staring up at him. Her lips were still parted, drawing in short, raspy breaths. The collar of her modest green dress was high and hugged her neck. He thought of the silky column of skin he could not kiss because of the material's presence. He wanted to kiss her—to touch her—all over. An agonized moan escaped from his mouth.

"Woman," he said, his voice breathy, "you make me crazy, out-of-control." He cupped her chin in his large hand, and looked down into her eyes. The moonlight cast silvery shadows over her face. Lance thought she had never looked more desirous. He moaned again, but the sound was filled with pain.

"What's wrong?" A dozen worried thoughts crowded into Torrie's head. His teasing smile did not erase them.

"Nothin' much," Lance said. "Except I've got a hankerin' to do things to you that aren't real respectable."

Torrie felt her cheeks grow hot. His words enticed the thoughts in her own head, and made her oblivious to anything else. "What's stopping you?" Her lips curved with a taunting grin.

Lance glanced toward the house. Through the cottonwoods that surrounded the house he could see Pete Wheeler standing on the porch. His gaze traveled to the surrounding buildings, then he sighed with frustration. "Want to go for a ride?"

Torrie also turned to the house. Her mood shifted. "I don't know if I should—I mean—they'll wonder where I went."

"Is everything going all right here? Mrs. Connor and the baby . . ."

"Oh, everything's fine," Torrie interrupted. "She says she'll be able to leave for Denver right after Will's funeral."

"I reckon that will be soon," Lance said, his voice sounded hoarse. His hands rested on her shoulders. He told himself not to kiss her again.

"In two days," Torrie said, quietly. She hoped the moonlight did not afford him with a glimpse of the agony she felt. His hands tightened over the tops of her shoulders for a moment, then he dropped his arms down limply at his sides. A silence deafened the night. Torrie cleared her throat.

"Have you found out anything about Canon?" Her attempt to change the subject did not make the ache in her heart go away.

Lance took a deep breath, he shrugged his shoulders. "No. But I think I might have learned who set fire to Jim Larson's place."

"Ben?"

Lance nodded. "I found some tracks leading away from Larson's ranch. They led straight to the Grand Mesa." Even in the faded light, he noticed Torrie's expression showed no surprise.

"I talked to Sheriff Kearny about the tracks."

Lance shrugged again. "I doubt he'll do anything about it." A thoughtful frown tugged at his face. He watched Torrie for a moment. Her expression was hard to determine in the faded light.

"Did you happen to notice if Wayne left here today?"

"I went into town to make the funeral arrangements. I didn't see him before I left this morning, but he had dinner with me and Elsa this evening." Her eyes narrowed slightly as she tried to see his face more clearly. "Why?" she asked.

"Just curious." He was tired of talking—and thinking—about the range war. He was even more tired of worrying about Torrie's impending departure. He reached out again, and pulled her to him. She did not resist. Lance felt her arms encircle his neck, her body pressed against him without hesitation. He brought his mouth down on her lips. She returned his kiss with complete abandonment. His mind kept repeating . . . two days . . . two days!

When—at last—their kisses grew too impassioned for them to continue, Lance pulled away. He could not be this close to her without wanting more than just her kisses. A disgruntled noise rang from his throat. He turned loose his tight hold around her slender waist. A hoarse cough followed.

"I reckon I'd better get going." His voice sounded controlled.

Panic raced through Torrie, her heart seemed to expand in her chest. "Where? I mean—aren't you going to stay here tonight?"

He shook his head. "I have a long ride ahead of me." He ran his hand along his damp brow.

Torrie clutched at the material of her skirt, her hands drew into tight fists. She shivered visibly. The temperature—to Torrie—felt as if it had just dropped to zero degrees. She wanted to ask him where he was going, but the words hung up in her dry mouth. He backed away from her. Another cold tremor shot through her body.

"How's your knees?" His voice sounded distant to his ears. He wondered if it was his imagination or did she just shiver as if she was cold? He ran his hand over his brow again. He was sweating like a hog in July.

"I can ride," Torrie said without thinking. Her voice sounded like a plea. Inwardly, she cursed at herself.

Lance took another step backwards. "G-Good," he said. He glanced around at the darkening ranch, his gaze did not settle on anything. "Well, I reckon I'd better go." He grabbed for Raven's reins, then twisted them around his fingers as he looked back at Torrie. She had not moved.

"I'd better get back in the house."

They nodded their heads in unison.

Lance swung up into his saddle, then nudged Raven forward. He stopped the horse in front of Torrie. Even in the dim light he could make out the sorrowful expression on her face. Would it get harder every time they saw one another? he wondered. He told himself maybe he should stay away for the next couple of days. He leaned down and gently touched her upturned face with the tips

241

of his fingers. "Take care of yourself, little darlin'," he whispered.

Torrie could not reply. She stared after him until the darkness of the night swallowed him up. There had been something in his voice—something in the way he touched her face—something almost final. A slow, devouring fear began to creep up through her limbs until it consumed her entire being.

You take care of yourself, Lance, she thought as she forced her numb legs to walk back toward the house.

Chapter Twenty-Four

Torrie stood at the window in Wayne's kitchen and stared out. She did not focus on anything, however. Her mind was consumed by thoughts of the previous night—by Lance's parting words. She'd hardly slept a wink, and she was up before the sun. But, Wayne was up even earlier this morning. Just as she was getting dressed she heard someone leaving the house. From her bedroom window, she spotted Wayne heading for the barn. She watched, and a short time later she saw him ride off on his light-colored palomino.

"A penny for your thoughts?"

Torrie jumped at the sound of Elsa's voice. She forced herself to smile as she turned around. "They're not worth that much," she said. "What are you doing up so early?" She noticed Elsa had changed from her robe into one of the dresses she had worn before her pregnancy. She seemed even thinner than she had back then. However, her skin coloring looked better today, and Torrie noticed she was beginning to walk with a normal stride again. The mixture of relief—and disappointment—Torrie experienced made her fill with a nagging sense of guilt.

"I thought I smelled coffee," Elsa said. She cast an anxious glance toward the stove. A relieved smile curved her mouth when she noticed the brewing coffee. They had always shared their most intimate thoughts over a cup of coffee.

Torrie grabbed two cups, but did not speak while she poured the coffee. She knew Elsa was probably wondering why she had not gone back to her room after Lance left last night. She hadn't wanted to discuss the way he had acted when he left, then, anymore than she wanted to talk about it now.

"Wayne headed out early," Torrie said.

"I guess you don't want to talk about Lance Farlo?" Elsa asked bluntly. She took the coffee cup Torrie was holding out to her. Her gaze met Torrie's as they faced one another.

Torrie tried to force herself to appear calm. Inwardly, she was a quivering mass. "There's nothing to talk about."

"What about last night?"

Torrie walked back to the stove and retrieved her own cup of coffee. "I didn't get to see Lance for long," she said. She swallowed hard and closed her eyes for a moment before she faced Elsa again. When she turned around, she knew Elsa could see right through her.

"I never used to worry much about Will when he'd go out to herd cattle," Elsa said as she sat down at the table. "I suppose it would be hard not to worry about a man like Lance Farlo, though."

Torrie approached the table. She was amazed by Elsa's perception—and even more surprised Elsa hadn't tried to reprimand her for falling in love with Lance. She sat down opposite Elsa, a weak grin tugged at her mouth. She started to tell Elsa how grateful she was for her friendship, but she was interrupted before she had a chance.

"I hope I'm not intruding. I knocked at the front door, but I reckon you didn't hear me." Lance glanced at Elsa's shocked face for a second, but his gaze settled on Torrie. She had gone pasty white at the sound of his voice. When she looked up at him, he noticed her emerald gaze illuminate with what he thought looked like excitement and joy.

Torrie jumped up from her chair. When she spoke, her voice conveyed the same emotions Lance had glimpsed in her eyes. "Lance! I thought you were going to . . ." her voice faded. He hadn't told her where he was going last night.

A sheepish smile parted his lips. He clutched his Stetson in his hands, unconsciously scrunching the brim. "Yeah—well—I came back." He looked down at Elsa again. "I reckon you must be Elsa Connor. I'm Lance Farlo."

Elsa rose slowly, her eyes never left his face as she nodded her head in reply. "It's a pleasure to meet you, Mr. Farlo." His gaze touched hers, briefly, before he returned his full attention to Torrie. Elsa felt a strange mixture of emotions invade her. Lance Farlo was exactly the type of man she had envisioned for Torrie—yet, he was so different from what she had expected a man of his reputation to be like. Her gaze flitted back and forth between Torrie and the handsome gun-fighter.

Torrie made no attempt to apologize for not introducing Lance and Elsa to one another. She was still overwhelmed by his appearance—and grateful. "W-Would you like c-coffee?" she finally managed to stammer as her senses began to return to normal.

"No." He continued to clutch his hat nervously in his hands. "There's somewhere I need to go. But—well—I was wondering if you would ride along with me?" He also wondered if he was blushing. He'd felt a hot sensation rise up under his beard. The idea made another rush of heat soar through his entire face. He wondered why he was surprised at anything he did lately. Coming back here now, after he thought he had convinced himself last night he wouldn't see her again, made him certain he'd already lost his mind.

Torrie gave her head a quick nod, then she glanced at Elsa. Her expression lost some of its excitement.

"Go on," Elsa said. "I'll be fine."

"We'll be gone until tomorrow," Lance stated in a bland tone. He heard a loud gasp come from Torrie, but he was facing Elsa.

Elsa met his piercing gaze. She was unable to look away for a moment.

"The funeral's tomorrow afternoon," Torrie said. She tried to hide her disappointment, but it was evident in her tone of voice.

"I'll take you straight into town when we get back."

Elsa dragged her gaze away from Lance. "Well —then it's settled." She turned to Torrie. "I'll see you tomorrow in Rifle." When Torrie started to shake her head in disagreement, Elsa added, "Don't go if you don't want to, but remember, we're leaving after the funeral."

Torrie's gaping mouth clamped shut. Once again she was overcome with the urge to tell Elsa how much she loved her, but time was wasting. She squeezed Elsa's hand as she hurried past her. Their fleeting gazes met. There was no need for words.

"I'll saddle my horse," Torrie said as she swept past Lance.

"I'll help," he retorted. Before he turned to follow her, he paused to look at Elsa again. His expression of gratitude spoke for him.

"Take care of her," Elsa warned. She felt foolish after she spoke. If ever there was a man capable of caring for Torrie, she knew it was Lance Farlo.

Lance nodded, then turned to leave. Torrie was already out the front door. When he stepped onto the porch, he noticed she was halfway to the barn. He saw Pete Wheeler was walking from the bunkhouse to resume his guard post at the house. He cast a surly look in Lance's direction. Lance shoved his hat down on his head, and rushed to catch up to Torrie without a word to the younger man.

"Where are we going?" she asked when he

caught up to her.

"Remember that cave I told you about—the one up on Horse Mountain?"

A confused look covered Torrie's face. Her steps never faltered. "That's where you were headed last night?"

"There's no sign of Canon anywhere on the Grand Mesa. But I was thinkin' about what you said—that maybe he was hidin' out somewhere. I remember once when he ran away from home when we were kids. He was gone for a couple of days. When he came back, he told me he'd been hidin' in the cave."

"What about his horse?" She threw a blanket on Ginger, then stepped back as Lance heaved the saddle on the animal's back.

He shrugged. "Maybe the horse got away from him." He shook his head as he finished saddling Ginger. "Canon was beat up, but he wasn't hurt bad enough to crawl off and die." His voice was firm, and his tone did not sound as if he were attempting to justify the fight. He turned back and raked his gaze over her attire. She was wearing her black riding skirt and white blouse again today. But it was apparent she had washed them since she'd worn them last.

"You'll need a coat," he said.

"Everything I need is in my saddlebags," she replied.

Lance was struck by the thought that she was starting to sound a lot like him. "Let's ride, then."

As they left the barn, Lance glanced over his shoulder. He noticed Wayne's palomino and fancy

248

saddle were gone.

The vast acreage of the Diamond G Ranch took Torrie and Lance most of the morning to cover. They skirted the town of Rifle, then rode along the eastern edge of the Grand Mesa. By late afternoon they reached the base of Horse Mountain. They rode hard all day, only stopping to water the horses and themselves.

Lance still could not justify to himself why he had decided to bring her along, so he quit trying.

"How far up there is the cave?" Torrie looked up at the towering mountain overhead. With an elevation of over nine thousand feet, Horse Mountain sprouted an abundance of aspens, spruce trees, lodgepole pines, and evergreens. Now, the white-trunked aspens were barren of leaves, but the pines were green and fragrant year round.

"Not quite halfway up," Lance answered. His gaze scouted the dense growth of the trees. He hoped he remembered how to get there, at the same time, he wondered if he were wasting time coming here. But sometimes he got these gut feelings. He had one now, and it told him to find that cave.

"We'd better get going if we're going to make it before the sun goes down."

"Are we going to spend the night up there?" A sense of foreboding crept through Torrie as she nudged Ginger forward. The forests of the high country always made her feel nervous. There were too many hiding places.

"We'll stay up at the cave if we don't find Canon there. Then, we'll have to make fast tracks back to

Rifle to get you there in time for the funeral."

Torrie didn't reply. She didn't want to think about tomorrow any more than she wanted to think about what they might find at the cave.

They stopped long enough to put on their heavy coats once they were deep in the trees where the chill of autumn was even more evident. Patches of snow blanketed the shady areas around some of the trees.

"We'll eat when we reach the cave and can make a fire," Lance said when they started riding again.

Torrie nodded, but she was sure she wouldn't be hungry. Her eyes kept imagining hundreds of shadows lurking behind the tree trunks. Finally, she had to ask Lance the question that had plagued her ever since they began this journey. "What if we do find Canon there?"

Lance could hear the fear in her voice. A shiver of dread ran down his spine. Unconsciously, he glanced around at the darkening forest. "No use worrying until we know if he's there or not."

His answer told Torrie he was as uncertain as she was about the outcome of this trip. Even as scared as she felt though, she still did not regret coming with him. The entire trip—until now—was another memory she would cherish for the rest of her life. All day Lance rode his horse beside Ginger. He was more talkative than usual, although his topics were not about anything serious—mainly about the lessons of survival he had learned in his many travels. Torrie knew most of what he spoke about, but she never let on. She was certain she would never tire of listening to his deep, slow drawl or his robust laugh.

The lengthening shadows seemed to close them in almost completely by the time Lance signaled for them to halt their horses. Torrie felt a nervous fluttering in her stomach as she glanced around.

"If I remember correctly, the cave is just ahead," Lance said. He pulled his 30-06 from its scabbard and handed it to Torrie. He knew it would be easier to shoot than the sawed-off shotgun that hung from her saddle. "You stay here. If you hear anything—shoot first—ask questions later."

Torrie clutched the gun in her sweating hand. "I want to go with you."

Lance lowered his head and stared down at the ground for a second. When he looked up, he nodded his head. "I reckon it wouldn't be smart for us to separate here. But, if Canon is in the cave, he'll see us long before we see him."

Torrie felt chancing an ambush from the cave was far more desirable than staying here alone. She slid from Ginger's back and tied her reins to a tree branch. She noticed Lance dropped his horse's reins on the ground. He motioned for her to follow him. Her hand tightened its grip on the rifle.

The entrance to the cave came into view within a couple hundred yards. The dark shapes of aspens and pines framed its sides. The black cave looked like a gaping mouth. The opening was about five feet high and three feet across. Lance remembered the interior to be deep—at least twenty feet. He motioned for Torrie to get down on the ground beside him. They watched the entrance for several minutes. Darkness continued to creep in around them.

They inched toward the cave on their bellies. Torrie kept remembering the day they had crawled beneath the cottonwoods on the south range. Will Connor's corpse haunted her thoughts, and the forest grew more menacing. She stayed as close to Lance as possible.

"I've got to go in before it gets any darker," he whispered.

"I'm going in, too," Torrie said, firmly.

"No. If Canon is in there, and he starts shooting, I'll need you to cover me from here."

Torrie wanted to argue with him, but she could tell he would not give in this time. She also knew she would be of no help to him if Canon did ambush him in the cave. But there was no logical plan. Before she had a chance to voice her opinion, however, Lance surprised her by leaning over and brushing his lips against hers. She returned his brief kiss at once. It was not a passionate kiss, rather one that bespoke of the ever-deepening bond between them.

"I'll be back for more of that," Lance whispered when he pulled away. He glimpsed the worried expression on her face in the fading light. He knew he wore a similar one. "I wanted to be with you again so much I never thought about the danger I was putting you in."

"No matter what happens," Torrie said quietly, her voice trembled as she added, "I'll always cherish every second we spent together."

Lance stared at her for a moment. He wished it was possible to see her face more clearly. He forced his attention to return to the cave.

"Ready?" he said, then sprang to his feet before Torrie had a chance to reply.

She clasped his rifle against her shoulder, and narrowed one eye as she stared down the long barrel. It was growing darker by the minute. In five minutes she would not be able to distinguish the cave entrance from the rest of the hillside. She saw Lance pause behind a boulder close to the opening. He threw a rock in front of the cave, and waited.

Nothing.

Lance ran the rest of the way to the cave. His gun was drawn, his actions sharp and calculated. He stopped at the side of the entrance, and waited again.

Still nothing.

Torrie slowly began to push herself up. She couldn't kneel on her knees because of their injuries, so she rose to her feet. She kept the rifle positioned and ready. Every muscle in her body felt tense. She heard the pounding of her heart over the stillness of the night. A gasp escaped from her mouth when she saw Lance slip into the cave. The dark hole seemed to swallow him up.

Fear kept her rooted to the spot and her eyes staring straight ahead, although she wanted to look around, to look behind her. The forest was shrouded in total darkness now. She willed herself to stare at the black hole in the hillside. The tiny hairs on the back of her neck felt as if they were standing on end. A creepy sensation inched down her back.

In the cave she thought she saw a flash of light. She reinforced her hold on the gun, and controlled her urge to call out to Lance. The light flashed again, it lasted longer before it died away. Torrie could not contain her growing fear.

"Lance. Are you all right?" she asked. Her feet took an unsteady step forward. The cave entrance now blended into its surroundings. "Lance!" she called out again.

She saw movement in the cave. Her finger curled around the trigger, her arms shook with the weight of the gun.

"I'm comin' out," Lance said. His footsteps were slow as he approached Torrie. In his hand he clutched the two matches he had just lit. When he was close he heard her give a sigh that sounded like immense relief.

"He wasn't there?"

Lance nodded his head slowly. "He's there all right."

Torrie could not stop the weak cry that escaped from her mouth. "Is he . . ."

"Dead," Lance said. "Somebody finished what I started. They did a real job on him." He tossed the matches on the ground, then shoved his hands on his hips and hung his head down.

As the meaning of his words sunk into Torrie's shocked mind, questions began to accumulate. "W-Was he shot?"

"His killer was too smart for that. He's beaten to a pulp."

"Worse than when he left the Connors' barn?" Torrie saw Lance's head rise up, but it was too

254

dark to make out his expression. His controlled tone of voice told her what she couldn't see.

"I know what you're thinking, and I reckon everybody else will think it too. I admit I beat him up good, but you saw the way he looked when he rode away. Whoever found him after he left the Connors' that night showed him a lot less mercy than I did."

Torrie spoke before she thought. "I didn't see him when he left. I was hiding in the stall." A long silence filled the air. Torrie wished she could retract her words—and the other thoughts she could not chase out of her head. To her way of thinking it was all beginning to make sense. Maybe Lance had found Canon the morning after the fight?

"Yeah—well—you think what you want," Lance spat. "If I had killed him, I sure as hell wouldn't have come all this way to recover the evidence of my crime. And, I sure as hell wouldn't have brought you along!" He stalked off, leaving Torrie alone.

For a moment she remained unmoving. Her mind mulled over his last words. She knew he was right, and she hated herself for doubting him again. She twirled around and peered through the dark trees. He could be five feet away and she would not be able to see him. Torrie opened her mouth, but only a choked cry escaped. A devouring sense of fear enveloped her, but it was not as much from the dark forest as it was because Lance was gone.

Her terror exploded in her body, and made her

too numb to move or speak. Her frantic mind tried to collect rational thoughts, but all she could imagine was how afraid she was of never seeing Lance again.

Then, he just seemed to materialize before her eyes. "I'm sorry," she said, her tone was barely audible.

"Our time together is too valuable to keep wastin' with this sort of nonsense," he said, his voice was almost as emotional as hers.

"I'm sorry," Torrie repeated. She let the rifle slip out of her hands. It landed in the dry grass at her feet.

Lance reached out and placed his hands on each side of her face. He noticed her skin felt cold against his fevered palms. "There's no more time for being sorry or for feeling mistrust."

"You're right. I'm sor . . ." Torrie stopped herself. She reached up and placed her hands on top of his—they trembled beneath her touch.

They stood facing one another for a few minutes longer. Torrie's fear faded, but it did not go away completely.

Lance slid his hands from her face and clasped ahold of her hands. There were so many things he wanted to say to her tonight—things he figured he wouldn't have the chance to say again. But he didn't know how to put his feelings into words. Instead, he just gave a heavy sigh.

"I reckon we'd better get some rest."

Torrie nodded her head in agreement. "What about Canon?"

"I'll make a travois for his body in the

morning.'' Lance's fingers tightened around her hands. "I keep thinkin' I should feel something— you know—about his death.''

Torrie's fingers tingled as she became aware of how tightly he was holding her hands. She thought about the dark cave where Canon's body lay. Her blood felt like it had froze in her veins.

"I know . . ." she said in a shaky voice. At this moment she felt closer to Lance than ever before, she felt closer to him than she had ever felt to anyone.

Chapter Twenty-Five

"Are you still cold?"

"No," Torrie answered. She hadn't been cold for quite a while now—not since he had made love to her for the first time last night. "Well—maybe just a little." His embrace tightened. She gave a contented sigh. The forest no longer seemed foreboding.

Lance planned to remove Canon's body from the cave last night so they could sleep in there, but Torrie refused. He finally consented to sleep under the shelter of a towering spruce. Its outer branches hung almost to the ground, but close to the trunk there was an area barren of branches. Lance lit a torch out of a pine bough while she cleared away the dry pine needles under the tree. There was enough room for them to spread out their bedrolls. The drooping branches created a natural tent around them, and the fresh scent of pine engulfed them in its heady fragrance.

Beyond the branches of the tree they had built a

small fire so they could heat up canned beans and coffee for supper. The last of the flames were gone now. Only a few faint orange embers remained in the circle of rocks.

"We'd better try to get some sleep," Lance said again. The warmth of his breath touched her cheek. The scent of coffee on his breath mingled with the smell of the trees.

Torrie sighed again. She was not sleepy—only worn out. "I'll have plenty of time to sleep after tomorrow." She tried to sound nonchalant. She didn't succeed. Lance's body tensed. He answered her by rolling her over and impaling her on top of his rigid manhood. He sank deep inside her, she felt a spiraling pain shoot through her. But it was a pain she welcomed with enthusiasm. As his hips arched up, she let him carry her with him. Then, she drove her own hips down when he receded.

When they reached the highest summit of this ritual, Torrie felt his whole body shudder beneath her. Her own body felt limp, and completely sated. She stayed on top of him, surrounded by his arms and the hanging pine boughs. She wished she had the power to hold onto this night forever.

"The sun's comin' up," Lance whispered in Torrie's ear. He hated to wake her. She had just dozed off a short time ago. He hadn't slept at all.

Torrie moaned softly. She heard his voice, but she hoped it was only a dream. It couldn't be morning already . . . it couldn't be their last day together.

"Come on, little darlin', we've got to get going."

She moaned again, louder this time. She felt his

260

arms around her, her backside was pressed up against the front of his hard body. They molded together as if they were one. Without him, she knew she would never be complete again. He kissed the back of her neck. Every inch of her awakened. She turned around, drawn to him like metal to a magnet. He kissed her lips, briefly, then pulled away.

A smile curled one side of his mouth. His hazel eyes glistened as he met her gaze. "If we stay here much longer, you may have to wait until tomorrow to leave for Denver." His voice held a tone of fevered hope.

Torrie's heart began to pound frantically in her chest. One more day—one more night. Her soaring hopes faltered, then came to an abrupt halt. "I have to be back in time for Will's funeral. Elsa will need me."

"She's lucky to have such a good friend," Lance said, softly. The memory of his friendship with Robert Farlo passed through his mind. He hated the idea, but he knew he had to get Torrie back to Rifle by this afternoon.

The briskness of the morning air caused them to dress in a hurry. Torrie busied herself making another fire and a fresh pot of coffee while Lance constructed a travois out of lodgepole pines. A deep frown tugged at his face as he surveyed his work and sipped coffee. Torrie watched him, but she avoided any further conversation about Canon. When he handed her his empty cup, their gazes met.

"I reckon I'd better go get him."

"Do you need help?"

"No." He noticed a fleeting look of relief cross her face. He grabbed the extra blanket from his bedroll and glanced up at the cave. The morning sun had not reached the slope where the entrance of the cave stood. It still looked dark and spooky. Lance thought of the day he and Canon had first found this place. It had been one of the rare times they had acted like brothers—and almost like friends. Now, the cave was Canon's grave.

Lance forced himself to enter the cave again. He blinked and waited until his eyes adjusted to the darkness. The gagging odor of days-old death hung heavy in the small enclosure. He pulled the handkerchief from his neck up over his mouth and nose as he approached Canon's decomposing body. After he threw the blanket over him, he rolled him up tightly in the shroud, then tied rope around it in several places. He didn't want Torrie to glimpse one inch of the corpse when he hauled it out into the open.

Rigor mortis made the body as stiff as a board. Lance grabbed the blanket by one end and dragged it out of the cave. He whistled. Raven pulled the travois to his side. The stallion gave a snort when he smelled the stench of death. As he loaded Canon's body, Lance was aware of Torrie's distance. She sat atop Ginger several hundred feet down from the cave. He looked down at her when he was finished. "Are you ready to go?"

Torrie nodded her head. She made an obvious attempt to avoid looking back at the rigid bundle on the travois.

Areas of the awakening forest were coated with a thin layer of frost—a definite sign of the approaching winter. In spite of this, and the lingering patches of snow from the last storm, it looked as if an Indian summer had claimed the Colorado countryside. Through the tops of the tall trees, a clear azure sky signaled another warm autumn day ahead.

Torrie was grateful for this small blessing. At least, with the sun shining, Will's funeral would not seem as bleak. Transporting Canon's body back to Rifle, however, made the day seem as gloomy as if the sky were heavy with storm clouds.

The trip back down the mountain was slow and treacherous. The horses had to choose their footing carefully, and Raven's progress was hampered by the weight he was dragging behind him. There was little time for conversation. But Lance seemed locked in his own private world, anyway. Every time Torrie caught a glimpse of his glum expression, she wondered if he was finally beginning to grieve for his brother. Another sharp pang of guilt shot through her. She still felt no real sense of remorse.

"When we get to Rifle would you do somethin' for me before you leave for Denver?"

Lance's voice broke into Torrie's guilt-ridden thoughts. She felt her body lurch upward in her saddle. "Sure—anything."

"I reckon Sheriff Kearny is gonna need to hear both of our accounts about what happened between me and Canon the other night."

"I'll tell him the truth."

"That's all I'm askin'."

They continued on in silence. As they began to travel along the edge of a high mesa that over-looked a section of the Grand Mesa's grazing lands, something shiny caught Lance's eye. He halted Raven. His eyes narrowed as he leaned over and peered out toward a distant plateau.

"What is it?" Torrie asked. She followed his gaze. The endless ranges, a scattering of cattle, and the flattopped mesas were the only things she saw.

Lance turned around and dug his field glasses from his saddlebags. He ignored Torrie as he surveyed the area again with the aid of the glasses.

An aggravated scowl masked Torrie's face. She focused in the direction he was looking again. A distant movement drew her attention to two dark dots disappearing over the far horizon. "Who is it?" she asked again.

Lance lowered the glasses. His expression was void of any emotion. "Does Gage always ride a roan?"

Torrie nodded. "Did it look like one of the horses was a grey roan?"

Lance shoved his glasses back in his saddlebags. "It was too far to tell for sure." He forced down the anger rising in him. He quickly regained his composure before Torrie noticed. When she was gone, he would deal with this new development.

His attempt to act nonchalant by the sight of the two riders did not fool Torrie. But she couldn't figure out why he would be so angered by seeing Gage and another rider on the Grand Mesa. She did not dwell on his attitude, however. There were

264

more important matters to think about.

Once she told Sheriff Kearny the reason Lance and Canon had fought, there was no way to avoid the gossip that would spread through Rifle. She didn't care what most people said or thought. Elsa would wonder why she had kept Canon's abuse from her all this time, though. Now, Torrie wondered the same thing.

"Are you ready?" Lance asked as they paused at the outskirts of Rifle. Torrie met his intense stare. He looked directly into her eyes as if he was trying to read her mind. She gave her head a firm nod. Three words hovered on her lips. "I-I lo . . ." She swallowed the urge. "I'm fine."

A strange feeling shot through Lance as he watched her—as he longed to say the words he sensed she wanted to say. He clamped his mouth shut. Some things were better left unsaid, and there was no use making her leaving more difficult.

He nudged Raven in the sides. The stallion was twisted around toward Ginger. The two horses were busy nibbling at one another's lips. An aggravated frown tugged at Lance's mouth when he had to yank on his horse's reins to turn him around. He dug his heels deeper in Raven's sides.

Torrie did not have to urge Ginger forward. The mare hung right at Raven's side as they started to move again. In spite of all the other things on her mind, Torrie could not help but to smile when she noticed Lance's irritation with the horses. Her plan was to leave Ginger in Rifle for one of the men from the Grand Mesa to pick up. Now—

although she wasn't sure why—she decided she wanted to take Ginger with her to Denver.

It was past noon by the time they stopped at the hitching post in front of Sheriff Kearny's office. The gunfighter, the woman who rode with him, and the body on the travois drew the attention of everyone who was in the vicinity. A crowd was already gathering on the boardwalk. Before Lance and Torrie dismounted, Sheriff Kearny was standing beside the travois.

He pushed his hat to the back of his head and scratched his forehead. His heavy blond mustache twitched at one end. He looked up at Lance, and squinted his eyes. "Canon Carrington?"

Lance gave his head a quick nod, then he swung down from his saddle. He helped Torrie down before he turned his attention back to the sheriff. "We found him in a cave on Horse Mountain."

Sheriff Kearny looked back and forth between Lance and Torrie. "What were you two doing up there?" The twitch of his mustache was more noticeable as his face contorted with a speculating frown.

Lance glanced at Torrie. She was staring down at the ground, her pale complexion was streaked with scarlet. He looked around at the curious— and growing—crowd. "Can we discuss this in your office?" he asked Sheriff Kearny.

The sheriff instructed his deputy to take the body to the doctor's office so the cause of death could be determined. Then he motioned for Torrie and Lance to follow him into his office.

"Seems strange Canon ended up way over on

Horse Mountain," he said as he sat down in the chair behind his desk. "Seems even stranger you two knew where to find him." He leveled his gaze directly on Lance.

"Me and Canon used to do a lot of exploring on Horse Mountain when we were young."

"Well—that still leaves a hellva lot of unanswered questions." Sheriff Kearny leaned back in his chair and crossed his arms over his protruding belly. He glanced at Torrie, then back to Lance. "Who wants to start?"

Torrie took a step backwards, but the brick wall stopped her. If it was possible she would crawl into one of the cracks between the bricks. She noticed Lance stepped forward.

He told the sheriff about the condition of Canon's body, but he left out the most grisly details. Without divulging the reason, he told the lawman about the fistfight between him and his brother at the Connors' barn. Lance finished his story by relating how he had gone to look for Canon at the Grand Mesa the following morning. "It was my intent to call him out for a showdown," he added.

"Well—that's a real interestin' story, Farlo. But the fact remains that Canon was beaten to death and you admit to fightin' with him. I have no other choice but to charge you with murder." Sheriff Kearny rose to his feet and faced Lance.

Torrie stared at the two men, her mouth gaped open. While he spoke, Lance had not mentioned her once. He hadn't even looked in her direction.

"Wait!" she cried out. She pushed herself away

267

from the wall and stepped forward. When she glanced at Lance, she was sure she noticed a look of relief filter through his face. She turned toward the sheriff again.

"I have something to add," she said.

Sheriff Kearny swaggered out from behind his desk and placed his hands askew on his hips. His gold badge hung limply from his shirt's breast pocket. He exhaled an annoyed sigh. "What?"

Unconsciously, Torrie clutched at the material of her riding skirt. She forced herself to look up at the sheriff's glowering face. "Lance didn't kill Canon when they fought in the Connors' barn. Canon got on his horse and rode off after the fight. And, the reason they were fighting was because Canon was trying to . . ." she glanced down at the floor for an instant, then made herself look up again. "He was trying to-to rape me." She felt a burst of heat erupt in her cheeks. The doubting expression on Sheriff Kearny's face stripped away her fleeting sense of bravery.

Torrie looked away from him. She stared down at the floor once more—she could sense Lance's gaze on her.

"That's a mighty serious thing to accuse a man of doin'," he said. "And Canon can't even defend himself against your charge."

Lance clenched his fists at his sides, he fought the urge to wipe the smirk off the sheriff's mouth. "I saw what Canon was trying to do," he added.

"I hope you're not the only witness," Sheriff Kearny said. He turned to Torrie. "Is there anybody else who can verify what you're saying?"

She shrugged. Her gaze moved to his unfriendly face, then back down to the floor. "No."

The sheriff gave an aggravated grunt. He focused his attention on Lance. "I'm gonna go look over Canon's body. I don't want you to leave town until I finish a complete investigation of his death." He looked at Torrie, adding, "You're not to leave town either."

"I'm leaving for Denver on the 5 o'clock train," she said.

"No you're not," Sheriff Kearny retorted. "Nobody's leavin' here until I find out who killed Canon—and why!"

Torrie gasped, her thoughts began to spin through her head. She looked at Lance in desperation. He offered no consolation. On his face rested a lopsided grin, his pale eyes were lit with an inner fire when he met her gaze.

Chapter Twenty-Six

With the noticeable exception of Wayne Gere, Jim Larson, and Shawn McLeary, most of the townspeople and ranchers from surrounding areas were present at Will Connor's funeral. Nearly all of the men from the Grand Mesa were in attendance, and so was Lance Farlo. He stood away from the rest of the crowd on a knoll a short distance from the gravesite.

Torrie held Will Jr. in her arms, and she stayed at Elsa's side throughout the service. She told Elsa about the things that had been going on with Canon for the past few years right before the funeral. She wished she could have waited until a time when Elsa wasn't under so much stress, but she wanted to tell her before she heard about it from someone else.

Elsa had been understanding, and sympathetic. She also made it plain her feelings were hurt because Torrie had not confided this devastating secret to her long ago. By the time they were ready to come to the funeral, however, Elsa said she understood the reasons behind Torrie's silence. Against the Carrington men no woman would ever stand a chance.

Now, Torrie's eyes were constantly drawn toward Lance. Every time she looked at him, then around at the rest of the people who were in attendance, the nervous knot in her stomach increased.

Ben and Gage stood opposite from her at the gravesite. Both of them kept casting deadly looks in her direction. She noticed Ben glancing over his shoulder every so often to glare in Lance's direction. He looked as though he was having a hard time concentrating on the funeral. Torrie knew Sheriff Kearny had informed him of Canon's murder when he had got into town today. Next to Gage stood Kenny Bower, his leering glare never left Torrie's face. The only friendly person she saw among the crew from the Grand Mesa was Mac Williams.

As the minister finished the service, Elsa stepped to the edge of the grave. She was cloaked entirely in black, even a black veil hid her face. In her gloved hand, she clutched a single red rose. The long stem had been twisted in her hands until the blossom dangled limply from the end. After she tossed the flower into the hole, Elsa paused to stare down at the wooden box which held her husband's remains. She stood on the mound of dirt at the edge of the grave—silent and still—for such a long time Torrie began to worry.

"Elsa, it's time to go," Torrie whispered.

Elsa didn't answer. Her slender form swayed as if her legs were about to go out from under her.

Torrie wasn't aware of crying out for help, but she did. Mac Williams was the first man to reach Elsa as she teetered at the edge of the grave. He clasped her arm and held her upright as he pulled her away from the deep hole. The entire crowd began to close around Elsa with concern. When Ben Carrington stepped toward her, Torrie noticed Elsa's spine straighten. An instant later she realized Lance was holding onto Elsa's other arm. The knot in her stomach tightened. She clutched Will Jr. against her so tight, he let out a cry of protest. Torrie loosed her grip on the baby, but her nervousness did not recede.

Elsa pushed the veil up from her face. Her eyes were swollen red, her face puffy. She looked directly at Ben Carrington.

He had stopped his approach when he saw Lance come to the widow's side. The old man's narrowed gaze was set on his son. The look of hatred on Ben's face was chilling and so explosive that those who noticed it fell silent and backed away.

"Mrs. Connor," Lance said quietly. His voice was firm, and his eyes never wavered from his father's cold stare. "It's time to go."

Elsa glared at Ben Carrington for a moment longer, then she turned and looked up at the tall gunfighter. He looked down and met her gaze. She was surprised to see such a look of tenderness filter into his eyes.

"It's time to go," he repeated.

Elsa nodded her head slowly. She wanted Ben Carrington to know what a selfish, hateful old man she thought he was, but Will's funeral was not the place. A heavy sigh rattled her thin body, gratitude toward Lance Farlo filled her grief-stricken heart. She took a faltering step, then a complete blackness engulfed her.

Lance felt her body go limp. He scooped her up into his arms before Mac Williams had a chance to grab her. Oblivious to anyone else, Lance pushed through the crowd. He headed out of the cemetery and toward the only doctor's office in town. Doc Richards was attending the funeral. He was at Lance's side within seconds.

Torrie's thoughts were spinning wildly through her head. She started to follow Lance and the doctor, but something stopped her in her tracks. Swinging around again, she leveled her enraged gaze at Ben Carrington. His contemptuous expression had not changed, but she refused to let him intimidate her. Her mouth opened, the same words Elsa had wanted to say, Torrie was ready to voice. A hand clamped around her arm—firm— but not hurtful.

"It is time to go, Miss Torrie."

Her attention snapped up to the man who was at her side. Torrie's first instinct was to try to pull away from Mac, but common sense quickly reclaimed her mind. A fierce shudder shook through her body. Will Jr. squirmed in her arms as if he had felt it too. Her head dropped down, she closed her eyes for a moment in an attempt to calm the fury that seethed through her. When she opened her eyes again, she did not look back at Ben. She tried to focus her thoughts on getting to Elsa as she let Mac lead her away from the cemetery.

"Thanks Mac," she said as they made their way toward the doctor's office.

"For what?"

Torrie glanced up at the older man. His weathered face hosted a slight smile. "For stopping me from making a fool of myself, and—" she took a deep breath. "Thank you for your words of wisdom the other day."

Mac's smile broke into a chortle. "Wisdom? I don't recollect saying anything wise the other day."

"I know why you told me about the girl from your past."

"Oh—that." He opened the door at the doctor's office and stepped back so Torrie could enter. Briefly, he met her gaze. Her expression told him she not only understood everything he had been trying to tell her, but he sensed she was also experiencing the same type of fear he had talked about. "If ever you want to talk again, Miss Torrie . . ."

Torrie paused at the entrance to the doctor's office. She gazed up at Mac's face. She thought of Lance—of how he would grow old alone—just like Mac. Her stomach twisted with pain again. She nodded, her voice felt strangled by the lump in her throat.

The doctor's office was the bottom floor of a large house. The upstairs rooms were used for patients who needed to stay overnight or under the doctor's care for long periods of time. The doctor lived with his wife in a small area at the back of the house. A waiting room was just inside the front door. Lance stood in the middle of the room.

"Mrs. Connor is upstairs," he said as Torrie turned away from Mac Williams. He noticed the troubled look on her pale face, his attention riveted to the old gunman. Mac was turning to leave, but Lance glimpsed his face as the door shut—his expression seemed compassionate.

"Are you all right?" he asked. In one long stride, he was standing before her.

"It's Elsa we need to worry about," Torrie stated. Her trembling voice belied her attempt to appear unshaken.

Lance felt his chest tighten. What had Mac Williams said to upset her? He reminded himself that maybe she was just worried about her friend. He was getting too defensive about her, and he knew he had to stop.

"I'm going up to be with her," Torrie said. She glanced down at the baby. He was looking around at his new surroundings with wide eyes. "Would you mind holding him for a few minutes?"

Lance stared at the boy. The baby's big blue eyes seemed to settle right on his face. He thought he noticed a slight smile on the tiny lips, the little arms waved out from the top of the blanket as if the child were anxious for him to hold him. In defeat, Lance reached out his arms—stiffly. As Torrie placed the warm bundle in his arms, he felt her push the baby against his chest. His arms curled awkwardly around the baby's squirming body. Abruptly, he jerked his head up, he opened his mouth to ask her what he should do next. She was already headed up the stairs.

Will Jr. made a cooing sound. Lance stared down at him. He looked like he was smiling again. Lance's body began to relax. It's only a baby—he told himself. He smiled back at the boy. Another gurgling sound escaped from the tiny mouth. Dribble trickled from the corner of the baby's lips. Lance cleared his throat in a nervous gesture.

He held the baby tightly in one arm as he untied his handkerchief from around his neck with his other hand. With one tip of the scarf, he carefullly dabbed at the drool on the baby's chin. Will Jr. made more contented noises. Unconsciously, Lance began to imitate the cooing sounds. His body rocked back and forth as his sole concentration became entertaining the baby in his arms. He noticed the boy kept glancing up at his Stetson. Lance cocked his head from side to side in an animated manner as he continued to gurgle and coo in a high-pitched tone.

During his performance, he happened to glance toward the staircase. He felt a hot blush color his face. The noises halted in his throat.

Torrie was not about to disturb Lance, and she wished he hadn't noticed her so soon. The sight of him playing with the baby was something she wanted to retain in her memory for all time. Holding the infant, Lance seemed even taller, his shoulders broader. Yet, for a moment there, he seemed almost like a little boy.

His obvious embarrassment over being caught made Torrie chuckle. The red hue darkened around his mustache and beard. She noticed a pout form on his lips. Torrie's love for him abounded.

"I-I was just . . ." he shrugged his shoulders, and held the baby out toward her. "How's Mrs. Connor?" he asked. His voice was serious sounding again.

"She's fine now. The doc said she probably passed out from all the tension she's been under lately. I suppose my confession about Canon was the last straw." Torrie heaved a guilty-sounding sigh.

As she let Lance deposit Will Jr. in her arms, she added, "She wants to feed him." She looked up. Lance's gaze was alternating between her and the baby. His expression was unreadable.

"Yeah—well—I'd better be on my way."

"Where?" she asked, then hated herself for sounding so nosey.

"Sheriff Kearny has ordered me to take him to the cave where I found Canon's body. I reckon he just wants to get me out of the way until Ben's outta town. Judgin' from the way the old man was lookin' at me, this town ain't big enough for the both of us."

A sinking feeling inched down through Torrie's chest and stomach. He'd be gone until tomorrow. She had hoped since neither of them were supposed to leave town she'd get to see him tonight.

"I'll see you tomorrow night," he said—almost as if he could read her thoughts. He leaned over, and gently clasped her chin. His lips descended on hers—kissing her always seemed so natural. He felt her respond at once. The baby in her arms prevented him from drawing her close. When he forced himself to pull away, he felt as though his heart had stopped beating for a moment. He didn't want to go.

Torrie was unable to look away from him. His kiss still moistened her lips, her body yearning for his touch. As he started to leave her, he let his fingertips gently caress her cheek. They left a fiery trail on her flushed face. While she watched him walk out the door another feeling joined her desirous longings—a feeling that was becoming as undeniable as her love for him. The knot of fear tightened in her stomach again.

Will Jr. unexpectedly broke into a loud wail. Torrie was jolted from her own agony. She cradled the crying infant to her breast and hurried up the stairs. Mac Williams' parting words echoed in her mind. She wanted to talk to him again, and she still needed to retrieve some of her things from the main house on Grand Mesa. Tonight Sheriff Kearny would not be around to see if she left town.

Doc Richards was coming out of Elsa's room just as Torrie reached the top of the stairs. He glanced at the howling baby, then stepped out of Torrie's way.

The sheets of the bed where Elsa sat were stark white. Torrie noticed how Elsa's pallor almost seemed to match. Her paleness was made even more drastic by the black dress she wore. She held her arms out when Torrie entered with the baby.

Will Jr. quieted the instant his mother took him.

"I guess he knows it's dinner time," Torrie said. Her voice sounded hollow to her own ears. She wondered how she would get to the Grand Mesa tonight without Elsa knowing about it.

"Doc Richards wants me to stay here tonight. I told him it's not necessary, but he insisted." Her attention was focused on getting Will Jr.'s mouth on the end of her swollen breast. She glanced up at Torrie, adding, "I asked him if you could stay here too. He said you could sleep in the room at the end of the hall."

"I could just get a room over at the hotel," Torrie retorted, quickly. In her head, she calculated how much money she had, which was very little. Everything had been provided for her while she had been living on the Grand Mesa. Her own funds were limited to the small amount of cash she carried with her for emergencies. She had already spent most of that money on the train ticket to Denver purchased earlier today. In her room at the ranch house, however, she had several pieces of expensive jewelry. She knew she could sell the jewelry and have enough money to live on until she was able to find employment in Denver.

"I really wish you'd reconsider," Elsa said. Her voice held a pleading tone, and her expression was the same. "But if you're planning on being with Lance tonight . . ." her voice faded. She was trying to be understanding about Torrie's relationship with the gunfighter. But, she wanted to protect her from more hurt too.

"He won't be in town tonight," Torrie answered, quickly. The idea of Elsa knowing how intimate she was with Lance made her feel awkward. She did not meet Elsa's gaze as she added, "I want to stay here with you."

She plopped down in a chair at the side of Elsa's bed. It probably wouldn't be wise for her to ride out to the Grand Mesa tonight, anyway, she told herself. If she did decide to go out to talk to Mac and collect her jewelry, however, there would still be the entire night once Elsa went to sleep.

Chapter Twenty-Seven

Elsa and Will Jr. went to sleep early. Torrie heard the doctor and his wife retire a short time later. Still, she was hesitant to go through with her plan. She knew it was a foolish—and dangerous—notion to ride out to the Grand Mesa alone at night. But, she might not have another chance to talk to Mac, and she desperately needed to retrieve her jewelry before she left for Denver.

Long after the house had fallen quiet Torrie continued to pace back and forth in her room. Mostly, her thoughts were with Lance. She kept telling herself his trip to Horse Mountain with Sheriff Kearny would reveal nothing incriminating, yet, she still worried. What if the sheriff discovered something that would put more suspicion on Lance—and on her?

As the night wore on, Torrie's anxieties increased. Exhausted from worrying about everything she finally convinced herself to give up on her idea of going to the Grand Mesa, and forced herself to go to bed. But after a restless night of tossing and turning she was up before dawn.

She scribbled a quick note to Elsa to tell her she was going to the ranch to pick up a few of her belongings. In the note she wrote she'd be back by midday. Torrie knew she could be gone longer, though, because Mac might not be close to the main house. If he was out on the range somewhere, she might spend most of the day looking for him. The idea of encountering Ben or Gage made her rethink her plan again. She couldn't forget the way they were both glaring at her at the funeral yesterday. A feeling of dread crept through her, but it was not enough to keep her from going.

By the time Torrie reached the livery stable where Ginger was boarded, the sun was beginning to cast a yellowish glow along the tops of the far mountains to the east. Torrie's nervousness did not fade as she saddled her horse. Yet, she knew if she just sat around at the doctor's house all day, she would be crazy with worry by the time Lance and the sheriff got back to town. Her hope was to be able to get to the main house at the about the same time Ben and Gage were out in the bunkhouses issuing orders to the men for their day's work. Neither of them did much of the menial work around the ranch anymore. Their main task these days seemed to be giving orders.

When she led Ginger out of the stables, she glanced in the direction of the doctor's house. The street was still quiet. As she climbed into her saddle, her gaze scanned over her saddlebags—and her shotgun scabbard. She had everything she needed.

A scattering of clouds dotted the horizon. Now, they were only wisps of white, but they could mean the advance of another storm. Each detail of the last storm still clung to Torrie's thoughts. She knew for the rest of her life every snowflake that fell would remind her of Lance and of the night in the line shack.

The fastest route was along the main road, but Torrie was not worried about encountering anyone on her way to the Grand Mesa at this early hour. The glimpse of a lone rider moving toward her, however, caused her to fill with uneasiness. She turned Ginger into the nearest grove of cottonwoods hoping the rider had not spotted her. The pounding of her heart felt as if it were trying to crash through her chest as she waited for the man to pass by. If he even glanced in her direction, he would notice her. Torrie held her breath as the sounds of hooves on the road reached her ears. She wondered if she should have her shotgun in her hands. It was too late to worry about it now.

Through the branches, Torrie caught sight of the rider. Her fear subsided, but something stopped her from calling out to him. She watched him until he had disappeared from her view. Wayne Gere never even looked toward the trees. He seemed completely engrossed in his own thoughts, and judging by the expression he wore, his thoughts did not seem pleasant.

Torrie nudged Ginger into the open again, then

stopped her once they reached the road. She stared off in the direction Wayne had just ridden. He was probably headed toward the Diamond G, yet, the sun had been up less than an hour. He must have been out all night, but where? She turned Ginger in the direction of the Grand Mesa as her thoughts dwelled on this strange development. Surely, Wayne had not been to the Grand Mesa. The McLeary ranch could be reached by traveling this direction. Maybe Wayne had business with Shawn McLeary. The idea of him spending the night at the McLearys' seemed unlikely to Torrie, but she could think of no other logical explanation.

As she continued on to the Grand Mesa, a dozen thoughts spun through Torrie's mind. Nothing made sense anymore. A part of her just wanted to get out of here—to get away from all this craziness. But another part of her wanted to prolong her departure for as long as possible, or at least, until Lance Farlo left. She tried to imagine each of them riding off in different directions—of thousands of miles separating them for the rest of their lives— but this was more than she was ready to cope with now.

At the main entrance to the Grand Mesa, Torrie met her first two obstacles.

"Sorry, Miss Torrie. But we've got strict orders not to let you on this property." The man who spoke was one of the gunmen who was hired recently. He went by the name of Yuma—just Yuma. With thick black hair and a black mustache, Yuma was a handsome man by most standards. But he had a dangerous aura that detracted from his good looks. Torrie had no desire to cross him in any manner.

His partner was a young gunman named Todd Wyman. The two of them had ridden into the Grand Mesa together. They said they hailed from Arizona, and it was obvious to everyone Todd was learning the tricks of the trade from Yuma. Now, Todd stayed at his post. He did not interfere with Yuma's conversation with Torrie.

"I understand," Torrie said. She was surprised her voice sounded so calm. The quivering in her body made her feel almost faint. Whether it was from fear, or from anger toward Ben for issuing this order, she wasn't sure. She did know she did not want this man to know she was looking for Mac Williams. He had become too good a friend for her to put him in a precarious position. "I was hoping to get some of my clothes and personal belongings."

"Sorry," Yuma said again. He stared up at her with a look that defied any further comments on the subject.

Torrie nodded her head. She didn't trust herself to speak. Her gaze rested briefly on Yuma's face. His handsome features appeared to be void of any emotion. Torrie felt as if an icy wind just whipped through her chest. She diverted her eyes from the gunman's face, and turned Ginger around without another word. There were other ways to get onto the ranch, but now she was hesitant to make an attempt to reach them. She had glimpsed something in Yuma's expression. It made a chill inch down her spine, and also gave her the feeling that he would follow her if she tried to go a different route.

Her instincts proved right. Several miles down the road, she glanced over her shoulder and caught sight of the gunman. He was keeping a far distance, but he was close enough to stop her if she tried to backtrack toward the Grand Mesa. A sense of defeat washed through Torrie as she decided to give up her idea of talking to Mac again. It really didn't matter, anyway, she told herself. What could he tell her that she didn't already know?

But she couldn't give up on her plan to get her jewelry from the main house. Without it, she would be penniless. She realized she would have to go back to the Grand Mesa again. Now that she knew where she stood, though, she would make sure she used more caution next time.

Torrie was almost back to town before she noticed Yuma turn his horse around. Elsa would be up by now, and she was probably worried sick about her. Torrie knew she had no other choice but to go back to the doctor's house. The town was beginning to wake up, too. As Torrie rode down the street, she became aware of the whispers and stares directed toward her. Speculation ran rampant about her association with Lance Farlo, and her possible involvement in Canon's murder. She tried to tell herself the gossip didn't bother her. But, she couldn't deny that it did.

She kicked Ginger in the sides to hasten her steps. As she neared the livery a commotion behind her made her yank on the reins. Riding hard and fast from the direction she had just come was one of Shawn McLeary's men. She had met him at church a while back. His name was Mike Ramsey. He started to dismount at the sheriff's office, but when he spotted Torrie farther down the street he headed straight for her.

"Where's Farlo?" he shouted.

"He's out of town with the sheriff. They won't be back until late." Torrie felt a rush of panic rip through her as she asked, "What's happened?"

"McLeary's place has been set on fire," the man gasped. "We put it out before it did much damage, but Shawn's madder than I ever seen him. He sent me to fetch Farlo. Shawn's headed over to Jim Larson's place. He said it was time Ben Carrington was made to pay for settin' fire to their places."

The cold, expressionless face of Yuma flashed through Torrie's mind. "They'll be killed before they even set foot on the Grand Mesa!"

"That's why I came for Lance Farlo," Mike said. He glanced around with a worried frown. A look of relief filtered through his flushed features when he saw Deputy Silt coming down the street. Mike related the story to the lawman.

"I'm going out there," Deputy Silt said. As he headed toward the livery to get his horse, he walked past Torrie. He paid her no attention as he stalked by.

Torrie turned toward Mike Ramsey again. "Does Mrs. McLeary need help?" She thought of the McLeary children; four little tow-heads with rosy cheeks. The oldest was barely six years old, the youngest just a few months.

"I think she'd appreciate it," he answered.

"But . . ." he glanced down at the ground for a moment. When he looked up again, his face was even more flushed than it had been. "I don't know that you'd be welcome. You know—being Ben's stepdaughter and all."

Anger flared in Torrie's breast. Her emerald eyes flashed with bolts of fire. She thought about trying to explain to Mike about her relationship with her stepfather, and about her banishment from the Grand Mesa. Instead, she remained silent. The entire valley was divided now; half still sympathized with the Grand Mesa, but now because of the two fires, the other half sided against the Carringtons. Torrie realized she didn't belong to either side.

Deputy Silt emerged from the stable before Torrie was able to sort through her angry—and confused—thoughts. As before, he completely ignored her as he motioned for Mike Ramsey to follow him. Torrie stared after them as they rode out of town. She was even more aware of the icy stares she was receiving from some of the people who stood on the street. In quick retreat, she led Ginger into the livery and unsaddled her.

The crowd had dispersed and the town had regained a somewhat normal atmosphere by the time Torrie made her way back to the doctor's house. She knew almost everyone she passed, but she received only a few mumbled greetings from some of the people. She quickened her pace, her anxiety increased with each step.

At the doctor's house she headed straight up to Elsa's room. She knocked lightly, then opened the door before she heard Elsa speak. "Ben has ordered his men to keep me off the Grand Mesa," she blurted out the moment she entered.

Elsa was bent over Will Jr.'s cradle. When Torrie burst in, she quickly straightened up. "Oh, Torrie! I was scared sick when I read your note." She crossed the room and stopped before Torrie. The anger came from Torrie like a pot boiling over on hot coals.

"I think we should leave as soon as possible," Elsa added.

"I can't go, remember? Sheriff Kearny warned me not to leave town until he knew who killed Canon."

Elsa wrung her hands together and shook her head from side to side. "That's ridiculous! It could take days—or forever—to find Canon's murderer." She twirled around and stalked over to the window. Her face drew into a thoughtful frown. She looked across the room at Torrie again.

"You don't want to leave yet, do you? I mean—because of Lance." Elsa's voice held a note of understanding, her expression had softened. When she saw Torrie's gaze move down toward the floor, she knew she was right.

Torrie jumped with surprise when Elsa laid her hand on her shoulder. She had been so engrossed with thoughts of Lance, she hadn't noticed Elsa cross the room again. When she looked into Elsa's eyes, a sense of guilt shot through her. She knew how badly Elsa wanted to go. "I just can't go—not yet," Torrie said.

They stared at one another for a few seconds,

then Elsa gave her head an affirmative nod. "You're right. You should be with Lance." A weak smile tugged at her lips when she noticed the way Torrie's complexion acquired a sudden glow.

"It wouldn't be for much longer," Torrie said. "This range war has come to a head, and when Lance's job is finished, he'll be headed back to Texas."

"After all that's happened between you, I'm sure he'll ask you to go with him."

Torrie glanced down again, her face lost its rosy glow. She drew in a deep sigh. "He made it clear the first time we were together. When he leaves— he will be going alone."

Elsa's heart felt as if it were shattering. The pain she could see in Torrie's face was immense. "Well—maybe you're wrong. I guess we'll just have to wait and see what happens."

Torrie tried to smile at Elsa. It was a wasted effort. She walked over to the window and stared down at the dusty street. Right now, she was filled with conflicting emotions. For Elsa's patience, she was once again grateful. But, she wished some of Elsa's optimism would rub off on her, because she had no doubt what would happen when Lance was ready to leave . . . and she knew she wasn't wrong.

Chapter Twenty-Eight

Rifle was host to one hotel, and one boarding-house. Anna May's Boardinghouse offered cheaper rates, so Torrie and Elsa decided this was where they would stay until they were ready to leave for Denver. By afternoon they had moved from the doctor's house to the boardinghouse down the street. Torrie hated letting Elsa pay for her room and board, but she had no choice until she could figure out a way to get back onto the Grand Mesa. Reclaiming her possessions was becoming more of a necessity as time passed.

The entire town was talking about the fire at Shawn McLeary's ranch this morning. A group of armed men rode out to join forces with Deputy Silt and the others. Torrie cringed at the idea of the townsmen—and the ranchers—clashing with the ruthless gunmen who guarded the Grand Mesa. She was certain Lance Farlo was the only man capable of confronting Ben's henchmen. He was only one man, though. She worried that too much was expected of him.

Down the hall, Torrie could hear Will Jr. crying. She thought about going to Elsa's room to offer her help, but she decided against it. In spite of her collapse at the funeral yesterday, Elsa seemed stronger than ever now. Torrie felt guilty making her stay in Rifle. She told Elsa to leave for Denver today. Of course, Elsa declined. She said she would not leave Torrie until she was certain Lance was taking her to Texas with him. Their conversation had ended on that note.

Too restless to stay cooped up in her room, Torrie decided she would go out and sit on the front porch. She could watch the street from there, and she could also watch for Lance's return. The autumn breeze held a crispness, which made Torrie shiver as she walked outside. Even though Elsa had offered her clothes to wear, Torrie was dressed in her same black riding skirt again. Not only was she more comfortable in her own clothes, but she was ready to ride if the need should arise. Torrie sensed with all the trouble in the valley she needed to be ready for anything. Her intuition proved right.

She had barely exited from the house when she saw Mac Williams come out of the doctor's house down the street. It was apparent he was looking for her when he swung into his saddle and headed toward the boardinghouse. As he came closer Torrie noticed his expression was drawn with worry.

"There's been trouble, Miss Torrie." He was almost out of breath when he added, "Where's Farlo?"

"What happened?" Torrie asked, although she sensed she already knew the answer. The first words out of Mac's mouth confirmed her thoughts.

"Jim Larson and Shawn McLeary's been shot." He glanced down the street in a nervous manner. "Where's Farlo?" he asked again.

The shock of what he had said was still sinking into Torrie's mind. "Are they dead?" she gasped.

"McLeary's dead. Larson is hurt bad. A couple of the men who were ridin' with them are dead, a couple others shot up. Where is Farlo?" he demanded once more.

Torrie pointed limply toward Horse Mountain. "Sheriff Kearny made him take him up to where we found Canon's body. Lance figured the sheriff was trying to avoid more trouble by getting him out of town until things cooled down."

Mac gave a disgusted grunt. "This might've been avoided if Farlo was here. Maybe he would have been able to talk some sense into McLeary and Larson. Against men like Yuma and the others those ranchers didn't stand a chance."

A sick sensation moved through Torrie as she thought of the tragedy today had wrought. She looked up at Mac as she tried to sort through her pain. "Were you—I mean—did you . . ." she didn't know how to ask Mac if he had fought against the ranchers.

"I got there after it was over," he said, guessing the rest of her question. "I won't be goin' back," he added. He slid down from his horse and leveled his gaze at Torrie. "I make a livin' with my gun. But I don't take to burnin' out innocent families. If

295

Carrington's gonna play dirty then I don't want no part of it."

Relief washed over Torrie. She thought of how similar Mac and Lance were in the way they viewed their professions. These two were a rare breed among men of any caliber.

"What now?" she asked.

"I'm headin' over to the Diamond G. McLeary's gone, and I suspect Larson won't make it either. That just leaves Wayne Gere. Once he's outta the way, Carrington won't have anyone left to accuse of squattin' on his land. I figure Gere might be needin' some extra help about now."

Torrie started to agree with him. She opened her mouth, but another thought passed through her mind. "Mac?" An intense scowl drew her auburn brows together. "I was headed out to the Grand Mesa at daybreak. About halfway out I saw Wayne Gere riding north." Her eyes widened, her mouth gaped open for a moment before she added, "He could've been coming from Shawn McLeary's place."

Mac stared at her for a second. A deep frown pulled at his face as he contemplated her words. "Didn't you talk to him?"

"At first I wasn't sure who it was, so I ducked into the trees. Wayne never even noticed me. He seemed preoccupied as he rode past." She drew in a trembling breath. "What if he's the one who started the fire at Jim Larson's, and at Shawn McLeary's?"

"That's a mighty big accusation, Miss Torrie." Mac stared down at the ground for a moment.

When he looked up again, his face was set with determination. "I aim to find out all about Gere before I offer to go to work for him."

Gratitude inched through Torrie. She wished Lance would get back. This thought reminded her of one of the reasons she was going to the Grand Mesa this morning. "I was coming out to talk to you, but Ben told the guards to keep me off his property."

Mac nodded his head. "Yeah—I got those same orders." He shrugged his shoulders and leaned against the porch rail. "I got time for talkin' now."

Torrie looked away from Mac's piercing stare. Her problems seemed so insignificant compared to all that was happening around her. She gave a shrug and glanced up at the aging gunslinger. "I was also going out there to pick up some of my personal belongings. There's some valuables in my room that I must have."

Her attempt to avoid the real reason she wanted to talk to him did not escape Mac. He knew she'd talk about Lance Farlo when she was ready. "How do you plan on gettin' your things?" he asked.

Torrie tossed her head back, her long red ponytail was flung over her shoulder with the gesture. "I'll have to sneak up to the main house."

A surprised chortle rang out from Mac. He was amazed she would actually think she could get past all the guards.

"I have to," Torrie said, her voice and expression were determined.

Mac did not ask her any more questions. He sensed no one would be able to convince her to give up her foolish notion, but he also guessed the reason she seemed so desperate to go back to the Grand Mesa. "Do you need money, Miss Torrie?" The red blush which colored her cheeks answered his question. "I'd be glad to help you out . . ."

"No," Torrie cut in. The scarlet hue in her cheeks deepened. "Th-Thank you. But I'll be fine once I get my things from the ranch."

Mac studied her for a moment. The stubborn tilt of her chin told him nothing—or nobody—was going to stop her from trying to get back whatever it was she thought she needed. He sighed with defeat. "Well—I guess I'll have to help you get your things." As the words fell from Mac's mouth, a sliver of dread shot through his chest.

A spark of light flashed in Torrie's green eyes as they grew wide like those of an excited child. "You will? When?" she asked.

Mac threw his hands up into the air, then let them drop down against his sides. "One time's as good as another."

"Let's get it over with then," Torrie said. If they didn't run into trouble, they would be back in time for her to see Lance tonight.

A look of uncertainty crossed Mac's face. "This ain't gonna be easy—especially in broad daylight." He scratched his whiskered chin, and slowly nodded his head. "I know where the guards are posted, so gettin' on the property won't be too hard. Gettin' up to the house is the tough part."

Torrie knew of a way, although the idea of going this way made her feel strange now that she knew how Lance's mother had died. The back of the mesa was the only route they could take, however, if they had any chance of getting up to the main house unnoticed.

"I need to tell Elsa where I'm going, and get my horse. Then, I'll be ready to go."

"I'll saddle your horse. Is she over at the livery?"

Torrie nodded as she turned to rush into the boardinghouse. It was midafternoon and they didn't have time to waste.

"Don't go," Elsa pleaded when Torrie told her where she was headed. "There's been too much trouble already. Don't worry about money. We'll make do." She wrung her hands together. Her thoughts were still in shock over the information Torrie had just relayed to her about Shawn McLeary's death and Jim Larson's critical condition.

Torrie stood in front of her friend, where she could see the torment in her face. She was torn between her decision to go to the Grand Mesa, or staying with Elsa. It was apparent this latest trouble expanded the heartbreak she was suffering because of losing Will. Still, Torrie knew she couldn't continue to be a burden to her friend.

She clasped Elsa's hand tightly as she spoke. "Mac will protect me. There's a back trail that leads to the house. Ben won't even know we've been there." She squeezed Elsa's hand again, then turned to leave before she changed her mind about going. Elsa's gloomy mood was beginning to rub off on her.

Before she was out of the boardinghouse, Mac was back. He entered the front door without

299

knocking and practically ran into Torrie in the foyer.

"You'd better not go out that way," Mac said, his voice was etched with urgency.

"What's going on?" A cold chill swept through Torrie as she glimpsed the strange look on the gunman's face.

"Deputy Silt and the others just rode into town with the men who were shot at the Grand Mesa. There's an ugly mob gatherin' in the street. I don't think it's safe for anybody they can associate with the Grand Mesa."

Alarm made Torrie's stance stiffen. "What should we do?"

"Sounds like Deputy Silt is gonna wait until the sheriff gets back before they make another move. They'd all be smart to wait for Lance Farlo." His gaze leveled on Torrie as he added, "I suppose anybody who gets close to the Grand Mesa is gonna meet trouble. Could be real dangerous, Miss Torrie."

"I have to at least try." Torrie noticed him shake his head as if he was going to attempt to change her mind. She quickly added, "If we get out there and it looks too risky, I'll give it up."

Mac eyed her suspiciously for a second. Then, he gave an exasperated grunt. He was wondering how Lance Farlo would feel when he found out about this foolish escapade.

"I'm gonna hold you to that," he said in a firm voice. He glanced over his shoulder toward the door. A heavy frown masked his face. "You stay here while I go fetch your horse. Meet me out back and be prepared to ride hard." He nodded toward the street. "Judging by the sounds of the crowd out there, Sheriff Kearny is gonna have a riot on his hands when he gets back. Our only chance is to get out to the ranch, and get off again before they come out to confront Carrington."

Torrie gave her head a quick nod in agreement, but Mac was already going out the door. She didn't dare go back up to Elsa's room and tell her what was happening.

She went down the hallway and slipped out the back door of the boardinghouse. Even from here she could hear all the commotion down the street. The angry voices of the men caused her fear to increase. Maybe she should just borrow money from Mac, she told herself. But how would she pay him back? Her thoughts were jolted by the approach of the gunslinger. He was riding his big bay, and leading her mare. He had both horses at a fast gait. They slid to a halt in front of Torrie.

Without a word Torrie grabbed her reins and climbed into her saddle. She kept telling herself she meant what she had said to Mac—she would abandon this plan if there was any indication they would encounter trouble. They headed south out of Rifle and took cover in the cottonwoods along the river until they were out of sight of the town. Even then, they stayed off the main road. Torrie knew the back roads almost as well as she knew the back of her own hand. She rode toward the most desolate part of the ranch where they did not run any cattle.

Mac wasn't even aware they were already on

Carrington land until he realized they were headed straight for the back of the mesa where the large house stood. Torrie had already gotten them past the areas where he figured they would encounter the most trouble. There were only a couple more open fields to cross before they were in the shelter of the thick brush at the base of the mesa. He didn't ask her how she intended to get through the heavy growth.

"I thought that the old man had the entire ranch fenced in," he commented as they slowed their horses to cross a dry creekbed.

A quick, humorless chuckle came from Torrie. "He's put claim to so much land, it would take years to fence in all of it." A weary sigh echoed from Torrie's lips as she glanced around at the sprawling countryside. This land had caused so much pain and death. She wondered when it would all end.

As they neared the back of the mesa they caught a glimpse of a group of men headed toward the south range. Torrie and Mac quickly hid in the sparse shelter of a clump of cedars until the men were out of sight. The riders were all gunmen, and it looked like they were armed for a war. A few minutes later they spotted another bunch of riders headed north.

"Ben's sendin' out the troops," Mac said as his narrowed gaze watched the men ride off in the distance. "It might not be as easy leavin' as it was gettin' here."

Torrie suspected he spoke the truth. It wouldn't be long before Ben's men had every corner of the ranch covered. Now it was too late to turn back even if they wanted to. She stared up at the rugged wall of the mesa. From here only the very tips of the huge cottonwood which sheltered the small graveyard were visible. She thought of the two women who were buried there. She studied the rocky slope again. A cold chill raced down her spine.

"There's a trail through these bushes." She glanced around at the tangled brush and low-hanging cedars. Lance had mentioned the trail so she knew it had to be here somewhere.

Mac looked at the dense growth and shook his head in a doubtful manner. He climbed down from his saddle and began to walk along the edges of the thick brush. He gave his head another negative shake. "If there's a trail in that mess, I don't know how we'd ever find it."

Refusing to give up now, Torrie slid down from Ginger and began to scour the area. Each time she attempted to push aside the branches of a rosebush, her hands would get torn by the sharp thorns. The sleeves of her white blouse were shredded by the sharp barbs when she would try to reach past the bushes.

"It ain't no use, Miss Torrie," Mac said after he had made another scan of the area. "If we waste too much time lookin' for this trail, we'll never make it out of here before dark."

"I can find my way around this ranch even at night," Torrie said with more confidence than she felt.

"Maybe. But if the trail is this hard to find in the

303

day, how hard would it be to find our way out at night?" He crossed his arms over his chest and gave her an unwavering stare.

A sinking feeling of defeat crashed through Torrie as she met his gaze. She clenched her fists at her sides, hating to give up, but she felt she had no choice. As she started to admit he was right, Mac glanced over the top of her head as if something had caught his eye.

"Well—would you look at that?" he said, his voice was incredulous.

Torrie swung around. She gasped with relief—and surprise. Ginger was nibbling on a large clump of range grass she had pulled free from the grip of the thick brush. The absence of the grass left a small opening in the bushes, and beyond this, was a barely visible trail. She clapped her hands together like a child. "Nothing can stop us now." Torrie rushed to the opening and peered through the branches and gnarled bushes. An eerie sensation passed through her. For a moment, she thought of telling Mac she had changed her mind.

Instead, she took a deep breath and said, "I'll lead the way." She swallowed hard and looked back at the trail. She wondered if she sounded braver than she felt at this moment.

Chapter Twenty-Nine

The knock on Elsa's door made her jump. In her lap was an open book. She had been staring at it for a long time without reading one word. When the knock sounded again, she rose from the chair and let the book drop on the floor, unnoticed. When she opened the door she looked up at the handsome face of Lance Farlo. For a second, she did nothing else. He tipped the brim of his hat.

"Howdy, Mrs. Connor. I'm lookin' for Torrie. The lady downstairs said she was gone," he said. His tone hinted of impatience. Glancing over Elsa's head he looked around the room. He noticed the baby asleep in his cradle.

"She hoped she'd be back before you returned." Elsa backed up for him to enter. He remained in the hallway.

"Where is she?"

Elsa took another step backwards. Her eyes never wavered from his face. She felt foolish admitting it to herself, but she almost felt in awe of this man.

Panic shot through Lance as he waited for Elsa to answer him. Her reluctance to disclose Torrie's whereabouts made him fear the worst. The words she spoke next confirmed his fears.''

"She rode out to the Grand Mesa." Elsa drew in a deep breath, then exhaled it loudly. "I tried to talk her out of it, but she insisted she needed to retrieve some things from her room."

Lance tried to fight down the acute sense of doom that rose in him. "Nothing could have been that important," he said, his voice was low, controlled.

"She was worried about money. I told her we'd make do, but—"

"Damnit!" Lance clenched his hands at the sides of his hips. He stepped into the room. His thoughts kept flashing back in time. He remembered what it felt like to be cast out without a dime. "That old bas—I mean—that old man would never give her any money."

"She didn't want anything from him. In her bedroom she has some valuables that she plans to sell. She said she knew of a way to get up to the house without being seen—a back trail or something." Elsa knew Torrie's plan was foolish, but telling Lance about it made it seem even worse.

Lance took a minute to absorb what Elsa had just said. He couldn't decide if he was more scared for Torrie's safety or if he was more angry at himself. If he had never told her about the trail leading to the back of the mesa maybe she wouldn't have gone. He placed his hands on his hips in a brisk gesture and gave an aggravated huff. His pale gaze settled on Elsa's worried face.

"How long ago did she leave?" he asked. There was no patience left in his tone. A short time ago he'd got back to town with Sheriff Kearny. They discovered nothing up on the mountain that would give any clues to Canon's murder. He felt the entire time had been wasted. Then, when they rode back into town and heard about the fire this morning—the killing of Shawn McLeary—and all the rest of the trouble, Lance was furious with the sheriff. He was disgusted with himself. So far, he had done nothing to help the men who employed him. The added fear for Torrie's safety was the last thing he needed.

"A couple of hours, but she's not alone." The flash of resentment that shot through the gunfighter's eyes made Elsa cringe. She quickly added, "She's with Mac Williams."

"He's one of Carrington's men." Lance's growing wrath was more apparent with each passing second.

Elsa drew in a raspy breath as she eyed the way Lance's hands were flexing at the sides of his fancy holsters. "Not anymore. He quit because of the trouble this morning."

Lance's gaze narrowed as he recalled the aging gunman. Before, he'd only looked at him as one of his father's henchmen. He had nothing more on which to base his opinion of the man, and he could not help but wonder why the old gunslinger had taken Torrie out to the Grand Mesa when there was a full-fledged war erupting in the area.

"I have to go," he said abruptly.

"Are you going after her?" Elsa's blue eyes were wide with worry. His obvious panic made her feel even more afraid.

Lance noticed the stricken expression Elsa Connor wore. He was struck by a pang of guilt. This woman had done her share of suffering lately, and he was not showing her any compassion. His gaze settled on her thin face. He allowed his anger and fear to fade to the back of his mind for a moment.

"I'll bring her back safe and sound," he said. He wished he felt as confident as he tried to appear.

"Then what?" Elsa asked. Her voice was low, but her meaning was clear.

Lance felt as if his throat had just closed up. He continued to stare at Elsa until her questioning gaze seemed to burn a hole through him. His broad shoulders gave a shrug, they hunched as if they carried the weight of the world on them. He cleared his throat. "Then . . . I guess she'll go to Denver with you."

He saw a look of crushing disappointment filter through Elsa's face, and he felt his own sense of plummeting despair. Twirling around, he stalked out of the room without any further comment. He couldn't have said anything else if he wanted to, because the lump in his throat was threatening to choke him.

The loud voices of the posse the sheriff was organizing reached Lance's ears. He pushed Elsa Connor's disturbing question from his mind as he made his way down the dusty street. He kept

308

wondering if he could have prevented this morning's tragic events if he had been here or if there was something he should have done to keep the range war from reaching this violent end. But—he reminded himself—it wasn't over yet.

Wayne Gere passed through his mind. Why wasn't he with his neighbors when the shoot-out at the Grand Mesa occurred? Lance scanned the men who were gathered in front of the sheriff's office. Where was Gere now?

Lance began to push through the crowd of men. When they noticed him—noticed the dangerous glint in his eyes—the group parted to make way for him to pass. He approached the sheriff, aware of how quiet it had suddenly become. "I'm headed out to the Grand Mesa," he said.

Sheriff Kearny motioned toward the men he had just deputized. "We're comin' with you."

Lance glanced around at the men. Most of them were shopkeepers and farmers. They looked awkward with their weaponry, and even more uncomfortable wearing the shiny gold badges. Lance gave a discouraged grunt. He directed his sole attention on the sheriff. "I'm going alone."

Sheriff Kearny met Lance's gaze with his own defiant glare. "Even a man with your reputation can't stand up against all Carrington's guns. Besides, I haven't cleared you of murder yet."

Lance gave another disgruntled huff. Impatience tore at his insides. He stepped closer to the sheriff. Their gazes were almost level. "You know what will be waitin' for you when you get there. Are you prepared to take the responsibility for these men's lives?" He noticed the sheriff's complexion grow noticeably pale. He remained unmoving, his gaze never wavered.

Sheriff Kearny made a gulping sound when he swallowed. He forced himself to look away from the piercing stare of the gunfighter. His attention became directed toward the men who were standing, mutely, waiting for his next command. He looked back at Lance. "Okay, they stay. But," he puffed up his chest as he added in an unyielding tone, "I'm goin' with you."

Lance hesitated for a second, then finally shrugged in compliance. He still wondered where the sheriff stood on this range war issue. At times, Lance speculated whether or not the lawman was being paid off by Carrington to overlook anything incriminating against the Grand Mesa. A crooked lawyman was always something that ate at his craw. Lance hoped this wouldn't turn out to be the case here.

While the sheriff gave Deputy Silt new orders, and told the rest of the men to go back to their usual business, Lance sat in his saddle and waited. His anxiety was rubbing off on the stallion. The big horse snorted and pawed at the ground as if he wanted a free rein to run. By the time the sheriff was ready to go, Lance had lost the last of his patience. He kicked Raven in the sides, and left the sheriff and his horse in a cloud of dust.

When Lance allowed Sheriff Kearny to catch up to him, he was not surprised at the lawman's haughty attitude.

"When we meet up with the guards at the Grand

Mesa, I'm doin' all the talking." Sheriff Kearny was out of breath, but he tried to inject a tone of authority when he spoke.

"We won't be seeing any guards," Lance stated. He yanked on Raven's reins and turned his horse off the road.

Sheriff Kearny stared at Lance's back for a moment before his mind snapped into action. "Where the hell do you think you're going?" He kicked his horse in the sides and quickly caught up with the stallion again.

"I'm going in the back way," Lance replied in a firm voice.

A snide chortle rang out from the sheriff. "There ain't no back way. Besides, I ain't gonna be sneakin' around on Ben Carrington's land." He rode in front of Lance's mount and tugged on his reins. The stallion collided with the other horse before Lance had a chance to halt him.

"You're gonna do it my way—or you're gonna get out of my way," Lance said from between clenched teeth. His pale brown eyes were no more than two narrow slits, his jaw squared with determination. He stared point-blank at the sheriff until he noticed the lawman begin to blink in rapid succession. The long tips of his mustache twitched slightly.

"Wo-Wouldn't it b-be better if we just rode up to the main gate and asked to see B-Ben?" the sheriff stammered. He couldn't tear his gaze away from the gunfighter's face. He was certain he'd never seen such cold determination in a man's eyes before.

311

"After what happened this morning do you really think they'd escort us up to the house?"

"They would me—I'm the law," Sheriff Kearny said in a condescending manner. The deadly glint in Lance's eyes made him grow humble almost immediately.

"The law doesn't seem to mean much in these parts." Lance loosed his reins. He felt Raven push against the other horse. "Now what's it gonna be, Kearny?"

Sheriff Kearny fidgeted in his saddle. The big stallion's weight against his smaller bay was making both the sheriff and his horse noticeably nervous. He wanted to remind Farlo who was suposed to be in charge, but he knew it would be a waste of breath. His eyes moved down to the six-shooters on Lance's hips, fleetingly. He jerked his gaze back up to the gunfighter's stony face. Their eyes met. A shooting pain gripped at the sheriff's chest. He pulled on his reins and backed his horse out of the stallion's way.

Indecision tore at the sheriff's mind. He thought of telling Farlo to go on without him. Yet, something inside told him it was his duty to continue on with the gunfighter. Ever since this whole damned mess started, he'd been trying to avoid being caught in the middle like he was now. As the sheriff of a little, one-horse town like Rifle, Kearny knew he couldn't have any effect on a powerful man like Ben Carrington when he decided to run off the families he accused of being squatters living off his land. But then Wayne Gere and the others had went and hired Lance Farlo.

312

Now all hell was breaking loose!

"What's your plan?" Sheriff Kearny asked. His voice lacked purpose, his gaze looked toward the ground. He wished he'd never taken this job two years ago.

Lance studied the other man for a few seconds. Until the past few days he usually trusted his instincts. He decided to trust them again now. Something told him Kearny was nothing more than a braggart who hid behind his badge whenever possible.

"My plan is to quit wastin' time," Lance spat. He nudged Raven forward. The sheriff kept his horse at his side. Lance led them along the same route Torrie and Mac had just taken. He had no doubt of this because he could see fresh tracks in the dirt.

Sheriff Kearny noticed them too. His nervousness seemed to increase with every step of their horses' hooves. He spent most of his time glancing around as if he expected an ambush at every bend or from behind every bush and tree. Lance ignored him.

Every time he thought of Torrie climbing up that slope—the slope he would only associate with tragedy—his fear abounded. He knew what his father was capable of doing if he discovered Torrie sneaking into the house. The idea made his heart pound frantically in his chest. The sense of doom, which had plagued him ever since he had returned to Colorado, seemed to claim every fiber of his being.

Up ahead, Lance could see the jagged ridge at

the back of the mesa. The thick brush that blanketed the valley floor at its base appeared more impassable than the last time he was here. Daily, the autumn wind stripped away more of the greenery. The spiny branches of the wild rose-bushes were a drab brown and the cottonwoods were almost the same hue. Only the dark logan green of the cedars lent the area any color.

Lance glanced up at the sky. The clouds that had been present earlier in the day were gone now. He squinted toward the sinking sun. It would be dark in a couple more hours. He looked at the mesa again. His thoughts became a tangled web of the past and the present. The pounding in his chest threatened to rip his chest apart. He had to get to Torrie. . . . He had to keep the past from being repeated.

Chapter Thirty

Torrie and Mac left their horses at the bottom of the mesa. On foot they made their way to the top without any mishap. The climb made Torrie's injured knees throb, but she was concentrating too hard on her destination to be more than vaguely aware of the pain. Before they scaled over the last ledge, Mac motioned for her to wait until he had a chance to check out the area behind the house.

He heaved himself over the rocky edge. For a time, he remained crouched on the ledge as he surveyed the back of the huge L-shaped house. The house and the courtyard in the center were completely quiet. Mac's gaze scanned over the tombstones under the cottonwood without a thought to who was buried beneath them. From here the barns and outbuildings at the front of the house were not visible.

Mac leaned over the ledge and gestured to Torrie. He took her sawed-off shotgun when she held it up to him. Then, with an outstretched arm, he clasped her hand and helped her the rest of the way up. When they were both standing on the flat surface, Mac turned toward Torrie. A troubled frown—the same one he'd been wearing all afternoon—hovered on his face. They were right out in the open. If there was anybody in the house, they only had to look out one of the back windows and they would see them.

Sensing Mac's thoughts, Torrie motioned for him to follow her. She headed straight for the courtyard. She was hoping Ben and Gage would be too occupied with their blood-thirsty war to be paying attention to the back of the house. This time of day—late afternoon—usually found them out talking to the hired hands as they began to filter back to the bunkhouse. Ben always tried to make it a practice to discuss the day's work with his men every evening. Torrie figured he would have a lot to discuss with them today.

The tiled courtyard seemed a hundred miles away, and as they ran the several hundred yards to reach the enclosure, Torrie imagined almost a hundred ways they could be caught. Her legs were shaking so violently she was surprised she could run at all. When they leaned against the wall she exhaled the pent-up breath she'd been holding with a loud gasp. Panic washed over her as she glanced around to see if anyone had heard the noise.

Mac was looking around as if he expected someone to burst out of one of the doors or through a window at any second. He held one of his six-shooters in his hand. His lean body was tensed and ready to move into action. He couldn't believe he had consented to come here.

They waited for a moment, then when there was no movement from the house, Torrie leaned close to Mac to whisper, "You wait here. I'll go to my room and get my things."

Mac's face scrunched up into a scowl. He glanced around the large courtyard. In the center was a circle of shrubbery and what had apparently been a flower bed during the summer months. Now, the leaves and stems were barren of blossoms. One cedar tree and a couple of rosebushes grew out from the dry flower garden. A long table with benches stood in the courtyard, along with several chairs scattered around the area. It was the kind of place that was perfect for parties and large gatherings, but Mac had never heard of any parties being held here. He wondered if the Carrington family had ever sat out here and eaten or lounged in the chairs. He couldn't imagine them doing anything together like a normal family.

He leaned toward Torrie. "Where's your room?" he whispered. She pointed at a pair of double doors across the courtyard.

"It's through those doors and just to the right."

Mac's frown deepened. She had to cut right through the center of the courtyard. She would be completely out in the open until she reached the doors. Then, she would be out of his sight. If she needed him, he might not be able to reach her in time.

"I'm going in with you," he said. He tried to make his low voice sound authoritative.

Torrie shook her head. "No. I can do it faster if I'm alone."

Mac figured she was right. She knew the layout of the house, and one person would make less noise than two. He sighed and gave his head a nod of consent.

Torrie also sighed, but it trembled as it escaped past her lips. She glanced up at Mac. Their gazes exchanged a silent kinship. She thought of telling him how grateful she was to have him here, but she sensed he knew. Now there wasn't time, anyway.

She took a firm grip on her shotgun. Setting her sights on the doors, she ran her tongue over her parched lips, then took a deep breath. She pushed herself away from the wall and charged forward. The doors loomed before her, yet, they seemed out of reach. She kept her eyes focused on her destination. She was afraid to look around her . . . afraid of seeing Ben or Gage lurking in one of the windows.

Torrie was running so fast she had to skid to a halt to keep from crashing into the doors. She paused to catch her breath, and to look back at Mac. He was in the same position. His gaze was moving back and forth between the windows. When he noticed she was watching him, he gave his head a nod and signaled for her to go ahead.

She turned back to the door, reached out, and placed her hand on the knob. Hesitantly, she began to turn the knob. It made a squeaking noise which was barely noticeable, but to Torrie it sound like it echoed across the entire courtyard. When she began to push the door open, the slight

318

scraping noise it made sounded like a cannon exploding. She pushed it open only halfway. Again, she waited, and listened, then turned sideways and inched into the house.

The house seemed deathly quiet. Torrie did not move for a couple minutes as she cocked her head and listened for sounds that would alert her to anyone's presence. The early evening sun shining through the windows in the foyer cast luminous yellow rays across the shiny wooden planks of the floorboards, and shadows were settling along the walls. Torrie took a step forward. She was standing in the hallway. Directly across from her was the front door. Ben's office door was less than twenty feet away.

Torrie's legs felt rubbery. She wondered if she could make herself move. She took a shaky step. It amazed her she could walk. The trembling in her legs was now consuming her entire body. She forced herself to take another step. Her gaze held the sight of her bedroom door firmly in focus. As it drew closer, her terror increased.

The knob to her door felt slippery. She realized she was sweating profusely. Her hands felt like she had just dunked them in a washbasin. Her whole body was drenched in sweat. She had to turn loose of the knob to wipe away a rivulet of perspiration that was running down from her forehead and was threatening to blind her. The shotgun in her other hand felt as if it were glued to her clammy palm. She clasped onto the knob again and twisted it to the side. She no longer wanted to take extra precautions—she just wanted to get out of the hallway and into the sanctuary of her room.

After Torrie stepped into the room and shut the door behind her, she took her first full breath since she had started across the courtyard. Her chest hurt, the breath seemed to hang up in her lungs for an instant. When she looked around the room her panic began to fade slightly. For eleven years this room had been her haven. Her mother used to come to this room, and they would sit and talk for hours about clothes and hair and all those types of frivolous things. There was nothing important for them to talk about because they were never included in anything concerning the ranch. Thinking about those times always confused Torrie. She still could not understand why her mother had seemed so content to be Ben Carrington's wife.

Torrie walked over to the bureau where her jewelry box sat. She paused and glanced around the room again. All her memories of the room would be good if it wasn't for the one night when Canon had come in here. Her gaze narrowed as she looked at the big brass bed. A sick feeling erupted in her stomach. She thought of Canon's stiff body tied on the back of the travois, and a sense of guilt joined her disgust. As hard as she tried, she still could not feel any remorse over Canon's murder.

She realized she was wasting precious time with memories best forgotten. She leaned her shotgun against the bureau and returned her attention to the jewelry box. The box was dark green velvet. Her mother had given it to her as a gift for her sixteenth birthday. She'd said it matched Torrie's eyes, and when Torrie opened it up, she had found it contained an exquisite gold and diamond brooch. She would not sell the brooch unless it became absolutely necessary. The jewelry box also contained a strand of genuine pearls and a ruby necklace. Torrie hoped these two pieces alone would be enough to provide her with the funds she needed to start her new life.

Her sweaty fingers left little dark indentations on the soft green velvet when Torrie picked up the jewelry box. She noticed her hands shook. Her panic once again descended on her like a giant cloak. Until now, it hadn't occurred to her that she might have done all this for nothing. She yanked open the lid. A heavy, relieved sigh slipped from her mouth. All the pieces were neatly arranged in the white satin interior of the box. She almost felt like laughing at herself for thinking that Ben or Gage would have thought to come in here and take her jewelry. It probably never occurred to either of them she would even have anything of value.

Torrie hugged the box against her bosom for a second, then she grabbed the shotgun again and turned away from the bureau. Fleetingly, she thought of getting a satchel from her armoire and packing a few of her clothes. But, that would take up more time.

Once again she cautiously turned the doorknob. She listened for sounds, but she heard nothing in the hallway. Still, her panic returned after she stepped into the hall again.

A sound—like a footstep—came from Ben's office. Torrie froze in her tracks. Wide-eyed she stared at the closed door. A dozen horrors filled her head. She imagined Ben bursting through the door, grabbing the shotgun from her hand, and blowing her head off. The smirking, red splotched face of her brother also taunted her morbid thoughts. She knew he would like nothing better than to rid himself of her once and for all.

As these thoughts raged through her mind, she waited—and stared—at the door to Ben's office. Her gaze fixed itself on the doorknob. She expected to see it turn with a menacing twist. Instead, nothing happened; more time was wasting.

She forced herself to start moving back down the hallway toward the double doors that led to the courtyard. Her feet inched backwards, though, because she was too terrified to turn away from the office door. She kept telling herself she'd only imagined the noise on the other side of the door. Her head felt light—like she was going to faint from her fear. She tried to calm the thudding in her chest by taking a deep breath when she reached the double doors.

With both the gun and jewelry box clutched tightly in one hand, she reached behind her with her other hand and turned the knob on one of the doors. It opened with no resistance. Torrie felt a wave of nausea wash over her. She thought she had closed the door tight when she entered. But maybe she hadn't, and her head was spinning too hard to sort out anything rational.

Torrie backed through the door. Her hand was still grasping the doorknob. She slid the door shut again. Her exorbitant heartbeat slowed. She drew in a breath which did not hang up in her dry throat. She shut the door again. Her shotgun dangled limply from her hand as she clasped her jewelry box with her other hand. She had done it!

An elated smile hovered on Torrie's lips as she swung around to face Mac. A cold sweat broke out on her body and across her brow. Her grip tightened on the butt of her gun, but she knew it was useless to try to raise the gun. Gage had one of Mac's Colt pistols leveled at her head.

Chapter Thirty-One

"I'll give you credit, little sister, I never thought you had the guts to attempt somethin' like this." Gage's green gaze was narrowed in two thin lines. His face was botched with dark purplish spots. He pointed one of Mac's six-shooters at Torrie. His other hand held Mac's second gun, and it was aimed at the old gunslinger. The Colts Gage wore at his own hips were still holstered.

Mac leaned against the wall in almost the same spot he had been when Torrie had entered the house. His arms were raised in a lame gesture at the sides of his head. The expression he wore was one of total animosity, and it was directed solely at Gage.

Instinctively, Torrie's hand tightened around the shotgun. Before she could make a move though, Gage began to shake his head in a negative manner. "That wouldn't be smart." He glanced down at her gun. "Drop it right where you stand, and then get over here."

Torrie hesitated. She tried to collect her run-away thoughts. He was her flesh and blood. Maybe she could reason with him. Her fingers loosed their hold on the shotgun. She bent down and laid the gun on the tiled floor.

"Gage," she said. She thought her voice sounded like that of a scared little girl. She cleared her throat and straightened her stance. "Gage," she repeated, her voice had gained strength. "I don't want any trouble between us." Her gaze riveted toward the graves—she wondered if their mother knew what was happening.

A cruel laugh rang out from Gage. His gaze followed Torrie's toward the grave, briefly, then his attention snapped back to the business at hand. He raised the gun higher until it was leveled on her face. "If you didn't want trouble why did you come back here?"

Torrie tried to calm the rapid pulsating in her temples, and the thrashing of her heartbeat. "I-I needed some of my things," she said. As she held out the velvet jewelry box she added, "This is all I came for."

He stared at the box. Torrie felt her fear giving way to anger. She glanced at Mac. His fury was apparent as he continued to glare at Gage. Rage began to dominate Torrie as she clutched the jewelry box in a protective manner. She took a step forward. Gage's body tensed, his reddish complexion grew darker.

"Good grief, Gage, I am your sister," Torrie said. Her teeth clenched as she spoke. A fiery glow consumed her cheeks. "I'm not gonna interfere with your scheme to inherit the Grand Mesa."

Her words seemed to throw Gage off guard momentarily. "W—What are you talking about?" He cast an anxious glance toward the double doors. "I don't have any scheme," he said, his sharp tone belying his words. "I deserve to take over for Ben someday." He took a step forward. His thin lips curled over his teeth in a taut manner as he repeated, "I deserve it!"

A cold chill raced through Torrie as she watched her brother. He sounded too anxious to convince her—and himself—he was worthy of being here. There had been so much happening lately she hadn't thought about Gage's newly-acquired position now that Canon was gone. Another icy shard shot through her body. She sensed nothing she said would sway Gage to let them go, but the next thought that passed through her mind made her grow numb.

"My God," she gasped. Before she thought about her next words, she added, "Canon! It was you wasn't it?" She noticed the color drain from Gage's face. He took another step forward. She could almost see the rage that poisoned his thoughts. At this instant he was a complete stranger to her.

Gage stopped his impulsive footsteps. He glanced back at Mac. With one of the guns he held he motioned for Mac to move toward Torrie.

Torrie held her breath as she watched Mac inch along the wall. Movement at the edge of the cliff caught her attention. Her eyes widened, the thudding in her chest calmed slightly. She forced herself to look at Gage. It was one of the most difficult tasks she had ever tackled. Her lips clamped together, she felt an avalanche of emotions tumble through her being. Outwardly, though, she willed herself to act as if Gage was her only focus.

Gage waited until Mac moved forward. His back was to the cliff, and his full attention was on his sister once again. A nonchalant shrug shook Gage's shoulders. His lips curled in a cruel smirk when he set his gaze on Torrie. "Canon couldn't run this ranch. He was too hotheaded to succeed with a big operation like this."

Even though she was hearing Gage's confession, Torrie's mind still resisted the realization that her brother was a cold-blooded killer. Her mouth gaped open as she tried to seek the right words . . . they had to be right to hold Gage's attention for a few minutes longer.

"So you finished what your brother started," Mac said. He spoke in a rushed tone. He forced his gaze to remain on Gage's face. Like Torrie, his only goal was to keep Gage distracted until Lance Farlo and Sheriff Kearny were close enough to hear what he was saying, and get the drop on him before he was aware of their presence.

Gage shrugged again. He glanced at Mac, then back to Torrie. It didn't matter if he told them; he had to kill them, anyway. "I was ridin' back from town that night when I met Canon. He wouldn't tell me who he'd fought with, but he said he was headed into town to lick his wounds." Gage gave a crude snicker. "He didn't want the old man to see him lookin' like a whipped pup."

"So you bashed his head in and took him up to Horse Mountain," Mac stated. His voice held a note of disgust.

Gage gave an indignant huff. "No. I didn't take him up on the mountain that night. I'd never have found the cave in the dark. Canon had only taken me up there once—years ago when me and Torrie first came here to the ranch." Gage looked at Torrie, his evil grin widened. "He told me only two people knew about that cave; him and his brother. But, we all thought his brother was dead, remember?" A humorless chuckle escaped from his mouth. "I thought I was somebody real special because Canon had showed me the cave. That's when I knew I was meant to be here—to be a Carrington."

"But you did kill Canon that night?" Mac asked. He kept his eyes set on the other man's smirking countenance.

"Yeah. I hid his body down by the river and ran his horse off. I figured everybody would think he'd been murdered by the same men who killed Leo MacFarlene and Will Connor."

Mac still held his arms in the air. He lowered them slightly as he shrugged. A confused expression covered his weathered face. "That don't make no sense. Why didn't you just leave him at the river?"

"I never found out who Canon had fought with that night. I suspect he had an encounter with Lance Farlo, but I don't know for sure." Gage glanced at Torrie. She showed no reaction on her tense face. He recalled how strange she acted on the morning he went to the Connor house to ask her about Canon.

Torrie met his gaze. She opened her mouth to ask him why he had decided to take Canon to the cave. Her mouth felt gummy, she wasn't sure if she could speak. Mac didn't give her a chance, anyway.

"When did you decide to take him up on the mountain then?" Mac's voice was growing impatient. It was getting more difficult to keep from looking over the top of Gage's head. Lance and the sheriff were standing only a hundred feet or so behind Gage. They were rooted to the spot as they listened to his confession.

Gage fidgeted with the guns he held in his hands. They were getting heavy. He was tired of talking. He had to get this over with before Ben came back. The old man had gone down to talk to the men who were guarding the road that led to the front of the house. Gage realized now they would have to start guarding the back of the mesa too. If he hadn't glanced out the kitchen window and noticed Mac Williams lurking in the courtyard, Torrie would have gotten away with breaking into the house.

Mac sensed the change in Gage's attitude. He raised his arms higher in the air and tried to inject a tone of desperation in his voice. "I know you're gonna kill us. At least explain to us why you took Canon's body up on the mountain."

Gage's hooded eyelids blinked in rapid sucession. His green gaze seemed to lack any luster amongst the ruddy hue that was once again coloring his face. He drew in an aggravated breath. "When I found out who Lance Farlo was, I panicked. I figured he would ruin everything. But, luckily, none of those idiots who work for us," he cast a debasing look at Mac as he continued to speak, "had found Canon's body at the river. I got to worrying more and more about Ben makin' up with his youngest son. Then where would I be?" He stepped forward, his anxiety to finish with this business was obvious in the way he was tensing up.

"I wanted to make sure this wouldn't happen," Gage said. "I know how Ben thinks. For eleven years I've studied him, prepared myself to take his place. He's almost as impulsive as Canon was, and when things drag out, Ben gets crazy. I knew if Canon's body wasn't found for a long time, and the suspicion against Lance continued to build up, Ben's hatred would grow. It would fester until it was irreversible." He paused, and leveled the guns at Torrie and Mac's heads.

"So," Mac said quickly, "you got Canon's body from the river and took it up to the cave a few days later."

Gage nodded. "It worked out just perfect too." A chilling smirk pulled at his thin lips as he met Torrie's wide, terrified gaze. "You and Farlo knew exactly where to look. Ben's been doin' a lot of thinking about that. When he finds out I shot you while you were breaking into the house, he's gonna be real pleased with me. That leaves just Farlo. He'll probably hang for Canon's murder if Ben doesn't get to him first."

331

"I don't think so." Lance's low, dangerous-sounding voice broke into Gage's reverie.

Torrie saw the stricken look wash through Gage's face before he swung away from her. His expression tore at her heart. For one fleeting moment, she had glimpsed regret in his eyes. She knew he realized he had made a terrible mistake, but he couldn't rectify his past actions now. Her body grew numb, her mind spun with tormented thoughts of the brother she had never really known.

Lance's unwavering gaze met Gage's startled eyes. The guns Gage held in his hands were now aimed at him. Lance had not drawn his guns, yet. Although he had never trusted Gage, he was still trying to absorb the outlandish story he had just heard.

"Don't make me draw on you," Lance said. He still did not make a move. His intense stare never moved from Gage's face. Lance knew his opponent's eyes would tell him when to draw his own gun. In Gage's eyes he saw a spark of golden flames illuminate his green pupils. Lance's right hand fell to his gun. Before his mind had a chance to think through his actions his gun cleared leather and fired. He felt one of Gage's bullets whiz by his head—another bullet grazed his upper arm as it flew past. The sulfur-like smell of gunsmoke filled the air as Lance holstered his Colt.

Torrie stepped forward when she saw Gage start to topple over to the ground. Her mouth opened, but no sounds escaped. Gage fell face down. The guns he had just fired spilled out across the tiled floor. The scraping sound they made was the only interruption of the silence that followed the gunfire. For a moment Torrie stared down at her brother. She could see the side of his face. His carrot-colored hair was tousled over his forehead. His eyes were open, and so was his mouth. A single stream of blood trickled from the corner of his mouth where it was pressed against the tan tiles.

Tearing her gaze away from her brother's body, Torrie looked over at Lance. He was also staring down at Gage. When his head rose up, their gazes met. The look in his eyes made Torrie feel like a soothing ointment had just been rubbed on her aching heart. Somehow, she knew he understood the conflicting emotions that were raging in her. She also knew he had come here for her.

Lovingly, she let her gaze rest on him for a moment. She wished it was just the two of them. She wanted to run into his arms, and let him take her away from here forever. But then, reality snapped her fanciful thoughts back.

"I ain't never seen nobody draw that fast," Sheriff Kearny said in a breathless voice. He slowly approached Gage's body.

Lance tore his gaze away from Torrie when the sheriff's voice interrupted their private interlude. He glanced down again. But he quickly looked up when he saw Mac Williams move to Torrie's side. His body tensed. His hand flexed at his side. He saw Torrie glance up at the aging gunman, and he noticed the tender way she looked at him. Lance moved his hand away from his gun. He felt a stinging sensation in his upper arm. When he glanced down, he saw a rip across the top of his shirtsleeve and a tiny ring of blood around the torn material.

Returning her attention to Lance, Torrie saw him look down at his arm. She noticed he was wearing the white shirt he had let her wear the night they were at the line shack. She wondered why something so trivial would enter her mind now. Then, she saw the tear in his sleeve—and the blood.

A frightened gasp flew from her mouth. She rushed forward. "You're shot!" In panic, she reached for his arm. His hand entrapped hers before she had a chance to touch him. Her gaze sought his. Her panic evaporated.

"It's only a scratch," he said in a low tone of voice. "Are you all right?" She nodded her head. Lance felt the tight sensation in his chest lighten up.

"He's dead for sure," Sheriff Kearny said as he knelt over Gage's body. He had rolled him over and was staring at Gage's unseeing green eyes.

"And you heard a full confession," Mac reminded the sheriff.

Sheriff Kearny gave his head a firm nod. He looked toward Lance and Torrie. They were not paying any attention. No one noticed the man who had just shoved open the double doors at the end of the courtyard until they heard the doors bang against the outside walls of the house.

Lance pushed Torrie aside. Sheriff Kearny and Mac stepped away from Gage's body. There was nothing between Lance and his father except the cold sense of burning hatred that was emitted from

334

the old man's narrowed gaze.

"What the hell happened here?" Ben demanded. He spoke to Lance. He didn't glance at anyone else.

"Maybe you should let the sheriff tell you," Lance replied. He noticed his father's hand was curved over the top of the handle of the gun he wore on his hip. A sick feeling inched through him. If Ben drew, he knew he would draw, too. But, he prayed Ben wouldn't.

Sheriff Kearny cleared his throat with a loud grating noise. The sound seemed to vibrate across the courtyard. He took a couple of shuffling steps toward Ben. "Gage admitted to killin' Canon. Now, why don't we all sit down and talk in a rational way?"

Ben mulled over the sheriff's words for only an instant. The problems with Lance went back much further than just the last few days. "I'm through talking," Ben spat. He walked around Gage's body without looking down. He stopped several feet in front of Lance. "You've caused nothin' but trouble. That's the way it's always been with you."

Lance eyed his father closely. The past few days had taken a noticeable toll on the old man. His white hair and mustache stood out starkly from his flushed complexion, and his eyes were rimmed with puffy patches of wrinkled skin. To Lance, he seemed to have aged another ten years since he'd seen him a few days ago. He also noticed a strange glint in the old man's eyes. He narrowed his own gaze and repeated the same warning he had just issued to Gage.

"Don't make me draw on you." His voice contained a note of regret when he added, "You know you'd never stand a chance."

Ben did not have to be told this. He didn't want to die either. But he didn't know how to back down. His indecision made him feel weak . . . weakness made him scared. He slowly eased his hand away from his gun. He couldn't just turn and walk away though. His pride would not allow it. Impulsively, he lunged forward. His outstretched hands grabbed for Lance's neck.

Lance stumbled backwards. The shock of the old man's attack left him too stunned to react for a second. When his mind began to function again, he tried to pry Ben's hands from his neck. Ben's hands held him in a death-like grip. Lance gasped for breath. His instincts told him to punch his attacker in the gut or to kick him in the crotch. But as Lance struggled to free himself, he realized he didn't want to fight his father any more than he wanted to shoot him. He had wanted revenge—or at least an explanation—for the events of the past. Killing his father was not what he sought.

The two men backed out of the courtyard. Lance grabbed his father in a bear hug and kicked the old man's feet out from under him. They both toppled to the ground and began to roll across the hard ground. The edge of the cliff loomed closer as they continued to struggle.

Torrie screamed. Sheriff Kearny started to move toward the men, but Mac grabbed his arm.

"From what I've heard this feud has been

brewing for a long time. They've gotta settle it themselves." Mac cast a look of warning toward Torrie.

She closed her gaping mouth and returned her frightened gaze to the sight of Lance and Ben rolling across the plateau. Only a few feet away from them was almost the exact same spot where Lance had told her his mother had been pushed. An eerie sensation crept through Torrie as she watched the old man and his son cling to one another on the ground. She could see Lance's eyes bulging from the pressure around his neck. Another scream welled up in her throat. She forced it back down. Why didn't he fight back? It looked as though he was doing nothing more than trying to get away.

They inched closer to the edge as Lance continued to pry at his father's crushing hold. Torrie could not stop the scream when it re-surfaced. Mac and Sheriff Kearny rushed forward when they realized the two men were going to tumble down the slope. They were a blur to Torrie's eyes. The last thing she remembered was seeing Lance and Ben struggling on the rocky ledge.

Chapter Thirty-Two

When Ben felt himself hovering on the edge of the cliff, instinct for his own survival made him turn loose of Lance's neck. Instinctively, he groped for something to stop him from falling. His hands clawed at the air.

Lance felt his father's grip slip from his neck. He also felt the edge of the rocky ledge cutting into his back. With every ounce of strength he could muster he pushed himself away from the cliff. His father continued to roll. Instinct made Lance grab for his father as the old man went over the edge. He clasped onto Ben's hand, but it was a weak hold. He could feel Ben's sweating fingers slowly sinking away from his own wet grip. He peered over and saw Ben groping at the loose dirt on the side of the slope. He was searching desperately for a foothold or something to grab ahold of with his other hand.

He ceased to struggle when he felt himself slipping from Lance's grip. His face tilted back, his old eyes were wide, and pleading. His son's icy stare met his frantic gaze. They stared at one another for only an instant. To Ben it seemed like an eternity. His extended arm felt as though it was being torn from its socket. But, it didn't matter. He knew he was going to fall to his death, anyway. He tried to tear his gaze away from Lance's face. He did not want the last thing he saw to be Lance's look of victory. But, he could not make himself look away. Nor could he understand why Lance was trying to grip onto his sweaty hand so tightly.

Lance's thoughts were alternating between the memory of his mother's death, and his strange feeling of compassion for his father. If he just let his hand slip away. . . . Lance forced this thought from his mind. He tightened his hold. Beside him, Mac Williams was kneeling as he tried to reach down to Ben and help pull him up. Lance attempted to scoot over so Mac's outstretched hand could clasp the old man's arm. He could only move a couple of inches—it wasn't enough. Ben's hand was growing flaccid.

"I'm gonna throw a rope down, Ben," Sheriff Kearny shouted. "Hold on a little longer."

Ben could not answer. He was certain his life was ebbing away. He almost wished Lance would just turn loose of him instead of staring down at him with such an accusing look.

As Lance became aware of the rope Sheriff Kearny was lowering down to his father, his thoughts became more clouded. Ben was hardly holding on. Lance knew it was solely his determination that kept his father from falling. If the old man fell it wouldn't be his fault. He imagined his father crashing down over the rocks—just like his mother had done all those years ago.

An eye for an eye. Isn't that what Torrie had said?

Lance saw his father reach for the rope the sheriff was dangling at his side with his free hand. His arm ached and his fingers were numb from the strong hold, but the worst pain was in Lance's heart. He watched as Ben wound the rope around his arm several times and clasped it tightly in his other hand. He felt Ben's fingers release the last of their hold so he could grab the rope with both hands. Lance clung to the ends of his father's fingers for a moment longer. Their gazes met for a last time. A heavy sigh shook Lance, he turned loose and inched back from the edge of the cliff.

For a moment he remained on his stomach. He felt drained of all his strength, and void of any purpose in life. Once again, he wondered why he had ever decided to come back here, to dredge up all this pain from the past. Then, he felt a hand touch his back—gently. With no more than this simple gesture, Lance felt reborn. He rolled over and stared up at Torrie. Her emerald gaze cradled teardrops that had not fallen. The expression on her beautiful face bespoke more than words.

Mac and Sheriff Kearny finished hauling Ben up the cliff. He collapsed in a heap on the ground beside Lance. His old body felt as if it had been torn apart at every joint. He took several deep breaths, then looked at his son. The question that hovered on his lips was simple. "Why didn't you let me f—"

Lance cut him off. "Why did you push my

mother?" His pale brown gaze flashed with bolts of gold and green as he pushed himself up to a sitting position. He was facing his father, but he was aware of Torrie kneeling at his side. Her hand rested on his shoulder.

Ben stared at him. He wanted to tell him to forget the past—not forgive him—just forget about it. But Ben knew Lance would never let it drop. He had come back after all this time just to have this one question answered. He exhaled sharply, and glanced down the slope where his life had just dangled. His thoughts wandered back to the day when his first wife had fallen to her death from this same spot.

"I didn't push her," he said in a tired voice. Those were the same words he had said eighteen years ago. He saw the same look of disbelief on his son's face. Now, he added the part he had omitted back then. "We had been fighting . . . again."

"Why?" Lance asked.

Ben huffed as if the memory still angered him. "Your mother wanted to help me run the ranch. She said she was sick and tired of doing nothing but putterin' around the kitchen and cleanin' house. She said she could take care of all the book work for me, and go to market to help me buy stock. Can you believe she even said she wanted to start helpin' with the branding and go on the cattle drives. She wanted to interfere with everything I did."

"That's why you killed her?" Lance asked in an incredulous tone. His pallor was almost the same shade as his white shirt.

"No," Ben answered, then gave an indignant

grunt. "But I did refuse to give in to her demands. She had her own work—woman's work. This is my ranch, and my life! No woman is gonna run either of those things."

Lance shook his head in disgust. Unconsciously, he reached up and clasped Torrie's hand on his shoulder.

Ben noticed the tender gesture. Surprise filtered into his expression. He looked up at Torrie when he spoke again. "Your mother knew a woman's place. She never tried to interfere with my work. Too bad you didn't learn from her."

Lance felt Torrie tense. He clasped her hand tighter. His gaze drilled into Ben again. "You still have more to tell."

Ben wiped his brow. He was still sweating from his recent brush with death. He looked back toward Lance. "Yeah—well—there's not much to add. We were standing out here that day—fighting about her stupid notion to . . ." he paused when he saw the look of unbridled fury enter his son's pale gaze. "Well—we were shouting at one another. She was standing too close," he motioned toward the cliff. His expression lost some of its hardness for a moment, but it returned when he started to speak again. "While she was carrying on like a crazy woman I guess she didn't realize how close she was. She swung around to yell at me again. Her long skirts became tangled around her ankles. I saw her teetering there on the edge, trying to regain her balance . . ." Ben swallowed hard and glanced down at the ground.

"You didn't push her. But you stood there and let her fall without even trying to help her," Lance said in a low, raspy voice. Ben didn't answer. He just shrugged his shoulders, and continued to stare down at the ground. Lance felt sick to his stomach. He clung to Torrie's hand with a desperate grip.

"This has been one hellva day," Sheriff Kearny said in an exasperated voice. There were confessions coming from every direction, and he wasn't quite sure what he should do about any of them.

"I wanna get outta here," Lance said. He did not look at Ben again. He had what he had come for, and he never wanted to look upon his father's wrinkled, old face again. With Torrie's help, Lance rose to his feet. He had used every fiber in his body to keep his father from falling. He hurt all over, but his physical pain was only minor compared to his mental anguish.

Lance draped his arm over Torrie's shoulder. He didn't mind leaning on her right now. Lying in the dirt was his Stetson, not far from the hat was the velvet box Torrie had been carrying. He led Torrie over to where they lay. When he bent down to retrieve his hat, he noticed Torrie grabbed the box and clutched it against her breast.

He glanced at Sheriff Kearny and Mac Williams. "We'd better get down to the horses before it gets dark. It'd be impossible to find that trail in the dark."

Both men nodded in agreement. They followed Lance and Torrie to the edge of the cliff. All of them stared down the steep slope.

"Going down is tougher than climbing up," Lance said. He studied the slope for a minute. "We can climb down over there." He motioned toward

344

an area that looked the least treacherous.

"What about Gage and—and me?" Ben growled. He pushed himself up from the ground. His movements were slow, agonizing. Only Sheriff Kearny acknowledged him.

"I want to see you in my office first thing in the morning." The sheriff pointed an accusing finger at the old man. "We've got a lot to discuss; McLeary's murder, and Jim Larson, and the fires . . ." The sheriff's voice faded. More and more, he felt overwhelmed by all this trouble, and he had to deal with his own guilt over the way he had handled things so far.

Ben did not answer, nor did he make a move while he watched them disappear over the ledge. He turned to stare at Gage's body in the middle of the courtyard. The pains in his joints and muscles were growing stronger. His head throbbed. He felt old—too old to face all this alone.

Torrie and Lance held onto one another's hands as they began to slide down the slope. Most of the way they had to scoot down on their seats to keep from tumbling down headfirst. Climbing over the jutting rocks was more tricky, but they took their time in spite of the fading daylight. No one spoke. All their attention and energy was spent trying to control their descent down the slope. When they reached the bottom, Mac glanced up toward the top.

"Do you suppose he'll send a lynch party after us?" he asked.

Sheriff Kearny's eyes followed Mac's gaze. He shook his head from side to side. "He's got himself in enough trouble already."

"That never stopped him before," Lance spat in a sarcastic voice. He whistled for Raven. The horse didn't come. He whistled again.

Torrie grabbed Lance's arm and led him toward the clump of cedars where Ginger was tied. She heard Lance give an aggravated grunt when he spotted the two horses standing with their noses pressed against one another. From somewhere in her sore and tired being Torrie found the energy to smile.

"It's startin' to get dark," Lance said. A frown tugged at his mouth. He wasted no time in pulling Raven away from the mare. He refrained from voicing the insults that crowded his thoughts.

They led their horses through the dense growth as quickly as possible. Overhead, the sky was a pale bluish-gray. The western horizon was streaked with different shades of orange where the sun had just dropped down behind the distant hilltops. The entire countryside had assumed a faded hue of gray by the time they were out of the thick brush. It would be dark long before they were off the Grand Mesa.

"I'm not going back to town," Lance announced as he swung into his saddle. He looked at Sheriff Kearny. His expression was set in determination.

Sheriff Kearny started to protest, but he quickly closed his mouth. He gave an indifferent shrug.

"I want to go with you," Torrie said. When she noticed the look of uncertainty that crossed Lance's face, she added, "I have something important to talk to you about."

"Is it something the law should know about?"

Sheriff Kearny asked. His thick blond mustache twitched slightly on one side.

Torrie hesitated. She glanced at Mac, then toward Lance. "No, it's personal."

Sheriff Kearny eyed her with a doubting scowl on his face. He looked back and forth between the two gunfighters. There was more going on, but he didn't care. He wanted to go back to town—he wanted this whole damned mess out of his mind until tomorrow. Then he could figure out what he should do next. Turning to Mac he asked, "You going with them too?"

Mac glanced at Torrie. He saw her give her head a quick nod. He turned toward the sheriff. "Yep."

An irritated grunt came from the sheriff. He set his attention on Lance again. "I don't want no more killing."

Lance's eyes narrowed as he stared at the sheriff. He didn't reply.

Without another word Sheriff Kearny kicked his horse in the sides and sent the animal into a gallop across the flatlands. He had enough to worry about just getting off this ranch without being shot. The rest of them could worry about their own hides.

The lawman's rapid departure was observed with little interest by the three people he left behind.

Lance was noticing the way Torrie's long hair hung in wild abandon around her shoulders. The black riding skirt she wore was coated in dust—her white blouse in tatters. Smudges of dirt decorated her silken cheeks. He thought she was beautiful. He wished Mac Williams had went with the sheriff.

"What'd you need to talk to me about?"

Torrie drew in a quavering breath. She couldn't miss the ravenous glint in Lance's hypnotizing eyes. "Wayne Gere," she said, her voice was hoarse.

Lance's head snapped up in an attentive manner. His lascivious thoughts evaporated at once. "What about him?"

"I think he was responsible for the fire at Shawn McLeary's this morning."

"I reckon that's a possibility. I reckon he might be responsible for some of the other trouble, too."

A sense of surprise filled Torrie. She had expected Lance to question her accusations about Wayne Gere. Instead, he acted as if he harbored the same suspicions.

Lance glanced at Mac Williams. "Where do you stand on all this?"

Mac returned the other man's piercing stare without hesitation. "I think Miss Torrie could be right." The two men stared at one another for a second longer.

"I reckon we're wastin' time then. We'd better head to the Diamond G." Lance turned to Torrie again. His expression softened. "I'm sorry about Gage."

A wan smile touched Torrie's mouth. Tears sprang into her eyes. "You did what you had to do." Their gazes locked. Time seemed to stand still. Torrie wished time would stop all together. Then . . . maybe she could be with Lance forever.

Chapter Thirty-Three

The road leading to Wayne Gere's ranch was guarded almost as heavily as the Grand Mesa. They were extra cautious tonight. The shoot-out at the gates of the Carrington ranch this morning was predominant in everyone's minds. The guards allowed the three riders to pass, but they all eyed Mac suspiciously. Most of them knew he worked for the Grand Mesa. But they were growing accustomed to seeing Lance Farlo and Torrie Carrington together. Why the older gunman rode with them tonight was a mystery.

They rode directly to the house. There were no lights on in any of the windows. The first thing Lance noticed though, was the absence of guards around the house. Pete Wheeler was a common sight on the porch or somewhere close by. Gere must've sent all his men out to keep watch over the herds and along the boundaries of the Diamond G. Lance wondered if Wayne felt no more fear for himself now that all the hostility had been shifted to the Grand Mesa.

"He must be in bed already," Torrie said as they reined their horses at the hitching post.

"Or out somewhere," Lance added. His voice was edged with suspicion. He scanned the area with an uneasy glance. If it turned out that Gere was the one who set the fires, he could also be the one who murdered the two cowboys from the Grand Mesa. Should this be true, Lance knew they were dealing with a cunning and dangerous man.

Torrie shivered. The night was growing cold. She thought about getting her coat from her saddlebags, but she dismissed the idea when Lance and Mac began to walk toward the house. She practically had to run to keep up with their long strides.

They stalked up the few stairs that led to the front stoop. Lance banged on the door with his fist. The house seemed quiet—empty. Lance pounded on the door again. Impatiently, he grabbed the doorknob and turned it. The door was unlocked. Lance shoved it open and stepped inside. He paused to let his eyes adjust to the dark. Before he had been in the house for more than a few seconds, a voice bellowed down from the stairs.

"Who the hell's there?"

"Lance Farlo."

A silence deafened the house. A light went on at the top of the stairs. Wayne stood in the light of the lantern that was attached to the wall by a brass bracket. Strands of his dark hair were hanging across his forehead. He wore no shirt or boots, the top snap on his jeans was unfastened. Heavy breathing made his chest rise and fall in rapid succession. In his hands he held a 30-06. "What's going on?" he asked.

"We need to talk to you." Although he was surprised to find Wayne at home, Lance forced himself to speak in a calm manner. Turmoil dominated his insides. He didn't like to accuse a man of something unless he was certain of the facts. Now, he wasn't certain of anything.

"Has something else happened?" Wayne lowered his rifle and began to walk down the stairs. He looked past Lance toward the doorway. His gaze settled on Mac Williams. A hostile expression claimed his face. "What the hell are you doin' here?"

Mac stepped forward and struck a bold stance. "I don't work for the Grand Mesa anymore."

Wayne looked to Lance, and received a firm nod as confirmation of Mac's statement. He still acted distrustful. "So why are all of you here?"

"We just came from the Grand Mesa," Lance said. He stalked forward just as Wayne reached the bottom of the staircase. Now, the two men stood face-to-face. "Gage Carrington is dead," Lance added in a blunt tone of voice. He noticed an ashen pallor claim Wayne's face—the grey hue inched down through his bare chest. His mouth gaped, and for several seconds he was speechless.

"H-How did it happen?" Wayne finally stammered.

"I shot him." Lance noticed Wayne's coloring grow even more sickly. He kept remembering the

351

day he and Torrie had been coming back from Horse Mountain. He'd seen two riders through his field glasses—he was certain one was Gage, the other one was Wayne Gere. The shiny conchos on his fancy saddle had been reflecting the sunlight like a beacon.

"I need a drink," Wayne gasped. Without looking up at Lance again, he motioned toward his den. "Why don't we all sit down and you can tell me what happened."

"There's no need to waste time," Lance said. His stance remained stiff. "I want to know what your relationship was with Gage Carrington?"

Lance's question surprised Torrie and Mac. It seemed to catch Wayne off guard, too. He quickly regained his wits about him, though. His hunched shoulders puffed back as he stepped back to glare into Lance's face.

"I've got the feeling I'm on trial here. You're the one who should be answerin' questions." His eyes narrowed. He clutched the butt of the 30-06 tightly in his hand. "You were paid damned good money to guard our land and cattle. Where the hell were you when McLeary was killed and Larson was shot?"

Lance's face turned to stone. His spine straightened, and his hands fell to the handles of his Colts without him being aware of his own movements. Wayne Gere did not back down. But—if possible —he did grow more pale.

"I could ask you that same question," Lance retorted. His voice was bland, a sharp contrast to the expression on his face and his lethal stature.

"I was out guardin' my own herds," Wayne spat. "We were stupid—no, they were stupid to think you'd be any help. All you did was make matters worse. You never once earned a penny of your wages."

Lance's pale gaze drilled into Wayne's face. His words had cut Lance to the bone. He felt a sharp pain shoot down through his chest and impale itself in the pit of his stomach. Wayne's words echoed through his mind again. They were almost identical to what he had been telling himself. All he could do now was try to compensate for the things he had not done.

Lance reached into his shirt pocket and pulled out a wad of money. He separated part of it from the bundle and held it out toward Wayne. "Take it," he commanded. "It's the wages you paid me. Take it!"

Wayne did not hesitate to grab the money. He looked up and saw a fiendish grin tilt up one corner of Lance's mouth. He wished he had a shirt to put on—he felt cold all of a sudden.

"Now, I don't work for you anymore," Lance said. "Now, I work for myself. And I aim to find out who set fire to McLeary's and Larson's ranches. Whoever started those fires is responsible for what happened this morning." Lance studied Wayne's expression, his eyes. He saw nothing but Wayne's look of staunch defiance. It was hard to read a man who felt so little emotion. Lance wondered if all the years Gere had spent in the Army had taught him to be so disciplined or if he was just a coldhearted excuse for a man.

He glanced over his shoulder at Mac and Torrie. "We're wastin' our time here." He saw Mac nod his head in agreement. Torrie showed no reaction as her gaze flitted back and forth between the three men. Before he turned to go, Lance cast one more leveled stare at Wayne. Their gazes met for a second. Lance knew he had been wrong about this man . . . in the beginning. He understood Wayne now, and he knew he had to find a way to expose him somehow.

"He's lying," Mac said as they walked back to their horses."

"I know," Lance said.

"What are we going to do?" Torrie asked. She almost had to run to keep up with the wide gait of their long legs.

Lance grabbed his saddle horn and swung onto his horse. He sounded impatient when he answered. "Mac's gonna take you back to town." It was too dark to see one another clearly, so Lance made certain the tone of his voice was enough to convince them that he would not argue about his decision when he added, "I need to finish this—alone."

Mac climbed into his saddle. He waited for Torrie to do the same. Neither of them said a word.

"Tell Kearny I'll be back when I've found the evidence I need." Lance spoke to Mac. He was all business. He clicked Raven's reins, kicked his sides, and sent the horse galloping into the night without another word to either of them.

Torrie felt stripped of all her hope. What had happened to change Lance so drastically—so fast?

"We'd better get back to town before Gere orders his men to shoot us for trespassing."

Torrie's body jerked at the sound of Mac's words. "What about Lance?" she said, her words were barely above a whisper.

"He'll be back when he's done with his business." Mac tried to sound confident, but inside, he did not feel so sure.

A flaxen moon had risen in the sky, but it was shrouded by a haze and offered little light. There was just enough of a reflection for following the road. Mac and Torrie were stopped by several of Wayne's guards as they rode from the Diamond G. Mac told them Lance had stayed with Gere. They would hear differently before long.

After they had reached the main road that led back to town, Torrie turned to Mac. Abruptly, she said, "I love him, Mac. And I'd go back to Texas with him if he'd ask me to . . . but he won't."

For a moment Mac was taken aback. She'd avoided talking about Lance all day. He was surprised she was being so honest now. "It's obvious how much you love him, Miss Torrie. It's just as obvious that he loves you."

"But he's the one who's scared, not me," she said. An angry tone crept into her voice.

Mac didn't answer. Her words had a profound effect on him. He felt as if something had just erupted inside him. His thoughts were jolted back thirty years. In his mind he was in Kansas again, he was riding away from the only girl he'd ever loved. He remembered how he'd told himself how her fear had kept her from lovin' him. But he also remembered the burning fear that had boiled through him. He had been scared, too, even more scared than when he faced another man in a showdown. He had wanted to go back to her, to tell her he'd hang up his guns, change his name—whatever it took to get her back. But, he was too afraid of makin' promises he didn't know if he could keep.

Mac continued to ride beside Torrie in the moonlight. He never replied to her insinuation that Lance was scared.

Lance knew Wayne would be laying for him, so he had no time to kill. After he left Mac and Torrie he rode around to the back of the house and hid Raven in the cottonwoods surrounding the house. He patted the horse on the neck.

"Now neither of us has any distractions, Blacky," he whispered. He dropped the stallion's reins on the ground and stalked through the dark countryside. At the side of the house he waited to see if Wayne Gere would do as he expected. He did not have to wait long.

Wayne stomped through his front door without taking the time to close it. On the front porch he paused and glanced around as if he were looking for someone. "Pete?" His voice lacked all patience.

Low curses were muttered, then he stalked away from the house. He buttoned his shirt and donned his coat as he walked to the barn. He came out a short time later leading his palomino. Even at night the conchos shimmered against the dark leather of the saddle.

Lance waited until he was sure of the direction Gere was headed, then he casually walked into the house. The open door—and the absence of any guards—made his entry simple. He went into the den, but did not light a lamp. He wasn't sure he'd find anything here, and he knew he didn't have much time. Wayne's men would tell him only two riders had ridden out.

As his eyes became focused, Lance glanced around the dark room. He knew it would be impossible to accuse Wayne of setting the fires or connect him with Gage if he couldn't find any tangible evidence. His gaze scanned the walls. A large picture caught his eye. Quickly, he moved to the wall and eased the picture down. His instincts had not failed him this time. Every rancher he had ever worked for had a wall safe where he kept valuables. Usually it was only a hole in the wall with no more than a box stuffed inside. Lance's hope sank when he saw the steel door on Wayne's safe. A small combination lock was in the center of the square door. If there were any clues to Wayne's activities in the safe, there still was no time to figure out the combination. Lance knew he was already walking a fine line with the law, and he was certain Wayne would see to it he was arrested for breaking and entering if he caught him here.

Lance replaced the picture and made his way to the front door. He could hear the pounding of approaching hooves. His heartbeat matched their pace. His feet wasted no time skirting the side of the house. He whistled as he ran. Raven met him before he reached the spot where he had left him. Behind them, he could hear the shouts of Gere and his men as they dismounted from their horses and began to scour the area for him.

The darkness—and the dense groves of cottonwoods—hid him within a few hundred yards. He checked his bearings in the dark, then headed toward Piceance Creek. He knew he could lose anybody who was trailing him once he reached that area. If Wayne or any of his men were following him though, Lance wasn't aware of it. He rode to the creek bed without any sign of trouble. The line shack where he'd spent the night with Torrie was only a couple miles downstream. He tried not to think about that night. His efforts were not successful. Her memory, and the memory of every moment they'd spent together kept dominating his thoughts. He reminded himself that this was part of the reason he had not been able to do his job. He tried to be angry with her. It was a lost cause. He kicked Raven in the sides, he was anxious to get back to town.

By the time Lance had reached the outskirts of Rifle he felt completely defeated. Mostly, because he couldn't prove anything on Wayne Gere—the man had covered his tracks too damned good.

It was past midnight. The streets of Rifle were deserted. The town's only saloon still hosted a few patrons, but they were a quiet crew. Lance headed straight for the sheriff's office. He forced himself not to look down the street where the boarding-house stood. To his surprise, he noticed a light still burned in the sheriff's office. Through the window Lance could see four men. He knew three of them. The fourth man was sitting in a chair with his back toward the window. Lance thought he looked familiar, but he couldn't place him right off.

He tossed Raven's reins over the hitching post and headed into the office. Sheriff Kearny, Deputy Silt, and Mac Williams acted as though they had been waiting for him. The other man eyed Lance, nervously.

"Have you met Pete Wheeler?" Sheriff Kearny asked Lance as soon as he entered the office.

The younger man sprang up from the chair he was sitting in, and swallowed hard. "Yeah—we met."

"Yeah, so we have." Lance's gaze narrowed with a scrutinizing observation of the other man.

"At—at the Diamond G. You asked me to look after Miss Torrie when she hurt her knees." Pete rubbed his sweating palms down the sides of his jeans. His face felt flushed and he could feel a cold sweat break out along his browline.

Lance remembered. He gave Pete a curt nod.

"You'd be interested in what he has to say," Sheriff Kearny said. He sat down behind his desk, and absently began to rub his thick mustache.

Setting his gaze on the young man's face, Lance crossed his arms over his chest and waited. He could see the beads of sweat erupting all over Pete's face. He sensed he was about to hear something pertinent.

"I-I usually stand guard at Mr. Gere's house,"

Pete began. "I see most of his comings and goings."

Now Lance gave his full attention to Pete Wheeler. "Did you see him leave early this morning?"

Pete wiped the back of his hand across his brow. "Yes sir, I did. I saw him leave early in the morning the Larson place was set on fire too."

Lance looked at Sheriff Kearny. He met the sheriff's gaze. The sheriff nodded his head toward Pete. "There's more," he said.

Pete glanced back and forth between the lawmen and the gunfighter. He didn't bother to wipe away the rivulets of sweat running down his face—it didn't do any good anyhow. "Gage Carrington and Wayne Gere had become real friendly lately. They were real secretive about their meetings, but I overheard them talking about being partners."

A thoughtful expression consumed Lance's weary features. He thought of the smaller spreads on each side of the Grand Mesa and the Diamond G; Shawn McLeary's land and Jim Larson's. They were all that stood in the way of a merger between the two big ranches. Lance figured Gage was thinking ahead to the time when he would inevitably take over the Grand Mesa. He must have known there was the possibility of a judge ruling against the old man's claim that the others were squatters on his land, so Gage was making sure they lost no more land than possible. A partnership with a shrewd man like Wayne Gere was a good move on Gage's part. Lance wondered if

Gage told Wayne he could retain title to his property if he helped him eliminate McLeary and Larson.

"We suspect Leo MacFarlene and Will Connor were just in the wrong place at the wrong time," Sheriff Kearny said. "They probably seen Wayne and Gage out on one of their secret rendezvous. Gage couldn't chance havin' Ben find out what he was up to."

Lance drew in a heavy breath, then exhaled hard. Fatigue made his actions slow. He glanced at Pete Wheeler again. "Why'd you decide to come forward with this information?" Pete did not meet his gaze at first. He stared at the floor. When he looked up again, he looked directly at Lance.

"I was sitting in church a few days ago. That's how I know Miss Torrie—we visit at church and—" Pete shrugged. "Well, anyway, in church the other day I saw Shawn McLeary and his wife and kids—the Larsons' too. When I heard what happened today, I knew I had to speak out."

A grin curved one corner of Lance's mouth. "You did the right thing. I reckon you'll be looking for a job though."

Sheriff Kearny rose from his chair and leaned on his desk. "He got one if he wants it." He glanced at Deputy Silt and added, "This town needs more lawmen, and honest men are hard to come by." He leveled his gaze on Lance. "If you ever decide you'd like to pin on a badge, I'd—"

Lance threw his arms up and shook his head from side to side. "No thanks."

Sheriff Kearny shrugged. "I could use help in

the morning when I go out to arrest Wayne Gere."

For a moment Lance thought over his request. He looked at Mac Williams and Pete Wheeler, then back to the sheriff. "I think you'll be able to handle it. It's time I cut a trail back to Texas." His attention was drawn toward Mac again. Lance looked away quickly. The strange expression on the older gunman's face made him uneasy.

Before he left, Lance reached into his pocket and pulled out the wad of bills. He held the money out toward the sheriff.

"What's that for?" Sheriff Kearny asked. He made no move to take the money.

"It's what McLeary and Larson paid me. I didn't earn it. I reckon their families could use it right about now."

Sheriff Kearny stared at Lance for a moment. Their gazes met again. He didn't speak as he clasped ahold of the large wad of money. As the gunfighter turned to leave there were things he thought he should say, but he remained quiet. Sometimes, men knew what each other was thinking.

Lance stepped out into the quiet town. His gaze moved down the street on their own accord. The boardinghouse was dark and silent. He climbed into his saddle. His energy was exhausted. He wanted to head out for Texas tonight, but he didn't think he had the strength. Besides, he sensed if he did start riding tonight, he'd only end up coming back in the morning. He had to see her one more time . . . he had to say goodbye.

Chapter Thirty-Four

Torrie tugged at the waistband of the turquoise dress she wore. It was another one of Elsa's, and she didn't think it fit her any better than the green dress she had borrowed the other day. When she got to Denver, she'd sell her jewelry and buy herself some new clothes. The thought made her stomach feel quivery. She needed a lot more than clothes . . . she would have to build a whole new life when she reached the city.

She clutched the train tickets in her hands and glanced down the empty train tracks. The train would not leave for Denver until late afternoon, but she had come to the depot early this morning to confirm their seats on today's eastbound train and make arrangements to have Ginger ride in the car reserved for stock. She held the tickets against her breast and continued to stare down the barren stretch of track.

Where was Lance? She'd stopped by the sheriff's office on her way here. He and his two deputies were organizing another posse. Mac Williams was also there, and he had filled her in on what had happened last night. He told her they were headed for the Diamond G to arrest Wayne Gere, and that he would be here this afternoon to see her and Elsa off on the train. He made no mention of seeing Lance at the sheriff's office last night.

A slow, yearning ache worked its way through her body. She had a feeling Lance had left for Texas. The pain settled in her heart like a heavy weight. She thought he would at least say goodbye. Maybe it was best if he was already gone. She wasn't sure if she could handle watching him leave and knowing she would never see him again. At least this way the hardest part was done.

"I reckon those are train tickets you're about to rip in two?"

Torrie swung around at the sound of the deep voice. Her previous thoughts evaporated at once. Joy exploded in her chest and dispersed the pain. Inwardly, she thanked God—outwardly, she tried to appear calm.

"L-Lance," she stammered. "I-I thought maybe you'd left already." Her emerald gaze sought his eyes for some sign that might suggest he had changed his mind about them going separate ways. His expression was unreadable.

"I couldn't leave without saying goodbye to you." He tried to smile. It felt unnatural to force himself to smile when he didn't feel like smiling. He took a step toward her. They were only a couple of feet apart. The sadness—the disappointment—in her expression made his insides hurt.

"I thought—well—" Torrie drew in a trembling

sigh. She wiped at the corner of her eye. Dust must have blown there; her eyes were stinging. The silence that followed was almost unbearable. She wished she could look away from his face, but she couldn't. It was the last time she would ever gaze at him, she couldn't let the chance slip away.

Lance cleared his throat. "Yeah—well—I'm leaving now." He tried to glance down at the ground, but his eyes were drawn back to her face. He was painting another picture in his mind to add to all the pictures he would carry back to Texas with him.

He'd told himself he wouldn't touch her, because it would only make it harder. But he couldn't control his actions any more than he could stop himself from breaking her heart. He reached out and ran his fingers along the silken strands of her copper-colored hair. Today, she wore the long tresses loose. Lance thought they hung down her back and around her shoulders like a shimmering waterfall in a red sunset. The turquoise dress she was wearing complemented her pale skin, and made her complexion appear even more alabaster. His fingers slid from her hair to her soft cheek. She felt like satin to his touch. He felt his groin tighten, his heart pounded like thunder in his chest.

"I-I reckon I'd better . . ." his voice faded. His arms reacted without his permission when they pulled her into their embrace. His lips descended on her mouth without hesitation. The entire length of his body resisted his previous commands. He crushed her against him until he was afraid he'd hurt her. She didn't seem to be hurt though. She was responding to his kiss and his enslaving hold in an almost desperate manner.

Torrie threw her arms around his neck when he pulled her to him. She let herself mold against his hard body. She sought his mouth like a starving animal seeks food. It didn't matter that they were kissing and holding one another with no regard to anything or anyone around them. Only this moment mattered, and she wished she could make it extend into eternity.

Their kiss lasted as long as was humanly possible. Eventually, they had to part for air. Torrie felt the burning sensation in the corners of her eyes again. She hoped the threatening tears would not fall.

"I have to go," he said. His voice was breathy, low. He stared down at her for a moment longer before he released his tight hold and stepped back. "Maybe if I'm ever in Denver I'll—"

"Yeah—well—I won't make you promise that," Torrie said. She attempted a smile. She couldn't pull it off.

A deep sigh rattled through Lance. He took another step backwards. He pointed at the tickets she still clutched in her hand. They were wadded into a twisted ball of paper. "I reckon you're gonna need to trade those in on a new set." He tried to make his voice sound calm, joking. Instead, his words quivered. He cleared his throat again. His gaze held her in its embrace for a moment longer.

"I reckon this is goodbye then." The abnormal sound of his voice reached his ears again. "Take care of yourself." He dropped his arms down at his sides and started to turn away.

"Lance!" Torrie gasped. She stepped forward, then halted when he turned back to her. "Take care of yourself too," she whispered. She didn't know if he heard. His expression was so strange—so unreadable. He twirled on the heels of his cowboy boots without another word, and walked to where his horse stood.

He felt the fire of her gaze on his back as he walked away from her. Nothing could make him look back again. It was over . . . she'd be better off without him. He climbed into his saddle and yanked on Raven's reins to swing the horse in the opposite direction. He willed his gaze to remain on the road ahead. Finally, his mind was able to gain control. Once he was gone from her, he would regain control of his life, he told himself.

He headed for the river where he'd spent the night down in the cottonwoods. Sleep hadn't come easy. Now—he told himself—he would be able to sleep again, too. When he got away from here, the past would finally be where it belonged. He knew he would never come back again . . . he'd probably never even come to Colorado again.

Raven crossed the Colorado River in a shallow spot. The Red River that cut a lazy trail by his cabin came to Lance's mind. He missed Texas. He missed Torrie and he'd only left her ten minutes ago.

After he left the river behind, he headed straight south toward New Mexico. If he wasn't side-tracked he'd be home in a week.

By nightfall, he was tired of trying to convince himself that he was doing the right thing by leaving Torrie behind. He camped at the foothills of Elk Mountain in southern Colorado. His body was exhausted, his mind even more fatigued. He knew he'd sleep good tonight.

Hours later—his hands wrapped around a tin cup filled with coffee that had been cold for almost as long—Lance stared into the dying embers of the fire. Nothing coherent claimed his thoughts. He was too tired to think straight, yet, he couldn't fall asleep. It was because he was still in Colorado, he told himself. A cold breeze whipped down from the mountain. Lance scooted closer to the fire. He hoped it wouldn't snow again until he was out of this area. The thought reminded him of Torrie. Every tree, every rock, everything seemed to remind him of her.

When he was back in Texas, however, he would be able to put her out of his mind once and for all. He planned to head straight for the nearest town—Wichita Falls—and buy enough whiskey to last him for the whole winter. He would hole up in his cabin and drink himself into oblivion. He'd wash away all the painful memories of his father, Canon, Gage—everybody and everything. By springtime he'd be healed. He would tackle his job with a new sense of determination, and he would make up for the way he'd messed up here in Colorado.

The wind whistled through the aspens again. Lance tightened his fingers around the tin cup. They gathered no warmth from the icy coffee. He exhaled a weary sigh. He would be in Texas soon. He could live without sleep for a few more days . . . and he could live without Torrie Carrington, too.

Chapter Thirty-Five

Torrie rubbed Ginger's heaving side with a damp rag. The horse eyed her from the corner of her eye. Another contraction gripped the mare. She had just lain down on her side, and her legs flailed against the ground. Torrie stepped to the back of the mare. Her movements were awkward, but she managed to escape from the deadly hooves. She rubbed her own aching back, but it didn't ease the dull ache which seemed to be her constant companion lately.

After Ginger's contraction had passed, Torrie kneeled down by the horse's rump. There still were no visible signs of the foal. A worried sigh fell from Torrie's lips. Ginger had been laboring for nearly three hours. It shouldn't have taken more than an hour—two at the most.

Torrie worried Ginger was in trouble. Elsa had gone to fetch the vet from town, but she should have returned by now. To make matters worse, even Elsa's parents were gone today. They had taken Will Jr. into town to buy him some new clothes. He was nine months old now, and he was growing like a weed. Elsa had to make him new clothes constantly. This morning her father had said they were gonna buy him some store-bought duds so Elsa could take a break from sewing.

Elsa's father checked Ginger before they had left. Although Ginger wasn't due for at least two more weeks, her teats were filling with milk. This meant the foal's birth was imminent, probably within the next three days. But since Ginger, and Torrie, both seemed fine, the Griswelds had decided to proceed with their trip into town with their grandson.

They hadn't been gone an hour when Torrie noticed Ginger was acting strange, and that the mare's water sac had broken.

Now she patted Ginger's sweating haunches. Then, instinctively, rubbed her hand over her own rounded belly. She shook her head in disbelief. For a long time, whenever she thought about the irony of her situation—and Ginger's—she thought it must be some sort of a joke. As time passed though, harsh reality set in.

She glanced out through the open barn door. She could see the tall, narrow frame house that rose up from the center of the beet fields. It had been her home for the past nine months. Elsa's parents, Mary and Warren Grisweld, were beet farmers. Their small farm was located on the plains north of Cherry Creek and the thriving metropolis of Denver. Torrie was amazed every time she saw how much Denver had changed since she had been born here in '78. It was still considered a mining town back then. Now, twenty-one years later, Denver was one of the fastest-growing areas in the country.

When Elsa and Torrie arrived here last fall, Mary and Warren Grisweld greeted them with open arms. They didn't even seem to mind that Torrie had shipped her horse over on the train with them.

It was Torrie's plan to find a place of her own as soon as she sold her jewelry. The necklaces brought her enough money to live on until she found employment. Elsa's parents insisted she stay with them. They said there was plenty of room, and Elsa could use help with Will Jr. while they worked in the beet fields. Torrie consented only after they agreed to let her pay rent.

Then everything began to fall apart. She began to get sick every time she ate. She had dizzy spells and felt faint at times. Elsa and her parents insisted she see a doctor. He confirmed her worst fears. She was carrying Lance's child. For weeks she didn't tell anyone. She panicked, then, and finally she confided in Elsa.

Elsa refused to let Torrie leave. Torrie refused to stay. She could not shame the Griswelds after they had been so kind to her. As she was packing her bags to leave, Elsa's parents came to her and asked her to stay. They said Elsa had told them everything, and they still wanted her to stay. After much discussion, Torrie finally gave in to their coaxing. Constantly, she wondered how she'd ever repay the Griswelds for everything they had done for her.

She was determined to leave once her baby was born, though. Another baby in the house would be too much of a burden, and Torrie felt she had to make a life for herself and the baby on her own. Lately, she'd been thinking a lot about going to Colorado Springs in the fall. Nobody would know her there, and she could say she was a widow.

Ginger whinnied. Torrie's attention was diverted away from her own worries. Something was happening. Torrie could see a dark patch sticking out from beneath Ginger's tail. She hoped it was a pair of hooves. Ginger seemed to be in so much distress, Torrie worried the foal might be coming out breech.

"It's gonna be all right, girl," she said soothingly. "Where's Elsa and the vet," she muttered. She felt her own baby give several rapid kicks. A gasp rang out from her mouth as she touched her stomach. She was constantly amazed by the fact that there was a real baby inside her—Lance's baby—a baby he would never know existed. The thought always made her fill with sadness. Would he want to know? she wondered.

Ginger raised her head slightly and looked back toward Torrie, briefly. Then her head collapsed back down to the floor. Her breathing was heavier, her eyes bulging with fright. A pang of sympathy seared through Torrie. She felt so helpless. The dark spot under Ginger's tail was larger, bulging. Torrie leaned down, she was sure it was a tiny hoof. She exhaled a relieved breath.

Fleetingly, she remembered Will Jr.'s birth. She'd known a lot less about delivering babies when she helped Elsa deliver him. A nervous fluttering erupted in the pit of Torrie's stomach. She tried not to dwell on the birth of her own baby. The idea of what she would go through scared her too much to think about it. Her greatest fear was that something would go wrong and she would lose this baby. Then, she would have nothing left of Lance but her bittersweet memories. She clasped her hands over her swollen stomach in a protective manner.

Ginger's breathing was even more erratic now. Another snort rang out from her nose, but she made no effort to move when another pain overcame her. Torrie scooted closer. She wanted this over with, and she knew Ginger did too. There was enough of the hoof sticking out for Torrie to grab onto so she could help pull the foal out. Her sole concentration was on this task. She didn't hear a horse approaching the house. Nor did she notice when the lone rider came toward the barn.

"Come on girl," she coaxed as she tried to hold on tight to the little, slippery hoof. Another contraction made it possible for her to grasp the second hoof.

"That's a good girl, Ginger," Torrie cried out. She was too wrapped up in the birth to see the tall man whose presence filled the doorway of the small barn.

Lance stared in silent shock at the sight that greeted his eyes. It took him only a second to realize Torrie was delivering a colt that had to have been sired by Raven. From where he stood though, he couldn't tell Torrie was also heavy with his

373

child. His first instinct was to call out to her, but he stopped himself. For a time, he just watched her. He was in awe of the entire scenario.

Torrie's long hair was tied in a loose ponytail. The thick red tresses hung over one shoulder—just like he remembered. He could tell her face was etched with concentration—a smudge of dirt was streaked across her sweaty cheek. His body ached with desire to hold her close again. But for now, he only stared at her.

He recalled the last time he'd seen her standing at the train depot in Rifle. He'd never forget the stricken look on her beautiful face when he turned to leave her. He'd never forgive himself for leaving either. The months he had spent trying to forget about her only increased his desperate need to be with her again. But, he hadn't given in to this need easily. Whiskey had poisoned his body, but it had not cleansed him of her memory. He wallowed in self-pity, turned into a hermit for a few months. When this didn't work, he wandered into Wichita Falls. He courted trouble, picked fights, and proved to himself—and others—that he was still the fastest draw in the west. He sought the company of other women in the saloons he frequented. Nothing could make him forget Torrie.

"Push Ginger!" Torrie shouted as she hung onto the wet hooves and pulled with all her might when another contraction shuddered through the mare's body. It appeared the foal was huge, but that didn't surprise Torrie. Raven was an extraordinarily large stallion. Engrossed with the fierce effort to pull the colt, she did not see Lance walk up behind her. When his hands clasped over hers, a startled cry escaped from her gaping mouth. Her head jerked up with surprise, but complete shock registered on her face when she met his pale brown eyes. No sounds escaped her parted lips— her emerald gaze shimmered with a sheet of tears.

"Howdy, little darlin'," he drawled as if their meeting was as casual as passing one another on the street. He gripped her hands tighter. They didn't have time to exchange greetings.

Ginger's whole body quivered as she strained to push the foal from her body. The hooves slid farther out, then long black legs followed. Torrie and Lance grabbed onto the spindly legs, then scooted back as they continued to tug on the foal. The shoulders and head shoved through the opening, the body pushed forward with a gush. The sudden explosion of the foal's body shoved Torrie and Lance farther back against the barn floor as their grips tore loose from its legs.

In silence they stared at the slimy black creature who was still draped in the transparent grey placenta sac. Ginger struggled to her feet almost at once. She turned around and began to eat the placenta off her foal. For a moment the foal lay completely still, but as her mother's rough tongue began to lick at her, she began to stretch out her long legs. The newborn filly was an exact replica of her father—right down to the white blaze on her face.

Torrie watched the mare and her filly, but her thoughts were spinning with the shock of Lance's unexpected arrival. She looked over her shoulder. He was staring at the horses. A tender expression rested on his bearded face.

When Lance noticed Torrie's attention was on him, he looked down into her eyes. They were the green eyes that haunted his dreams, and his waking hours, for the past nine months. He could see her surprise, sense her joy. He wanted—no needed to hold her. He rose to his feet and walked in front of her. His gaze fell down to the bulge at the front of her flowered dress. He felt a hot fire ignite in the pit of his stomach. His knees went soft. He thought he might fall down.

His mouth gaped open, but no words came to his mind. He couldn't tear his eyes away from her stomach. His mind fought to accept this reality. Torrie was pregnant, his stunned mind kept repeating. Not one doubt entered his mind about the role he played in this development, and the sense of guilt that flooded over him made him feel sick.

"I didn't know," he said. His voice came out in raspy tones. He was still gaping down at her stomach. She held her hands up so he could help her stand. He reached down, clasped her hands, and pulled her to her feet. She rose slowly, awkwardly. Lance's mouth fell open again, but he couldn't think of the right words to convey his feelings.

"I can't believe you're really here," Torrie said in a hoarse voice. Tears of happiness streamed down her face. They left little trails on her grimy cheeks.

Lance reached out and gently wiped them away from one side of her face. He glanced down at her round belly again. His face filled with tenderness. "I never would have left you if I'd known. I never should have left you anyway. I'm sor—"

Torrie pressed her fingertips to his lips. "None of that matters. You're here now." They stared at one another in silence for a moment. Their gazes bespoke all that was in their hearts.

"Good grief! It is you!" Elsa's voice rang out from the doorway.

Torrie and Lance were jerked from their moment of quiet rapture by the sound of her shocked voice. Elsa rushed into the barn. The vet followed her. He headed toward the mare and her new foal. Elsa's eyes never left Lance.

"I saw your horse out there, but I still couldn't believe it."

A crooked grin curved Lance's lips. He shrugged and tipped the brim of his hat toward Elsa in greeting.

A bright scarlet blush rose in Elsa's cheeks. She glanced toward Torrie, then looked at the foal. "Looks like you got here just in time."

Lance glanced down at Torrie. His pale gaze shimmered with untold happiness. "Just in time," he said.

As Torrie met his loving gaze, she felt a strange pang in her abdomen. She tried to ignore the shooting pain. She told herself it was just the excitement of Lance's return, and the strain of Ginger's delivery. It would be too ironic for her to give birth now.

"Are you all right?" Lance asked. He noticed the paleness that had pushed away the flushed color in her face.

She smiled. "I think I need to sit down for a minute." The worry in Lance's face touched her heart, but it had to crowd in with all the happiness that was already contained there. She felt his strong arm slip around her shoulders as he began to lead her out of the barn. It felt like he'd never left.

Elsa stayed right at Torrie's side. "Her baby is due any day," she announced.

"That's obvious," Lance retorted. He ignored the patronizing glare Torrie cast in his direction.

As they entered the house Torrie felt another twinge low in her abdomen. It was like a tightening sensation, but it was strong enough to make her gasp. Her barely audible noise induced a moment of panic among Lance and Elsa.

Lance grabbed her arm and peered into her face. "Is it the baby?" he said. His voice was almost harsh. Fear clutched at his chest and made him feel out of control.

"Take her upstairs," Elsa commanded. She sounded as frantic as Lance looked.

Torrie looked back and forth between them. An amused smile curled her lips. "Good grief, I'm only having a baby. With all the practice I've had, this should be easy." She chuckled. Lance gave her a glowering stare. Elsa wrung her hands together.

"You'll have to go for the doctor," she said to Lance.

Lance groaned at the thought. He'd spent the

378

last four days in Denver looking for Torrie. When he had finally found out who Elsa's family were, and where they lived, he'd raced out to this farm. He had no intention of going back to Denver now.

"I'm not leaving her," he said. He clutched Torrie's hand in an enslaving grip. She returned his tight hold.

Elsa stared at their defiant faces. "Oh, all right. I'll ask the vet to go for the doctor," she said in an exasperated tone.

Torrie felt the tightening sensation beginning to well up in her stomach again. Instinctively, she pressed her hand to her taut belly, and glanced up at Lance. "I think you'd better get me upstairs."

He wasted no time in sweeping her up into his arms. He glanced around the house until he located the staircase against the wall in the narrow foyer. Without a word he headed up the stairs.

"That's my room," Torrie said as she motioned to the door at the top of the stairs. She was surprised that she no longer felt scared about giving birth to Lance's child. In his arms, she felt completely secure, and capable of conquering any feat.

Lance placed her down on the bed as gently as possible. He reached up to fluff the pillows under her head. Torrie grabbed his hand. She held it against her swollen breast. His palm was wet with sweat. "Now that you're here I don't need anything else."

Beneath his fevered palm Lance could feel the rapid beating of her heart. He felt his own heart beating in unison with hers. Another pang of guilt rushed through him and clutched at his chest. If he hadn't come back—today—she' would have gone through this alone. He wanted to tell her all the things he should have told her months ago, but had never taken the time.

Torrie's grip on his hand tightened. The color drained out of her face as her body tensed against another pain. Elsa flew into the room at almost the same moment.

"The vet is going for the doctor." She leveled her blue gaze on Lance. "You'd better leave now." He returned her look with a deadly expression that made her stop dead in her tracks. Her mouth hung open, then she snapped it shut.

The contraction passed, and Torrie released Lance's hand. She cast a weak smile at him when he looked down at her. "I'll be all right," she said. Their gazes met again. A part of her wanted to ask him to stay with her. She was almost afraid to let him out of her sight for fear that he would leave again. Another part of her didn't want him to watch what she knew she would go through to give birth to his child. The decision was made for her when Mary Grisweld swept into the room.

"We just met the vet," she cried. "How's Torrie doing?" Before she received an answer she noticed Lance. "Who are you?"

Lance pulled himself up to his full height and glared down at the older woman. "I'm the baby's father."

A fleeting look of surprise passed over Mary's face. Her eyes—the same shade of blue as Elsa's—narrowed with contempt. Although he had apparently showed up to face his responsibility, she still told herself she'd give him a piece of her mind later. "Well, you'll have to wait outside. A man's got no business here."

Torrie nodded in resignation when Lance looked to her for confirmation. He leaned down close to her face. His warm breath brushed her forehead when he spoke. "I'll be waitin' right outside the door." His lips touched hers in a light, brief kiss before he stalked from the room without speaking to Elsa or her hostile mother.

As she watched Lance leave the room, Torrie experienced a strangling sense of panic. She knew she could never escape completely from this feeling, but she vowed to herself that she would learn how to cope with her fears.

Torrie didn't have time to dwell on much of anything for the next nine hours except giving birth to Lance's child. She was aware of the doctor's presence and of Mary Grisweld fussing over her, but Elsa was her main source of strength. As she crushed Elsa's hand in her own one, she tried to concentrate on her friend's soothing voice. In the long hours which passed, Elsa—and the knowledge that Lance waited outside her room—were the only things that offered her any solace.

The racking pains eventually wiped all thoughts from her mind. She could only concentrate on bearing down with the unbearable contractions which were almost constant now. Torrie felt as if she was being ripped apart. She was sure she couldn't take any more when another acute pain seared through her body. Around her she could hear excited voices. She felt something slippery slide from her body, the pressure began to ease away.

"It's a girl," the doctor shouted. He held the baby up so Torrie could see her. A weak cry rang out from the little heart-shaped mouth.

Torrie tried to focus her weary gaze on the tiny, wet girl, but tears were clouding her vision. She swallowed the heavy lump in her throat. "Where's Lance," she whispered.

Elsa patted her arm. "I'll get him as soon as the doctor finishes up with you."

Torrie didn't argue. She was too tired. But she wasn't too tired to hold her daughter when Elsa placed her in her arms after she'd wiped the newborn off and wrapped her in a blanket. Nor was she too tired to see Lance when he was finally permitted to come into her room.

As soon as everyone filed out of the room, Lance slipped through the door. He paused at the foot of the bed, and stared in awe at the sight of Torrie and his new daughter. The shock of returning just in time to discover Torrie was having his child seemed minor compared to the array of emotions he was feeling now. He moved to their side and sat down on the edge of the bed. Nothing was going to stop him from saying all the things he should have said long ago.

"She's beautiful—and perfect," Torrie said quietly. She pulled the white blanket back. The baby was sound asleep. Her tiny head was covered with light auburn fuzz. Long, dark lashes fanned out across the tops of her rosy cheeks. Miniature lips pursed into a pout as if she were dreaming about something too intense for one so new.

Lance's eyes grew wide as he looked down at his daughter in awe. She was the second most beautiful thing he'd ever gazed upon. "She's just like her mother."

In spite of her exhaustion, Torrie still found the energy to smile. Her smile faded though, when she saw the serious look cross over Lance's face.

"I have to say a few things—things that I should have said before now."

"Can't it wait?" Torrie asked. Her hopes plummeted when Lance shook his head in a negative gesture.

"I have to tell you why I left you in Rifle."

"It doesn't matter now."

"I was scared," Lance blurted out. "I was scared of the way you would have to live if I took you with me."

Torrie pulled the blanket up around her baby's head. She already knew the things he was telling her. A sense of dread crowded her joy.

"I'm still scared Torrie." He motioned toward the baby, adding, "Even more so now. And I still don't make promises I can't keep. I can't promise you'll have an easy life with me. I'm a gunfighter, and you know what that means."

Torrie nodded. She tried to hold back the tears that blurred her vision and made her eyes sting. The baby felt heavy against her arm. Fatigue settled over her like a giant shroud. She didn't want to hear him say these words again.

"I love you, Torrie, and I want you and our baby

to be with me forever. But because of what I am—who I am—that's asking a lot."

Torrie's heavy eyelids opened wide, she blinked, and her vision cleared. An engulfing sense of fulfillment overcame her fatigue. A radiant smile claimed her lips.

"I love you too," she said. Her ears savored the words she had longed to say—and hear—for so long. Nothing else he said mattered.

Outside, a full moon had risen in the sky. The temperature was warm and balmy on this mid-summer night. In the barnyard a proud stallion stood guard over his new family.

In an upstairs bedroom in the house, Lance and Torrie made a promise they could both keep. From this moment on they would always be together.